REVENGE OF THE DEADLY DOZEN

PETER BERRY

BLOODHOUND
— BOOKS —

For Debi with love.

1

Chris Tinker teased open the heavy, plum-coloured felt curtains by no more than an inch and peered south-westwards towards the cemetery. Of course, even from the third floor of the Kensal Green three-storey house, he wasn't expecting to see any actual gravestones, and particularly not the one he had visited every last Sunday of the month for the last six and a half years. However, the former surgeon liked to believe that he could just about make out the tops of the trees to the east of his wife Alison's final resting place and this thought inspired a gentle smile to develop in a moment of fond reminiscence.

He had woken absurdly early. Again. And with an abruptness that was unusual. Although it was getting light outside, at this time of midsummer it barely got dark and so Chris estimated that it was somewhere between three and four in the morning. The horizon to the east, as far as he could imagine without opening a window, leaning out and looking left, was already hesitantly brightening in anticipation of dawn. Through the gap at the top of the sash window, left open in a futile attempt to keep the bedroom cool, he could hear the sparse traffic on the Westway to the south. Rush hour was still distant.

Chris turned to look at the bedside clock which confirmed his suspicions. 3.28am. Miraculously, his sleeping companion appeared untroubled by his sudden jolt awake a few minutes earlier. It was one of the many things he liked about Anna. She slept deeply. Especially after sex. He smiled again, this time more broadly as he remembered the passionate events of the previous evening. The two of them had had to adapt their behaviour slightly since his injury three months earlier but, with time, the physical scars had mostly healed and now there was just the occasional twinge of discomfort if he moved in a certain way or if Anna accidentally pressed on his shoulder when the two of them were in certain positions.

The mental scars, however, were taking longer.

These early awakenings were, he knew, the result of increasingly dark dreams. About Alison's death. About his own. About how close he came to the end of his life, dirty and dishevelled on an Underground train in the middle of suburbia; the latest victim of a merciless and fanatical murderer. If it hadn't been for a few basic martial arts skills casually learned from an Eastern European champion who had also been stabbed by a serial killer, it was highly likely that Chris's loss of blood would have proved fatal. During his long career in various London hospitals, he had seen numerous people with less serious wounds not survive.

The dreams always featured a lot of blood, cascading like rapids across the floor of the Underground train. Filling the carriages. Soaking the seats in crimson waves. Lapping at the windows.

What was strange was that for the first few weeks after the incident, first in hospital and then recovering at home with regular visits from his three daughters and from Anna and, of course, from Monica and Thomas and other members of The Twelve, he had felt pretty good. Almost indestructible. Then, towards the end of May, he had been on an Underground train late at night after attending the opera and suddenly there was a feeling of being overwhelmed. He felt like he was drowning.

Luckily, his travelling companion, a jovial locksmith named Terry Wilson, had taken care of him. As another member of The Twelve, Terry had been assigned to keep an eye on his friend just to make sure there weren't any lasting effects of his near-death experience. The opera trip to see Pagliacci at Covent Garden hadn't particularly been Terry's cup of tea – and he did wonder whether the stabbings in the final act were an appropriate method of death to raise Chris's spirits – but The Twelve had paid for the tickets and it was more important to keep Chris safe.

The locksmith had manoeuvred the surgeon off the train and they had rested on a wooden bench on the platform for twenty minutes until Chris felt able to continue. 'We'll get a taxi,' Terry had suggested. 'It's not far to yours and I can walk home from there. Or stay in a guest room, if you'd prefer.' Chris had gratefully accepted the latter option.

Every night since that incident, Chris had been woken by these intense and terrifying dreams.

Sleeping pills hadn't worked. A medicinal whisky before bedtime hadn't worked. Sex had worked for a couple of nights – hence the moving into Anna's place in Kensal Green – but then the images had returned more vivid and disturbing than ever.

Chris stepped away from the window leaving the curtain to furl back silently into place, darkening the room slightly as a result. He crept to the bathroom to empty his nagging bladder and, after washing his hands, returned to bed, lying himself on top of the thin sheet rather than under it as he had realised he was sweating.

'Happy birthday,' mumbled Anna, sleepily.

'You're awake. Sorry, was it the running water?'

Anna rolled over to give him a kiss on the forehead. 'You feel hot,' she said, concerned and ignoring his question. She placed her palm on his head, checking different areas and then wiped his perspiration on a corner of white sheet. 'I mean ill hot. Not summer hot. How do you feel?'

Chris thought for a moment. As usual after waking early after disrupted sleep, he was now feeling distinctly drowsy. 'I feel okay, I think,' he suggested. 'I suppose I feel seventy. And if this is what seventy feels like then I can't realistically complain.'

Anna pushed herself up on a pile of pillows and turned on a dimmed bedside light so that they could see each other more clearly. 'To answer your question, I was aware of you by the window. You were thinking about death again, right?' She swung her legs out of the bed, grabbed some knickers from the floor which she quickly pulled on and tiptoed across the room to open the bottom of the window marginally for the purposes of airflow. 'I wouldn't normally wake up but I suppose I was in a light sleep phase for a change.'

'Do you remember that song that was on the radio all the time about forty years ago? The one about the best dreams being the ones where you're dying? Tears for Fears, I think the group were called. I'd beg to disagree regarding their controversial views on dreams.'

Anna climbed back into bed and stroked his hair, pushing a wispy grey strand behind his ear. He felt grateful that their occasional and casual physical relationship based on need and the fact that they were both essentially single – Anna's husband, Alan, had been confined to a care home with dementia for the past three years – had developed into something more formal and committed in recent weeks.

'I should try to get another hour or two of sleep,' he said with a sigh, easing his head back on the pillow. 'Sometimes I can drift off for a bit. If I'm lucky.'

'Would some birthday morning sex help? I could probably summon the enthusiasm after a wee and if I clean my teeth.' Anna pressed his earlobe between her thumb and forefinger, in two minds regarding whether she could, in fact, muster the required energy.

The ex-surgeon leaned over and kissed her on the cheek. 'You're so good to me,' he said. 'But I think I'll just try to doze off without that divine pleasure. Just having you beside me would help, though.' Twenty minutes later, after Anna's own bathroom break, she could sense from his breathing that Chris was in a deep sleep. They were still holding hands but his grip had loosened somewhat.

Anna looked at the clock and took a deep breath in. It was nearly 4am and a selection of birds could already be heard chattering in the trees. 'Trust a pathologist to fall for men who break,' she whispered softly to herself.

Roughly a mile to the east, Monica Lodhia was also awake in her St John's Wood apartment, wondering how she was going to ask her own lover to do something that she suspected he wasn't going to enjoy. A retired chemistry professor, herself rapidly approaching seventy, Monica had, a month earlier, taken over the role of leader of The Twelve from Lexington Smith, a stylish, erudite octogenarian who had finally decided that planning and organisation of the group's assassinations should probably be in the hands of someone a bit younger and more dynamic. Monica ticked both boxes, especially the second.

A few weeks into the new post and the full scale of the task was causing Monica to also lose sleep. In addition to the sheer amount of paperwork involved in running The Twelve's extensive finances, insuring its vast art collection and maintaining its many diverse London properties, there was the nagging worry that Chris was simply not going to be capable of continuing for much longer as a functioning member of the group.

She was going to require someone to monitor a potential new member, a sixty-four-year-old cardiologist named Richard Wisby whom she herself had been observing sporadically for just under a year. With the previous case taking up a lot of time earlier in the year, Monica had rather let this part of her job slip since February. These days she simply didn't have the time and with Chris's abilities diminished, Dr Wisby's importance was increasing daily.

The ideal person to take over monitoring was Thomas Quinn, a retired sports trainer in his late sixties who had joined The Twelve the previous autumn. Fortunately, he was at that moment sleeping peacefully beside her.

Unfortunately, he was also Chris's best friend.

2

A short distance to the north, in a spacious home overlooking a park in Willesden, seventy-year-old retired plumber David Latham was the third member of The Twelve who was also wide awake. The day before, he had been invited to the suburban Surrey home of his good friends Diana and Henry Morris for a conversation which he had been hoping never to have but somehow, at the same time, had been anticipating for a couple of years.

David had arrived in London from Trinidad in 1971 and had, after a couple of false starts with employers who seemed to think the colour of his skin meant that he could be paid less than other young workers, found himself a reasonably well-paid plumbing job alongside another recent arrival from the Caribbean, Henry Morris. Quickly they became the closest of friends, the sort who shared secrets and could be trusted completely.

Both in their early twenties, the two of them spent the first few years of the 1970s enjoying life in the bars and cafés that were proliferating through west London. They worked hard and used their pay to date a variety of young women for a few days or weeks at a time until Henry found one who made him rethink what he ultimately wanted out of life.

Petite and blonde with a good job teaching primary school children in Shepherd's Bush, Diana Batchelor wasn't necessarily looking for love when her eyes caught Henry's across a not-so-crowded Ealing pub on a wet Tuesday in March 1977 as Leo Sayer's 'When I Need You' played on the jukebox. Henry certainly wasn't. He already had four casual girlfriends on the go. Nonetheless, the two of them started talking and Henry felt a connection that was both strange and new to him. They started dating and, by the end of April, Henry had furtively ditched his other girlfriends. He told David, while they were both working on a challenging U-bend in a third-floor flat in Cricklewood, that Diana was the girl for him.

The couple were married in a registry office the following summer with David as the best man – his short, uneasy speech made no reference to the four abandoned girlfriends, even though David himself was stepping out with one of them at the time. David was proud of his speech's reception. It was the first he had ever given. Diana kindly told him that she couldn't tell.

When David met his future wife, Charmaine, in 1978, Henry and Diana were there to help the relationship flourish during double dates to the cinema and dancehalls. When David and Charmaine married in 1981, Henry reciprocated the best man role with Diana as chief bridesmaid. And when Charmaine died in childbirth in 1986 along with the couple's unborn daughter, Henry and Diana were there to guide their friend through years of pain despite their own growing family. For his part, David revelled in the role of uncle, knowing that he would probably never have a child of his own.

Thelma Morris was born in early 1980 and she was followed two years later by a sister, Althea. Both were, according to other mothers in the west London community, "easy" babies who slept through the night from an early age and even sailed through the "terrible twos" without too many issues. When Justin came along in 1991, he was something of a surprise, but with his huge brown eyes and gentle nature, he won over everyone who came to visit the house in Acton with the bright curtains and the plumber's van occasionally in the driveway when Henry wasn't working to support his young family.

Justin excelled at school and had plans to become an actor. He took drama at A-level and joined a theatre group where he was spotted by an agent who not only suggested he apply for some scholarships at drama colleges but also kindly put in a good word for him at each one. She had seen potential, a spark, something out of the ordinary.

In November 2010, Justin was out celebrating with two of his friends; he had, that day, received a letter offering him a scholarship to one of Britain's most prestigious dramatic arts academies. His friends had already been accepted at universities to study electronic engineering and computer science respectively and so the three of them were naturally in high spirits.

The pub they had intended to visit was full. It often was on a Friday, so the three of them decided to try a place they'd never been to before. It was a short walk away and down a side street so it might, they assumed, be a bit quieter. Sometimes those out of the way places were only frequented by a handful of elderly regulars nursing pints in cosy corners. They could maybe have a couple of drinks before finding somewhere to have a dance.

They were wrong.

On entering the pub, The White Hart, Justin and his friends were welcomed initially by menacing silence from the thirty or so all-male customers and then, almost immediately, by words which chilled them.

'Wrong fucking pub, boys.'

At once, Justin and his friends turned and ran. They weren't alone. Justin was aware of heavy booted footsteps behind him. Four or five of the thugs from the pub were chasing them. He knew he could outrun them – he was fit, after all, and wearing new trainers – but he wasn't sure where he was going. In the confusion, the three friends had run in the opposite direction to the way they'd come. Not back towards the original pub but into a warren of residential streets with semi-detached houses built after the war.

Justin tried to calculate the quickest way to get back to a main road. He could hear a siren in the distance to his left which usually suggested a police car or ambulance speeding towards something so he figured that that direction would be best. Any road to the left should suffice as a cut-through. There was one coming up. The sounds of boots behind him seemed to be fading away. His friends were a few yards ahead of him. 'Left!' he managed to shout but they were already just past the turn. He turned left anyway. They carried on.

Instead of the main road, Justin found himself running down a short crescent that curved to the right. Back to the road he'd just left. He had only run a few metres when his way ahead was blocked by two leather-clad skinheads. Both had drawn knives.

'Wrong pub. Wrong road too,' snarled one. 'Not your evening is it, mate?'

Justin turned to see the other thugs blocking the way back. There were three of them. All skinheads with one wearing a thick blue jacket while the others were in leather. He tried to make a run for it through the group of two but there wasn't enough room between the cars parked both sides of the crescent. He shouted for help but they were already upon him.

'When the police came to the door around midnight,' Diana

explained over tea in their well-maintained suburban garden, 'I think I told you at the time, David, I simply couldn't believe it. Not my baby. Anyone but him. He was so sweet and so harmless and he had so much to look forward to. He would have been a wonderful actor. You met him. You saw him perform.'

David agreed that the young man had been one to watch. He had seen Justin in an amateur production of *As You Like It* where his Touchstone had stolen the show. He had only been seventeen at the time but already his teachers were intimating that the stage might be something he should seriously consider. In fact, as David recalled, even his headmaster had described the performance as "assured", while Justin's drama teacher had preferred the more emotional term, "fucking brilliant".

'Anyway, you know what happened afterwards,' continued Henry quietly. 'The police messed up the original investigation, losing evidence, failing to take witness statements, not checking for fingerprints in the pub. Basic stuff. But eventually, after almost two years of campaigning and media coverage, we managed to bring the five of them to trial and four of them are now in prison for at least the next twenty-five years.'

'A huge success and a testament to your love for your son,' said David.

'Exactly,' agreed Diana. 'Yet one remains free. The man in the blue jacket. Paul Storey. As you'll remember, the jacket was found a few days after the incident. It was burned almost to a crisp on a piece of wasteland near the river but there was just enough blue material left to make out what it was. Sadly, the forensic team at the time couldn't retrieve any DNA apart from Justin's. Drops of his blood were found on the material which apparently came from the top of the sleeve of the jacket which Storey claimed had been stolen from him. Furthermore, at the trial, the other defendants wouldn't say whether or not Storey was with them on that crescent. Likewise, nobody in the pub would identify him, despite the fact that he was a regular. It was as if everyone was afraid of him.

'The jury in 2013 had no choice but to find him not guilty. But he is. I know it. I feel it here.' The mother clutched a fist to her heart. 'And he's still free. He hasn't paid for killing my son.'

David sipped his tea. He had sat with the Morrises many times over the years both in their Acton house and in the one in the Home Counties to which they had moved in 2019. Sometimes these occasions had been filled with joy and laughter; other times they had been days of unimaginable pain, tears, grief, darkness. This conversation felt different. It was increasingly evident to David why that might be.

'I'm reluctant to ask the next question,' he said slowly. 'But why are we talking about this again now?'

Diana leaned forward in her armchair and looked out over her extensive garden. The apple blossom had finished long ago but the climbing roses and philadelphus were filling the borders with midsummer colour. 'A couple of years ago,' she whispered, 'you mentioned in confidence about this organisation to which you belong. The Twelve. You said that the role of the group was to assassinate London criminals and that you yourself had killed four of them. A couple of serial rapists and a drug dealer and I forget the other one.'

David nodded solemnly. He could sense what was coming.

'I wonder,' Diana smiled, squeezing her husband's hand while turning away from the shrubs and looking directly at David with intense and hopeful eyes, 'I wonder whether you might consider getting rid of Paul Storey for us, please. To finally obtain justice for our son.'

3

Thomas turned in his sleep so that he was facing away from Monica and this gave her the opportunity to ease herself slowly out of bed without disturbing him. It was still only six something, but her mind had been fully awake for at least three hours zigzagging through the different possibilities and options regarding who best to monitor Dr Wisby with a degree of urgency. Just in case his expertise was required sooner rather than later.

So far she had always come back to the same answer. The one which presented the largest number of potential problems. She padded barefoot over to the bedroom door and lifted her summer dressing gown from its hook. Then she gently opened the door and crept stealthily down a short corridor and into her open-plan living room. The curtains were open and Monica smiled, blinking, as she saw that the sun was already high and warm, even at this early hour.

She stopped for a moment and stared longingly at her cello in the corner furthest from the window. It hadn't been played in a while but Monica knew that the simple act of pulling the bow across the D-string would help to calm her mind. An entire

Bach suite would be heavenly. It was tempting. It was also too early.

Instead, she fetched a notepad from a side drawer and settled down on her sofa to jot some notes. This sofa always held happy memories. It was the place she had seduced Thomas on Christmas Day, almost six months earlier. She had been unsure what his reaction would be but decided to be daring and, as it turned out, their first kiss had been the start of a blissful and passionate journey which had taken them both by delicious surprise. Whatever she decided about Dr Wisby, it mustn't jeopardise their relationship. Maybe there was another option.

Of the other members of The Twelve, Veronica Madison was too new – the former television presenter had only joined the group a month earlier and hadn't yet been involved in any cases. Monica felt sure that Veronica would agree to helping in any way but her experience told her that it was probably best to wait until there was at least one assassination bit part under her belt. Possibly more than a bit part. The two women could discuss how involved Veronica wanted to be whenever there was a new project on which to work.

Catherine Daniels, an ex-newspaper editor and feature writer, could possibly do it but she was already monitoring two potential Twelve recruits. In fact, everyone else was on double monitoring duties apart from Chris, of course, and Anna who was only observing one, a slightly kooky, purple-haired yoga instructor in her sixties named Corinne Brooks. As well as being a former pathologist, Anna was trained in yoga so it was fairly easy for her to keep an eye on Corinne as she had been attending her classes for three months.

Anna wouldn't be right to monitor Dr Wisby, though. She was too close to Chris. But then so was Thomas. And that was the problem.

The notepad wasn't helping. Monica looked at her working

of the previous ten minutes and saw only problems and crossings out. She heard a noise from the bedroom but it was only momentary so she assumed Thomas had half woken and then gone back to sleep.

There were only two options as Monica saw it. Ask Thomas to do it and carefully explain the reasons but swear him to secrecy, especially when it came to Chris. God knows, if the ex-surgeon found out that he was potentially being replaced, his already troubled mental health could take a turn for the worse.

The alternative was to ask one of the others to take on a third monitoring role. David would be the ideal candidate for that. His two observation subjects were more long-term propositions so he could reasonably shift away from one for a short spell. Hopefully Chris would return to full mental capacity and the whole problem would melt away in a few weeks. Monica crossed her fingers momentarily and made a silent wish.

Besides, there had been no ongoing cases since March so everyone in The Twelve was a bit more relaxed than normal. This was unusual but after the previous challenging case it was something of a relief to have a few months off. Monica looked at the wall clock. It was nearly seven. Time for a coffee. She wandered into the kitchen area and fired up her coffee machine. The underused cello glowered from the corner.

As she stood waiting for her morning pick-me-up, Monica looked out across the city rooftops with a feeling of quiet contentment. If David could pick up the Wisby job, then as long as there wasn't a case for, say, a month or two, then that should give enough time either for Chris to get back into shape or for them to begin to approach the cardiologist. She would never need to involve her lover whom she could hear softly stirring a few metres away. This leading The Twelve business wasn't as tricky as she'd once imagined.

Just as the last drop of espresso plunged into her cup, Monica's phone vibrated. David Latham was calling.

'Good morning, David,' she half-whispered in case Thomas wasn't fully awake. 'You're up early. It looks like it's going to be another hot one.'

'Morning, Monica,' replied the plumber with his customary joviality. 'You're not wrong. It's a good job I fitted air conditioning in my house a couple of years ago. Otherwise I'd be melting at night.'

'I know exactly what you mean.' Monica sipped her espresso. It was still on the hot side. 'I'm actually really glad you called as I was just thinking of you. You know how we haven't got a case on at the moment? I wondered whether we might talk about a bit of extra monitoring for you. A recently retired doctor by the name of...'

'Monica, I'm sorry to interrupt you,' David's tone had noticeably shifted in seriousness, 'but I think we need to talk. I suspect we're about to get quite busy.'

4

Having pulled on his dressing gown, a recent five-month anniversary gift from Monica as he was staying at her place more often than not these days, Thomas Quinn ambled sleepily into the living area. Monica was on the phone which, at this hour, would almost certainly mean something serious. Thomas hoped it didn't concern Chris.

'David,' she mouthed at him from across the room and gave a thumbs up to suggest the plumber wasn't in any sort of trouble. Relieved, Thomas wandered over to the sofa where Monica was sitting and gave her a kiss on the forehead.

'Coffee?' he mouthed back, miming a mug approaching his face. Monica pointed at her now empty espresso cup and nodded, her eyes widening gratefully.

'Okay, David,' she said, concluding the call. 'I'll gather everyone together over the next few days and we'll see what we can do. I think we also need to involve Suzanne at an early stage of this case because you know how funny the Met get when there's a bit of history. And with the Morris case, there's a *lot* of history.' David said that he understood and would let the Morrises know that the Metropolitan Police commissioner,

Suzanne Green, would need to be kept updated. It's possible that she may even be able to help; after an inauspicious start, Suzanne had become a fan of The Twelve, partly because of the sheer efficiency with which they dispatched London's criminals but also because, as people, she genuinely liked them, particularly Monica.

'Thank you, Monica,' replied the plumber. 'I'll await your text.'

Monica slumped back on the sofa and let out a long breath. So much for David taking on another observation job. There was only one remaining option.

'It's Chris's seventieth,' said the option excitedly as the coffee machine trilled its monotone song. 'We should text him. Although probably not quite yet. He might still be asleep. Maybe at eight. What do you think? Eight? Is that too early?'

Thomas's childlike enthusiasm for wishing his friend a happy birthday would have been endearing under normal circumstances but today it simply augmented Monica's sense of impending dread. She turned towards him just as he arrived with two fresh cups of coffee, one espresso and one cappuccino. Her expression was one of love but also of pity for the burden she would soon have to place as delicately as she could upon his shoulders. 'It's going to be hot again,' he said with a mischievous grin, almost puppyish in his sense of excitement about the day. 'How is David this morning? It's early for him. Was it anything important? I'm guessing it was important.'

Monica took her espresso cup and substituted it for the empty one on its saucer on a side table. Thomas was more wired than she was and he hadn't even had any caffeine. 'He has a case for us,' she began, feigning enthusiasm. 'I thought this hiatus would be too good to last. You remember the Justin Morris murder back in 2010?'

Thomas sipped his cappuccino and Monica experienced a

fleeting concern that it might render him completely hyperactive coming on top of his already heightened sense of joie de vivre. 'Oh absolutely. Everyone knows the Justin Morris case. Young kid, talented actor. Lovely family. Friends of David's, I think. Murdered in cold blood by skinhead thugs. Police messed it up and then finally, after a couple of years of relentless campaigning by family and friends, they found the killers and banged them up. That's about it, right?'

'Almost,' said Monica, slightly exhausted. 'Four of the killers are behind bars but the jury didn't convict a fifth man named Paul Storey. There were sources within the police who suspected that he was the ringleader but there wasn't enough evidence to convince the jury. None of the other suspects would point the finger at him and there was no DNA evidence to connect him. A blue jacket belonging to Storey was found a few days after the murder but it had been doused in paraffin and set alight so there was barely any material left. The only part that survived was the top of one sleeve. Forensics found some specks of Justin's blood on the sleeve but, at the time, couldn't identify any other DNA. Storey said he'd had the jacket stolen by a stranger the day of the attack and the jury believed him.'

Thomas thought for a moment. It had been three months since the end of the previous case and since March so much had happened that he had almost forgotten the main role of The Twelve which was to assassinate London's criminals as efficiently and surreptitiously as possible. It was a duty that various permutations of the group had performed with spectacular success since their foundation in 1831 and, before the retirement of Lexington Smith and the arrival of Veronica Madison, Thomas had been the newest recruit to add his expertise and abilities.

There had been a change of leadership with Monica squeezing seemingly effortlessly into Lexington's impressive shoes. In addition, at two Sunday lunches around his sixty-ninth birthday at the beginning of June, Thomas had introduced Monica to his daughter, Emily, and her nine-year-old twin girls, as well as to his son, Simon, who had, in turn, announced his own engagement to a delightful woman named Akiko. She was Japanese and did something clever and highly paid at the London branch of a Japanese bank which Thomas didn't fully understand.

Everyone had loved Monica, especially the twins Flora and Lucy, and Thomas had ended both Sunday lunches with his children basking in the sense of paternal harmony and quiet satisfaction that only comes with age. Now, though, the serious business was about to begin again. 'Back to the day job, then.' He beamed. 'Is it still too early to text Chris?'

Slightly exasperated, Monica decided to distract Thomas in the best way she knew. She took him by the hand, pulled him into the bedroom, slowly removed his dressing gown and dragged him into the shower.

After they were both dressed, and with the time now gone eight, Thomas sat on the edge of the bed, texted his birthday greeting and then stared at his phone impatiently for a reply. Chris's response a couple of minutes later was friendly but subdued and ended with the line, *See you at the joint party on the 30th x.* Monica's seventieth fell on July 12th so the friends had decided back in April, while Chris was convalescing from his injury, that they should host an event together.

Thomas had half hoped that his friend would invite him over for a birthday drink that evening and Monica noticed his slightly wounded look despite a valiant effort to conceal it. She sat beside him on the bed, leaned on his shoulder and kissed him on the cheek, her wet hair dampening the side of his face. 'You know he's in a funny place at the moment,' she reminded him. Thomas nodded, his earlier excitement waning by the minute.

'But he'll pull through it. Just give him time. Besides, you'll see him at the meeting once I've organised it.'

'You're right,' he said, turning to kiss her on the lips. 'It's just difficult at the moment.' The two men had become close over the few short months they had known each other and Thomas felt that the former surgeon was a friend with whom he could share everything, a rarity for men in their senior years.

Monica sighed. Today was clearly not the day to ask her lover about the Wisby monitoring job. In all likelihood, tomorrow wouldn't be the day either. She would have to pick her moment with consummate care.

Luckily, with the start of a new case, at least there would be something else to occupy their minds for a while.

5

Monica texted the group at 10am to ascertain their availability for a meeting about a possible new case. After rejecting the ensuing two days due to various clashes – Graham Best and Owen Pook were going to the cricket; Belinda Olorenshaw had a spa day booked and Veronica was visiting her eighty-nine-year-old mother in Lincolnshire as well as getting her hair coloured from its natural dark blonde to a lighter shade of brown – they decided to meet on the 20th.

Once the date had been settled, Monica called the commissioner to let her know the gist of what had been discussed with David over the previous few days and explained that they had arranged an initial meeting to discuss it. 'I'll be there,' said Suzanne with a surprising sense of urgency. Monica was a little taken aback that the commissioner of the Met could free up time so speedily but Suzanne was emphatic. 'The Morris case is, as I'm sure you can appreciate, Monica, one of extreme importance to the Met. If you're going to get involved, I won't stand in your way, but you'll need help. It's not as straightforward as you might imagine. There are elements of the case that you won't know. Certain details that have never been in the public domain.'

The location for the meeting would be Clarges Mews. It was one of the more central meeting places for The Twelve, tucked away behind an anonymous grey door in a short Mayfair lane. As such, it was convenient for the commissioner and it also allowed Monica to pick up some bits and pieces from Fortnum & Mason – she was craving some of their marmalade and, as Thomas knew well, if Monica had a craving, it wasn't long before that itch needed to be scratched.

Beyond the grey door was a dark corridor of around twenty metres which opened out into a spacious meeting room. The centrepiece of the room was a large oak table, hewn from one giant slice of tree, but there was enough space for a collection of comfortable suede chairs and two-person sofas. As usual with Twelve spaces, the walls were liberally sprinkled with fine art, mostly Dutch as Thomas had found out in the spring, as well as a Constable. He was trying to make out the signature on a particularly dour picture of a dog pining for its dead owner when he became aware of someone behind his right shoulder.

'Landseer,' said Veronica. 'And one of his later ones by the tone of it. He was more cheerful when he was painting stags in the 1850s. This is probably mid-1860s at a guess.' Thomas turned towards the former TV presenter and nodded. 'Sorry to be boring but you don't spend four years on an antiques show without picking up at least some arcane knowledge.' She drew Thomas into a friendly embrace. 'It's my first proper meeting,' she whispered, eyes sparkling. 'I'm nervous and excited at the same time.'

'I'm tempted to start a pub quiz team,' joked Thomas, waving at the commissioner who had recently arrived and was chatting with Monica. 'Looking around this room, I think we have pretty much every subject covered apart from maybe pop music.' His cursory survey of the space, however, made him realise that there were two absentees – Anna and Chris.

'We should probably start.' Monica had raised her voice just enough to be heard above the general chatter. 'I know Chris and Anna aren't here yet but Anna's texted to say she's en route and that we should carry on without them as the commissioner doesn't have all the time in the world. David, would you like to begin? I think it would be helpful to explain your connection to the Morris family and just explain your conversation with them a few days ago.'

The former plumber spent the next twenty minutes concisely running through his friendships with first Henry and then Diana, followed by the events surrounding the murder of Justin Morris as he understood them. The rest of the group sat in silence apart from the occasional chomp of a white chocolate and raspberry cookie which Terry had baked fresh that morning. 'As a result,' David concluded, 'Henry and Diana have politely asked us to assassinate Paul Storey. Any questions or thoughts at this point?'

Suzanne Green raised a hand. 'Why now, David?' she asked. 'I've known the Morrises on and off for many years. They've always been, if not forgiving, certainly understanding of the reasons why the jury didn't convict Storey alongside the others. Has something changed?'

David's head drooped. He began to rub his temples with his fingers as he contemplated how to express what needed to be said. 'Henry has had a health scare,' he said, finally. 'Quite a big one. With his prostate. They think he'll be okay, with treatment, but I suspect that just in case he isn't okay, they want to tie up some loose ends before...' The plumber closed his eyes momentarily to maintain his composure. 'Does that make sense to everyone?'

'It makes perfect sense,' said Suzanne while everyone else in the room nodded and muttered in agreement. 'Please send my best wishes to them both and let me know if I can practically help in any way. On the matter of Justin's murder, nobody would rather see the back of Paul Storey more than me. By most accounts, he was a nasty, vicious little thug from the age of about thirteen and he grew into a nasty, vicious, racist thug by the time he was twenty-one. At this point, I suggest everyone refills their cups, grabs one of Terry's delicious cookies if you've not had one, or takes a toilet break as what I'm about to say may take a while. I'll just text my PA to get my next meeting moved. It's with the Shadow Home Secretary. She won't mind. We generally meet more for gossip than policy anyway.'

Once ex-taxi driver Martin Francis had returned from the bathroom, the commissioner explained in depth how the initial investigation run by a detective inspector named Brian McMullan had lost evidence and taken witness statements which were later found to be false or obtained under duress. McMullan claimed that the stress of the case and the relentless media attention had contributed to the problems so instead of being sacked from the Met, he was suspended while the furore over the failure to arrest any suspects blew over. He was later quietly moved to more of a consultancy role at West Mercia police where, it was felt, he couldn't get into any trouble before taking early retirement a couple of years ago. Monica couldn't help noticing that every time McMullan's name was mentioned, Suzanne Green flinched almost imperceptibly.

In 2012, a new investigation began under a highly rated forty-year-old detective inspector, Ted Black. Black essentially started from scratch, reviewed all the available evidence, discarded everything that was questionable and finally made a breakthrough when one of the other drinkers in the pub that night came forward with new evidence. Ellis Richardson had been part of a skinhead gang in 2010 but, nine months after Justin's murder, and having been helped into a good job in a local warehouse by a West Indian friend of his mother, Richardson had begun to have serious doubts about his friendship group.

At the beginning of 2012, having grown his hair and smartened up a bit, Richardson had confided in his new girlfriend that he had been in The White Hart on the night of the Morris murder and that he had seen four of the men who attacked Justin return to the pub after the attack, their faces speckled in blood. The girlfriend had persuaded him to go to the police.

Under witness protection, Richardson's statement reinvigorated the investigation and, just over a year later, four of the five men were convicted. Richardson's evidence hadn't involved Paul Storey, simply because he claimed he couldn't remember seeing Storey that night. Storey was nonetheless charged and appeared in court because he was known to be a part of this group and failed to provide a decent alibi. There was also the matter of the blue jacket.

'There were definitely five assailants, not four?' asked Graham Best, himself a former police chief inspector.

'Both of Justin's friends gave evidence to say they were chased by five, one in a thick blue jacket which would have stood out, even on a dark night. Of the four who were convicted, none of them owned such a jacket. Further statements from people in the pub who eventually came forward to the new investigation stated that they were never seen in anything but black leather.' Suzanne took a breath and used the opportunity to finish off a biscuit.

'Bloody hell, Terry. I seriously don't know how you...' Her face contorted in an expression of unadulterated joy. 'Anyway, once the new evidence was gathered together, five names were in the frame. A series of dawn raids gathered more evidence including the four leather jackets which, stupidly, the men had kept. Obviously they'd washed them, or at least wiped them down, but forensics were still able to pick up traces of Justin's blood. Often criminals aren't that bright as we know.'

At the word "forensics", both Thomas and Monica looked hopefully towards the door for signs of Anna.

'Storey was cleverer. He must have known not to return to the pub and he also must have known to get rid of as much evidence as possible. Ted Black believes he returned home to his mum, Tiffany, who immediately told him to change clothes and thoroughly shower just in case the police came calling that night. As it transpired, she didn't have to worry because it took almost two weeks for the original botched investigation to get round to the Storey house. She was interviewed under caution three times but always maintained that Paul was home with a fever on the night of the murder. On the night of the murder, someone, probably Paul or Tiffany, then walked down to the river with the clothes – the Storeys don't own a car – covered them in paraffin and set light to them. In the morning when a local resident went to investigate, all that was left was a small piece of blue material.'

Thomas asked how they knew it was Storey's clothing and Suzanne explained that the jacket was quite rare in London at the time. Paul had bought it from a market trader in Notting Hill who, as a prosecution witness, said it was one of a kind. The trader remembered selling it to Paul a couple of weeks before the murder and Paul even kept a photograph of himself wearing it on his bedroom mirror.

'But none of Storey's DNA is on the fragment,' said David. 'Only Justin's blood.'

'Forensics has moved on a bit in the last few years,' said a new voice from the doorway.

Everyone turned suddenly towards the door, Terry letting out a muffled squeak as he had the furthest to twist.

'Maybe I could take a look at it,' said Anna, breathlessly.

6

Slightly dishevelled as if she had been running, Anna tied her wayward hair in a high ponytail and collapsed like a Jenga tower into the nearest chair, a burgundy sofa, next to Terry who was rubbing his neck and grimacing. 'Sorry I'm late,' she gasped, adjusting her legs so that she was sitting on her right foot with her left knee pointing ceilingwards. 'And before anyone asks, Chris is fine but he won't be attending this particular meeting. Monica, perhaps I could have a word afterwards.' Monica nodded and gave a friendly wink. Anna responded with a weak smile and reached for a bottle of still water which Martin quickly passed to her to save the pathologist from disentangling any limbs.

'That would be great,' said Suzanne, returning to Anna's initial question. 'I'll put you in touch with Ted Black as he'll have access to all the paperwork and evidence. In fact, thinking about it, he should probably attend the next meeting if that's acceptable to you all?'

Before the gathering ended, there was one more piece of information which the commissioner felt it was important to share. Two years after the trial, the Storeys had moved house.

Not too far away but to a run-down, detached building overlooking a cemetery in Ealing. In the crowded architecture of west London, the house, set slightly away from its neighbours, was a bit of an anomaly but the investigating team, which was still keeping an eye on the Storeys, assumed that they wanted a bit of privacy without having to leave the area entirely. Ironically, the house's position allowed the team to set up inconspicuous CCTV to monitor the comings and goings from the house twenty-four hours a day. 'For about a year, that just amounted to Tiffany going shopping every couple of days, collecting her benefits and occasionally meeting a friend for coffee at a local café. Paul rarely left home and, when he did, it was just to walk a few metres to the edge of the cemetery where he would look out over the plots for about twenty minutes before returning.

'After about a year,' explained the commissioner, 'he even stopped doing that. The house gets no visitors and Paul hasn't left the place for over five years. You can still see him moving around inside when Tiffany is out but that's it. He's basically a prisoner in his own home. Not that you should feel any sympathy for the racist little shit. Excuse my French.'

Monica's initial thought was that it wasn't going to be the easiest of tasks to assassinate a man who never leaves home, particularly as The Twelve's rules forbade the use of guns or knives. 'We'll need to give a bit of thought to how we're going to do this. Perhaps we all go away and do some research and David, maybe you could please keep the Morrises updated with our progress.' The plumber raised a hand in agreement.

'A quick reminder that there's no yoga while this heatwave continues so let's reconvene in a week if Ted Black is available.' The commissioner promised that she would seek him out as soon as she returned to Scotland Yard, her meeting with the

Shadow Home Secretary having been shifted to the following day.

'A quiet word, if I may.' Graham Best had gently touched Monica on the elbow as the rest of the group tidied away plates and cups into an adjacent kitchen area where Martin had begun the washing up. The former police chief beckoned Monica around the oak table and into a shadowy corner where one of the Vermeers was hung, an austere portrait of a woman sewing at a small table. 'There's something you should know about McMullan,' he whispered. 'I didn't know him well, in fact our paths barely crossed, but pretty much everyone in the force knew that his nickname was The Handyman and not because he was good at DIY. He had a reputation for inappropriate touching. If he were still around today, he'd be drummed out of the force in a heartbeat.'

'Well, let's hope so,' said Monica. 'Do you remember who his preferred targets were, by any chance? Young female colleagues?'

Graham lowered his voice even further. 'And male. Apparently he wasn't fussed. I remember a friend who worked closer to that side of the force expressing surprise when he got given the Morris investigation and it was no surprise to anyone when he fucked it up. Anyway, it might not be relevant but I thought I'd mention it. Let me know how Chris is.' They could both see that Anna was loitering impatiently to grab her moment.

The former police chief ambled off in the direction of the kitchen to see if he could help with the drying up and Monica gave Anna a hug as she looked like she needed one. 'He's okay,' said the pathologist unconvincingly, 'but we had a talk and we think it's probably best that he sits this one out if it's all right with you. The last case took more out of him than he anticipated. Physically, he's pretty much back to fighting fitness but the mental side is taking longer.'

Monica was torn. Her first case as leader of The Twelve looked like being a complex one. Already the group would consist of the untried Veronica as well as Thomas who only had one role in an assassination under his belt. To lose a key member of the team would be a considerable blow, especially as Chris was the expert when it came to lethal injections if such a method were required. Her attention returned to Dr Wisby. Naturally he would be even more of a rookie, assuming he was a good fit in the first place, but it would be better than nothing.

'Don't worry about the drugs side of things,' assured Anna, reading Monica's thoughts. 'I can cover all that. If we decide to go down that route with Storey.'

The drugs are only part of it, thought Monica. It was the fact of having a vital component of the group unavailable and the possible disruption to other members, notably Thomas. 'May I speak frankly?' she asked, straightening to her full height of just over five foot two. 'I'm just thinking medium to long term really. You know as well as anyone that we need someone exceptional on the medical side of things, probably more so on this next case if that meeting is anything to go by. We could delay starting on it to give Chris some time but then what if poor Henry Morris doesn't have time? As well as that consideration, it would look bad in front of Suzanne if we didn't give this our full attention having started the ball rolling.'

'Sorry, "look bad"?' Anna bristled. She wasn't sure where exactly this conversation was going but she was beginning to take a dim view of Monica's tone.

'It's a delicate balancing act with the Met as we know.' Monica was consciously attempting a more conciliatory and empathetic approach. 'At the moment everything's rosy but that could change. I don't want to give any incoming commissioner an excuse to start tinkering in The Twelve's business, or worse.' She touched Anna gently on the arm. The pathologist flinched.

'Monica, we're talking about a man's mental health.' Anna's volume had increased, causing a few heads to turn. 'Please trust me when I say that I will fix him but I need time.'

The former chemist was slightly exasperated. Anna had been a good friend for the four-plus years they had known each other, yet this was not entirely the direction she hoped this conversation would go. 'All I'm saying is that I may – and I stress "may" – need to look at alternative options. That's all.'

Anna took a step forward. The room fell silent and even Martin, hands encased in yellow Marigold gloves, poked his head round from the kitchen.

'I. Will. Fix. Him,' hissed Anna, her face inches from Monica's. The two women glared at each other for a few seconds before Anna grabbed her water bottle and turned towards the door.

'Anna, wait,' implored Monica but the pathologist had speed-walked down the corridor and out into the June heat.

7

Although the day was overcast with high, white cloud, it had remained very warm; somewhere in the high twenties and very humid. 'Are you okay?' asked Thomas as the two of them meandered out of the empty mews towards the bustle of Piccadilly.

'Sure,' Monica replied. Thomas had learned, even in these few short months, that Monica's "sure" in response to the question "are you okay?" generally suggested that she was anything but okay. He also knew that after a silence of around thirty seconds, "sure" would be followed by a sentence which typically began with the words, "the thing is". It was a waiting game.

'The thing is,' said Monica with a sigh as they hit the main thoroughfare and turned left towards Monica's marmalade destiny, 'that she doesn't understand. She thinks it's easy organising everything and staying on top of it all. But it isn't. It's bloody hard. There's so much paperwork and so many things to stay on top of. You understand, don't you, darling?'

On the one hand, Thomas did understand; how could he not when it was obvious how busy Monica had been in the last month, often working well into the evening and at weekends, scribbling notes and muttering under her breath that there was a backlog on the group's annual medicals because only Anna was available to do them. And yet a significant chunk of his thoughts and empathy were with Chris whose previously regular contact with Thomas had dwindled recently. Texts had gone unanswered. Answers, when they came, had been if not unfriendly then certainly more abrupt than usual. Thomas felt as though his friend was withdrawing, not just from him but from everything.

'The best thing to do with Anna is just to leave her for a couple of days.' Monica was now striding purposefully towards her destiny with something to spread on her toast. 'I've known her for over four years now, since she joined The Twelve, and she can be feisty. I'll just let the dust settle until we can get another meeting in. Once we know how DI Black's fixed.'

Thomas was keen to pay Chris a surprise visit but Monica advised caution. 'Besides,' she said as they finally reached Fortnum's, 'I need to ask you something first and it's not going to be easy for either of us but you're simply going to have to trust me. Okay?'

After buying a couple of jars of marmalade and some granola to which Thomas took a fancy because of its high seed content, the two of them walked towards Haymarket, politely declining offers from enthusiastic tourist bus employees, to have coffee at a Danish bakery. Monica was no longer striding but Thomas could tell she was preoccupied, not just with thoughts around the Morris case.

'Naturally,' began Monica as they sat side by side on a grey-blue banquette with cappuccinos and pastries in front of them, 'I want Chris back as much as anyone. He and I have been friends for a long time. He joined about a year before Anna, as I'm sure you know. I'm also fairly certain that he will come back and I'll give him all the support I can to speed up that process, whether it means some more time with Mrs Mendoza or whatever it takes, frankly.' Thomas took a bite of sweet pastry as he could tell Monica was building up to something. 'However, I also need to consider the rest of The Twelve and the next case and the case after that, whatever it may be. We can't really function as just eleven.'

Monica paused to gauge Thomas's mood before opening the bomb bay doors. 'As you know, The Twelve monitors potential recruits constantly, sometimes over a few months and sometimes for much longer. One of us, according to Lexington, has been observed on and off since the early 1960s before being invited to join a few years back.' Thomas raised his eyebrows. Fifty years of covert observation seemed rather excessive but then few things surprised him these days. After all, he'd spent the night with a dead body in a shed on a golf course and had also been seduced on a sofa on Christmas Day, all within the last six months.

'There's a chap named Richard Wisby I'd like you to monitor, please. It doesn't take too much of your time and I'll come with you for the first one; I was watching him myself for a while up until the last case somewhat overwhelmed the diary. All you have to do is make sure he's not into anything that might make his presence in The Twelve challenging. Prostitutes of either sex, gambling, religion, poetry, that sort of thing.'

'Religion?' Thomas repeated, surprised.

Monica took a swig of coffee. 'Probably the worst thing you can be into as far as The Twelve is concerned. Admittedly it hasn't been tried and tested properly since the 1880s but, if you think about it, although the God of the Old Testament killed far more people than The Twelve could ever dream of, most Christians tend, understandably, to lean towards the more benign teachings of the New Testament. Loving one's neighbour, curing the sick, that sort of malarkey. And, as a result, they tend to be put off by the thought of assassination regardless of who happens to be the target.'

'Doesn't Catherine go to church occasionally?' asked Thomas. He felt sure she had mentioned it in passing during one of their casual chats earlier in the year.

Monica swigged the last of her cappuccino. 'Catherine goes to Mass at Christmas and Easter. She also goes to confession after each case because it makes her feel better. She says it cleanses her filthy soul. Beyond that, her beliefs are pretty flimsy, if she's honest, otherwise she wouldn't be able to do the things she does. And by that I'm including her threesomes with Owen and Graham. I don't recall any of the gospels advocating some of the shenanigans that those three get up to in their spare time. "Flee from sexual immorality" said Paul in his first letter to the Corinthians. Most of us run towards it.'

These arguments seemed eminently sensible to Thomas and yet they begged another question. How did Monica justify The Twelve's work with her Hinduism? 'Well, for a start,' she giggled, 'I'm not exactly the most devout Hindu, am I? Do you see any statues of deities dotted around the apartment? You do not. But when I think about the targets of our work, I comfort myself with the thought that, if reincarnation does exist, they'll be reborn as a moth or a slug or something and they'll have to begin the slow and arduous journey back to being human. And hopefully a better human next time around.

'Anyway,' Monica continued, 'back to Doctor Wisby.'

Thomas flinched at the title. '*Doctor* Wisby?'

'Yes,' said Monica, a tone of regret in her voice. 'He's a retired cardiologist. In case we need to replace Chris.'

8

Despite Monica's best intentions to coax Thomas gently towards this moment, it still came as something of a shock. 'Can I think about it?' he asked, slightly dazed and glad he could at least take solace in the remains of his pastry, although even that reminded him of Chris; the former surgeon was renowned for finishing Thomas's sweet treats whenever there were leftovers, and often before Thomas himself realised they were, in fact, left over.

Monica leaned over and kissed him on one cheek while tenderly stroking the other. 'I would love to be able to say yes, Thomas,' she smiled, 'but with this Morris case about to start, there's going to be a degree of urgency to ensure The Twelve gets back to being, well, twelve. We're already eleven for the foreseeable future and, after what's just happened, I can't be certain that we're not in fact ten and a half.

'Naturally, I don't want to change things, especially so soon after Lexington's departure but if it has to be done then... you know...' Thomas leaned forward, his elbows on the table, his hands massaging his temples. 'I know this will be difficult,' said Monica, rubbing his back, 'but it's part of what we do. I had to monitor Belinda, and Graham for that matter. Plus a dozen or so more who never quite made the grade. It may well be that Dr Wisby won't be appropriate anyway but he's worth our urgent attention right now. Okay?'

Thomas nodded, uncertainly. He knew Monica was right and yet admitting that Chris may not be able to continue as part of The Twelve was, he felt, a step that he wasn't quite willing to take. 'I won't like him,' Thomas said quietly. 'This Wisby character. But you can tell me about him anyway.'

'Thank you, darling.' Monica beamed. 'One final thing. It's probably best not to tell Chris. Not quite yet anyway.'

The following day, Monica and Thomas were seated on a bench a few metres up Primrose Hill, casually watching the impressive home of Dr Richard Wisby. Thomas's initial thought was that clearly cardiologists made an enormous amount of money for the good doctor to be able to afford to live in this area. However, Monica explained that most of his fortune had been inherited and that the four-storey townhouse had, in fact, been in the family since between the wars. The doctor's great-grandfather had bought it with money he had made in the Anglo-Persian Oil Company in the 1920s.

According to Monica, the family had continued working in the oil industry and, indeed, two of Dr Wisby's brothers, both younger, were executive directors at BP which is what the Anglo-Persian eventually became. Richard had never expressed any interest in the fossil fuels business and so went into medicine, working his way up to senior cardiologist at the Royal Free before retiring at the age of sixty-two a couple of years previously.

He had been married three times, for progressively fewer

years each time. His third wife, Bryony, a beauty therapist over twenty years his junior, had divorced him after ten months on the grounds of irreconcilable differences. 'He doesn't automatically sound like the ideal candidate for The Twelve,' suggested Thomas with the faintest note of animosity.

Monica sighed. 'Just because a very wealthy heart surgeon struggles in matters of the heart, ironically, that doesn't make him a bad person. Anyway, he lives on his own now. Doesn't have children, so I suspect something wrong with his sperm count but that's no longer relevant. He likes to take walks up the hill which is why we're here. Also, he likes to wander down to the village to have a fry-up at one of the cafés on Saturdays so it's worth doing a bit of observing there – I'll show you the best vantage point. There's a patisserie opposite. The coffee is good and the tartes are exquisite.'

'Where do I go if I need the loo?' asked Thomas. At that moment, the Wisby door opened and the doctor trotted animatedly down four stone steps, waited between two parked cars for a space in the traffic before crossing and entering the park. He was shorter than Thomas with close-cropped grey hair and small, round glasses. Thomas also noticed he was a little out of breath as he passed them, despite only a light jog across the road followed by a brisk walk up a slight incline.

Monica frowned, reading the former sports trainer's thoughts. 'Possibly he just has a cold,' she muttered unconvincingly. 'Anyway, let's follow him at a safe distance.' Thomas's overriding thought was that the doctor should possibly rein in the fry-ups and start doing yoga, something he'd end up doing anyway if he became a member of The Twelve.

Dr Wisby made two increasingly laboured circuits of the park, smiling at acquaintances and once or twice stopping to stroke small dogs belonging to middle-aged women. After his second circuit, he left the park and strolled slowly into the village to visit a bakery where he collected a baguette and a slice of tarte Tatin before returning home. 'What is it with surgeons and sweet treats?' mused Monica. 'Anyway, let me show you where to visit the toilet.'

That evening, Thomas returned to his own house in Colville Square as he was expecting a visit from a gas engineer the following morning. 'Between eight and one they say,' he told Monica, 'so you can bet it'll be about 12.50pm by the time they get to me. Luckily it isn't urgent. Just the annual check.' It was unusual these days for him to spend the evening alone; more often than not, he was at Monica's. Nonetheless, sometimes he needed his own space and Monica understood that. 'Only child syndrome,' she explained. 'Perfectly normal. It's one of the reasons we get on so well.'

He poured himself a whisky, put on a CD of Keith Jarrett that Monica had given him on their four-month anniversary in April, and settled into his comfy armchair. The urge to text Chris was almost overpowering but he managed to resist, knowing that it was probably best to give his friend some space, particularly as Anna would certainly have told him about the tense meeting in Clarges Mews. Besides, if they got into a text conversation, Thomas couldn't be completely confident that he wouldn't blab about this Wisby fellow and that really could cause a problem.

In the morning, the gas engineer arrived at just after 8.30am and then left just before 9, having completed the annual checks. As he wasn't due to meet Monica until lunchtime, Thomas decided to take a walk before the sun got too high.

Letting his feet direct him, Thomas drifted north under the flyover and on towards Harrow Road. As he was heading in the rough direction of the cemetery, he thought he may as well visit the grave of his late wife, Alice. As he stood over the stone, having placed a bunch of hastily bought supermarket flowers on the plot, Thomas remembered that this was the place he'd first got talking to Chris the October before, a few days after joining The Twelve. That conversation had been pivotal in Thomas's understanding of his new role as well as marking the beginning of their friendship. He looked around cautiously, half-hoping that Chris was somehow in the vicinity and half-hoping he wasn't.

There was no sign of the former surgeon, only a couple of gravediggers in the distance off to the left and an elderly lady standing over a stone in the opposite direction. Relieved, Thomas said goodbye to his wife and stepped across the long grass carefully back towards the exit. He was just at the gates when a familiar voice appeared from nowhere, accompanied by its owner. 'Good morning, my dear,' said Chris. 'We simply must stop meeting in graveyards like this. People will talk.'

9

'I'm pretty sure I'll be okay,' said the ex-surgeon, 'but it may take a little time, that's all.' The two of them had settled into a table at the back of the same café where they'd first properly spoken before Christmas. Predictably, Chris was tucking into a sticky bun and Thomas had struggled not to say something about the incongruous connection between doctors and pastries which would have required the hasty acquisition of a spade with which to dig himself out of a Wisby-shaped hole.

On meeting at the cemetery gates, Thomas's first reflex had been to hug his friend as tightly as possible. 'Did you miss me?' enquired the surgeon, revelling in the warmth of the welcome. 'It's only been three weeks.' To Thomas, it had felt like a lifetime.

The owners of the café had nodded at them both in recognition as they arrived a few minutes later and there was a new employee, a young lady with numerous facial piercings who was on table service, a duty she performed with a radiant smile.

Chris had self-diagnosed as having a minor case of PTSD,

clearly brought on by being attacked back in March. 'I'm seeing Mrs Mendoza,' he explained, referring to The Twelve's octogenarian in-house psychotherapist whose house in east London was visited regularly by each member of the group to rebalance their mental health, often after a successful assassination. 'That's helping. She's an incredibly wise and understanding woman and it was her, really, who suggested I take a short break from active service if a case came up. I was reluctant, naturally, because I think what we do is important and generally I have a key role to play; but equally, if I'm not firing on all cylinders, then I might be a liability to the rest of us. And that's not ideal.'

Thomas agreed that a struggling Chris would arguably be worse than no Chris at all. 'I'm glad we bumped into each other, anyway,' he said, withholding a tear. 'I've missed you, especially on your birthday. What a happy accident that we were both at the cemetery.'

Chris sheared off a corner of cinnamon-rich pastry with his fork and chewed it with delight. 'No accident, my friend,' he slurred through his mouthful. 'I followed you from home. At a distance, of course.' Thomas's mind whirred. 'It was just like old times. I told you that Lexington got me to observe you for a few weeks before making the final decision on inviting you to join the group, didn't I? I'm sure I did. Rooting through your bins and everything. Anyway, I was on my way to see you and I was just coming round the corner to your square and I saw you wandering off in the other direction. I thought, either I can shout at him or I can follow him. The mischievous side of me won that battle. You look slightly nonplussed.'

'I... suppose I am, in a way,' stammered Thomas. He wasn't sure he liked being followed without his knowledge but then, as his friend had pointed out, it wasn't the first time.

'Talking of surveillance,' said Chris innocently, 'how's the Wisby observation going?' Thomas's descent into bemusement took a further unexpected dive. Chris wasn't supposed to know that he was watching the retired cardiologist. 'Oh, don't worry,' continued the surgeon amicably, noting Thomas's look of horror. 'I know Monica put you on urgent Wisby-watch in case I can't come back. I'm seventy years old so I'm not some trainee straight out of crazy school. Most of us know the people on the watch list and Monica herself had mentioned old Wisby back at the beginning of the year.' The extravagantly decorated waitress wandered over to assess how the two elderly gentlemen were getting on, noted their half-drunk coffees and retreated to the front of the café where a group of sixth-form students were discussing an impending exam over plates of pancakes.

'I'd assumed that she would be too busy to continue watching him and that you'd almost certainly end up with the delightful job.' Chris polished off his pastry and briefly considered indulging in another. 'It's absolutely fine, though,' he placed a hand on Thomas's forearm reassuringly, 'I'd do exactly the same in Monica's position. In fact, I was monitoring a possible replacement for her a couple of years ago. A biologist named Peg Copeland. She seemed sensible enough until I started reading her tweets and realised she believed in secretive organisations ruling the world. Lexington felt he couldn't risk or justify inviting her into an actual secretive organisation, internationally powerful or not. She might not have been able to resist the temptation to tweet confidential information to her forty-three followers.

'It's all part of the cut and thrust of life in The Twelve. Everyone's replaceable. But,' he slurped the last of his coffee and looked Thomas directly in the eyes, 'rest assured, I will be back in the fold as soon as I'm repaired up here.' He tapped his head and then realised that his finger was still slightly sticky from the cake.

'You gents all finished?' the waitress asked, beaming. At that moment, both Thomas's and Chris's phones pinged, indicating a Twelve-related WhatsApp message. 'Are you work colleagues then?' she asked politely, displaying a tongue piercing in the process.

Chris looked up from his screen and smiled. 'Indeed we are,' he said calmly. 'We're assassins and this text is just letting us know who to bump off next.'

The waitress giggled and started clearing away the crockery. 'Let's hope it's not me, then, eh?' she joked.

Chris diverted his attention back to the text. It was from Monica to the group and it set the time, date and location of the next meeting to be attended additionally by DI Black. 'Oh dear,' he said, sorrowfully. 'I'm afraid it *is* you.' The waitress feigned shock. 'But my friend here will leave a generous tip so at least you can buy yourself something fun before... you know...' He drew a pretend knife across his throat and stuck his tongue out.

'Oh well,' the waitress said with a sigh, arms laden with the table's cups and plates. 'It's been nice knowing you. Brief but nice. Pay at the till, please.'

Thomas thanked the waitress and turned his attention to Monica's text. 'You won't be attending, will you?' he asked.

Chris agreed that he wouldn't but that he'd keep on top of the case via Anna. Furthermore, if Mrs Mendoza felt that he was on an upward trajectory mental-health-wise, he would tentatively start paddling in the shallow waters of the case. 'I'll always be keeping a toe or three in the water. I like David enormously so any friends of his are friends of mine. What's happened to the Morrises over the years has been truly awful.

'Anyway, please let Monica know that I fully intend to return,' he said, looking window-wards at a passing bus. 'I just need to prioritise this for a bit.' He tapped his right temple once again having first licked his finger and dried it on his trouser leg. 'You should still monitor young Wisby, though. It'll keep Monica happy. It's best not to add to her stress. And I'll see you at the birthday party, of course. Can't escape that one, even if I wanted to.'

10

Three days later, just after six in the evening, DI Ted Black was formally introducing himself to each member of The Twelve at a meeting house Thomas had never visited. It was in a residential crescent of terraced houses a short walk from King's Cross station. The inside of the house had, at some point, been knocked through so that the entire ground floor, apart from a small kitchen area, was one large meeting space with the usual variety of eclectic, comfortable armchairs.

In terms of art, the only painting in the downstairs space was a giant canvas mostly consisting of broad brush-strokes of incrementally and subtly changing shades of blue which took up much of one wall and which Veronica reliably informed Thomas was a Rothko although 'not one of the really expensive ones. Probably the low millions if I was to hazard a guess.' Two of the other walls were home to vast bookcases of the sort that might be found in upmarket country hotels. The wooden floors were covered in a thin, patterned rug and, if he listened closely, Thomas could hear the distant rumble of an Underground train several metres under the house. It was most likely the Northern line, although he would need to ask David to be absolutely sure.

This noise, innocuous though it had been for the first sixty-eight years of his life, would now always remind him of his first case and the unfortunate victims travelling on the Underground network.

Ted Black, who had arrived early with the commissioner, was a bright-eyed, smartly dressed man approaching fifty with short blond-ginger hair and a neat moustache. He had clearly been fully briefed by Suzanne as he approached every incoming member of the group with ebullient enthusiasm. 'You must be Belinda,' he excitedly greeted the slightly shy linguist as she closed the front door behind her. 'I've heard so much about you. I hear you're fluent in ten languages. That's most impressive. I'm barely fluent in one!' Belinda blushed, smiled and shook the detective inspector's hand before scurrying towards the safety of Catherine who was loitering nearby. The two women immediately found a quiet corner in which to settle into a whispered conversation.

Owing to the relative lateness of the hour, chosen because both senior police officers had full days of meetings, a couple of bottles of vintage Saint-Émilion had been opened and even Commissioner Green had agreed to a large glass. 'After the day I've had, I don't think even the home secretary would begrudge me this,' she said with a sigh. 'Chin-chin!'

Anna was the last to arrive and shared a polite, slightly frosty nod with Monica before settling into a corner chair in an attempt to separate herself slightly from the group. This didn't prevent Ted Black from bounding over to her to enthuse about her brilliant career in forensic pathology. 'We should get started,' said Monica, sensing that Anna wasn't in the mood for small talk with a stranger. 'I understand that what DI Black has to say may take some time.' Anna breathed a sigh of relief and mouthed a 'thank you' towards Monica who responded with a reconciliatory wink.

Once he got started, Ted Black's outline of the Justin Morris case and subsequent investigations was so thorough that, after ninety minutes, Owen had to ask for a toilet break which quickly turned into a relay up and down the stairs to the bathroom for seven of the assembled group.

As Suzanne had explained previously, the original investigation under DI McMullan had been flawed from the start with inexperienced officers put in charge of key evidence gathering and a series of failures when it came to safeguarding even the evidence which had been accrued. Black had brought along as much of the available paperwork as he could realistically carry; copies of witness statements from both investigations as well as photographs relating to the case.

The detective also outlined the current situation with the Storey family, Paul and his mother, Tiffany. 'They've very much kept themselves to themselves over the last few years, especially in Paul's case. As far as we can see, he hasn't left the house at all unless he has some secret passage under the building which is highly unlikely. We've tried to visit a few times but on each occasion the door has been opened by Tiffany and she's very suspicious, as you can imagine. She usually just says Paul's asleep and that's the end of it.'

'Are you sure he's still alive?' asked Catherine. 'It would save us a job if he wasn't.' Black confirmed that the CCTV facing the house showed that Paul was indeed alive and often could be seen through an upstairs window, moving from his bedroom to the bathroom and back. 'Does he ever venture downstairs?' continued the former journalist. Black said he would have to check. He was currently involved in a number of active cases and, as a result, didn't necessarily have all the details on a case that was essentially dormant.

It was almost nine when he finally wrapped up and asked whether anyone had any further questions. 'How easy would it be for me to do some work on the piece of jacket?' asked Anna from the back of the room. Suzanne explained that obviously this vital piece of evidence needed to stay within Scotland Yard but that she would personally make sure that Anna had access to it as well as a secure room in which to carry out some forensic work. Black would also permit Owen and Graham to have access to the surveillance feed on the Storey house in case they noticed anything which could help towards the next steps for The Twelve.

'It looks like we'll have to assassinate Paul in his home,' said Monica. 'And that will involve getting Tiffany out of it, I would imagine. She's an innocent party so we can't exactly arrange a gas explosion like the Tookey case a few years back.'

'Boom!' recalled Terry under his breath. The locksmith was one of only three people in the room who was involved in that particular case. Along with Monica and Martin, he had arranged for a low-level arms dealer to be killed in a gas explosion at his home in Deptford, something which was only possible because of the distance between the house and its neighbours. Monica had needed to methodically calculate the amount of fuel needed to contain the damage as well as ensure that the immediate residents were away on holiday thanks to their winning a competition which a former member of The Twelve, Norman Stevens, had arranged with a compliant travel company.

Cabbie Martin had been unusually quiet since his toilet break as if something had troubled him. 'Could I take a look at the photographs of Brian McMullan again, please,' he murmured. DI Black sifted through his documents until he found a group of six A4-sized photographs of the retired detective. Martin flicked through them until he found the one he was looking for – a shot of McMullan smoking what looked like a celebratory cigar and surrounded by a group of eight or nine men, some in police uniform – and studied it closely. 'Do you know where this was taken, please?'

He handed the photograph to Black who, in turn, passed it to the commissioner. 'It looks like one of our meeting rooms at the old Scotland Yard building in St James's,' she suggested. 'By the looks of it, this would be around the time McMullan was transferred so perhaps it's his leaving drinks. Is there any particular reason why it interests you, Martin?'

The retired taxi driver looked thoughtful. 'Probably nothing,' he said. 'Just a face in the background that looks familiar. I can't place it at the moment but I'll give it some thought and let you know if it's relevant.'

'Any final questions?' asked Black. 'Otherwise I'll love you and leave you and hope that we all meet again soon.'

'Just one,' said Anna, deep in thought after what she'd heard. 'Do you personally believe one hundred per cent that Paul Storey was involved in the murder of Justin Morris?'

'I do,' replied the detective inspector. 'For some reason there's been a wall of silence around his involvement but he has as much motive as the men in prison and just because he had a better lawyer in court, it doesn't mean he should be allowed to get away with it. If you, Anna, or anyone else can find some new evidence then that's great but, in my mind, he deserves whatever fate you guys have in store for him. And I hope it's painful.'

'What about you, Suzanne?'

The commissioner leaned forward, enjoying the residual warmth of a second glass of wine and hoping that there wouldn't be an urgent call from the Home Office any time soon. 'Ninety-nine per cent,' she said. 'There's always that nagging doubt that there's more to this than any of us have uncovered, especially with the involvement of that,' she paused, as if finding her next words distasteful, 'man, McMullan.'

11

After DI Black and the commissioner had left, the detective inspector displaying the same desire to individually thank all eleven members of the group just as he had on greeting them much earlier in the evening, Monica asked everyone else to please stay behind for a few moments. 'At the risk of making this into an OAP version of *Twelve Angry Men*,' she said, 'please raise your hand if you're one hundred per cent certain that Paul Storey is guilty.'

Under the rug, the floorboards vibrated almost imperceptibly as, deep below, a Morden-bound train trundled east before veering south below the river towards its terminus. A discreet smile spread across Monica's face as no hands were raised. 'As I thought,' she said quietly. 'Not even you, David. You who knew Justin well.'

The plumber stretched his arms over his head and groaned. 'I would love to be able to say I'm one hundred per cent sure but,' he paused, 'from what I've just heard, it's a puzzle with too many missing pieces and I would feel extremely uncomfortable killing potentially an innocent man.' Martin observed that it was the quickest version of *Twelve Angry Men* that he'd ever experienced, as well as, thankfully, the most feminine.

'We have two tasks then,' said Monica. 'We begin planning for the death of Paul Storey while, at the same time, exploring reasons not to do so. It's unorthodox for The Twelve, I appreciate, but it looks like we have no choice.' She asked David, Terry and Graham to research the best way to kill Storey making sure that nobody else came to any harm and then turned to Anna. 'You mentioned there were advances in forensics which might prove useful in this case.' The former pathologist nodded. 'The jacket may be our best hope of helping Paul Storey. We'll await your news.' Anna assured the group that she would make an appointment to work on the jacket fragment first thing in the morning.

'One more thing, Anna,' continued Monica, cautiously. 'How is he?'

Anna's response was quiet and measured. 'He's better. He's seeing Mrs Mendoza regularly and that's helping. I'll keep him updated on the basics of this case. He's even talking about maybe getting involved later on, if the case is still going. We'll take one day at a time, if that's okay. He understands about the renewed interest in Dr Wisby but he very much hopes that option won't be necessary.'

Monica eased her way to the back of the room and hugged Anna warmly. 'We all hope he recovers soon,' she said, 'and if there's anything more that I can personally do, he just has to ask. Now, is there anything else anyone needs to say before we go our separate ways?' Terry had already started filling the dishwasher with glasses and gathering the empty wine bottles for recycling.

'There was a face in that photograph that I'm sure I recognise,' said Martin, yawning ostentatiously. 'I can't place it at the moment but it'll come to me. I'll let you know.'

As the formality of the meeting crumbled, both Belinda and Catherine asked if they could speak to Monica privately, by which they meant without the men. Anna joined the small group as they assembled in one of the upstairs bedrooms, decorated in blue to perhaps reflect the painting below. Catherine spoke first and explained that she had been working as deputy editor on a Sunday newspaper at the time of the Morris murder. Although she hadn't been directly involved, she recalled attending a number of meetings with the crime desk, none of whom were convinced that Paul Storey was guilty. The newspaper had offered the Storeys a six-figure sum for an exclusive interview "telling their side" and "putting the rumours to bed once and for all". The offer had always been refused with Tiffany even saying on one occasion that they were "all right for money". 'The main crime editor is dead now but I could track down the junior reporter to see if she can remember anything more.'

Belinda's ask was a more personal one. Her husband, Malcolm, had been deteriorating rapidly and she simply wanted to alert Monica to the fact that she too may need to spend less time on the case depending on what happened. Malcolm, living with dementia, was being well looked after and yet the senior staff at the hospice in Windsor had been clear that Belinda may need to be available at very short notice. 'If Chris were well enough,' she said, tearfully, 'I'd ask him to help speed things up but I don't want to add to his load.' Anna gave her a hug and said that she was sure Chris would understand and that she would speak with him when it seemed most convenient. The hug expanded into one of the group variety and Monica rubbed Anna's back to show that any tension following the Clarges Mews meeting was behind them.

'If it's all right with you,' she said, her arm around Anna's waist, 'I'll still ask Thomas to monitor Dr Wisby. I completely trust you when you say that Chris is on the mend but I think it's good for Thomas to get a bit of monitoring experience, even if it's ultimately going to be unnecessary at the moment. Now I think of it, it's probably the ideal way to get into the monitoring. Without too much pressure.'

Despite it being past 9.30pm when Monica and Thomas finally left the crescent house, it was still light and the King's Cross area was busy with commuters and travellers. Thomas suggested a quick drink at the St Pancras Hotel bar, a place they had visited often before Christmas when the two of them were on surveillance in the early stages of the previous case. 'We should stay here sometime.' Monica smiled. 'It feels almost like a home from home considering the amount of time we spent here. Plus it looks classy.'

Thomas rolled an ice cube around his glass. 'Why don't we stay here tonight?' He grinned. 'You've been working so hard these last few weeks. Maybe you deserve a treat.'

'I don't have any of my stuff,' said Monica, half quizzical and half intrigued. This impetuousness and spontaneity wasn't like Thomas at all. 'Toothbrush and toothpaste and all that.' Thomas pointed out that there were plenty of twenty-four-hour shops in the area that could cater for most of their overnight needs. 'I doubt they'll have any rooms at this time of year,' returned Monica, unconvincingly trying to present obstacles to Thomas's idea.

'Wait here,' he said, and scampered off in the direction of the hotel reception. He returned a few minutes later with a cheeky look on his face. 'They have rooms,' he said, beaming. 'Suites in fact. Shall we? My treat. Consider it an early seventieth birthday gift.'

Monica purred, 'I suppose a treat might not be such a bad idea. I don't have anything to wear in bed but then again I have the distinct feeling that I wouldn't be needing anything anyway.'

———

The following morning, as Thomas and Monica were still half asleep in each other's arms, Chris was climbing the stairs to Mrs Mendoza's second-floor consulting room in her ramshackle terraced house just off Brick Lane in the east of the City. The first-floor landing, he noticed, had a new acquisition; a stuffed squirrel in a perspex box. Mrs Mendoza had a fondness for the creatures so clearly this was something she had seen in an antiques shop and to which she had taken a shine. Chris thought the elderly psychiatrist must be the easiest person in the world to buy gifts for. Anything relating in some way to the furry-tailed animals would delight her.

'I must say, dear,' said Mrs Mendoza as she poured from her teapot which was white with, predictably, tiny squirrels dotted all over it, 'that I'm rather enjoying the current frequency of our visits. Usually it's every few months, apart from Terry of course, who pops in for tea and biscuit deliveries every fortnight or so. With you, at the moment, it's every couple of days. I appreciate that it isn't under the jolliest of circumstances but nonetheless.' She reached for a milk jug. 'It's just a dash for you, isn't it, dear? You don't like it too anaemic.'

Chris watched as the octogenarian dribbled the tiniest amount of milk into his tea turning it the colour of wet sand at twilight. 'And how are you feeling today? Any change with these dreams you've been having?'

The former surgeon slumped back in his chair. 'The dreams are better,' he said. 'Yesterday night I slept all the way through.

'However,' he looked out of the window into a now familiar

cloudless sky, 'there's a new problem. I'm starting to distrust my friends.'

12

Mrs Mendoza sipped her tea which, with the addition of triple the quantity of milk that Chris found acceptable, was already a drinkable temperature. 'Traumatic stress can be a terrible thing,' she comforted, 'and it can affect people in many different ways. I wonder, before we delve deeper, whether I may tell you a story? It may help.'

The surgeon nodded silently. He felt strangely tearful. 'Perhaps a cookie while I tell it,' said Mrs Mendoza kindly, sensing a need to distract him with food. She reached uneasily under her chair and retrieved a small, rectangular Tupperware box containing delicious-looking brown biscuits in the shape of squirrels. 'They're chocolate fudge,' she said proudly. 'Terry brought them round fresh out of the oven a couple of days ago. They were lovely and gooey at first but they've calcified somewhat with the passage of time. Much like myself. Still yummy though.'

Chris reached into the box, pulled out a cookie and bit its head off. Mrs Mendoza raised a quizzical eyebrow which further deepened the lattice of lines across her forehead but decided it would be wisest not to comment.

'Many years ago,' she began, 'there was a young man in his mid-sixties, so, not much younger than you are,' Chris smiled, bashfully, 'and he found himself in something of a terrible state. He had joined The Twelve aged sixty-three and the leader at the time, a somewhat forthright lady named Wilmot, had great hopes for him. However, he arrived with rather a lot of baggage.

'We are of that survivor generation whose mantra is "don't make a fuss". As children we survived the war and its aftermath. We were taught not to get emotional about things. This young man was very much cast from that mould. Like many of his – our – time, he was caned at school and told to deal with it like a man. Fragility was unacceptable.

'It was his second case for The Twelve and the job was to get rid of a drug dealer. Not one of the big players, you understand, but one of those middle management types who seem to have become more and more prevalent over the last couple of decades. The ones who get a little bit of power and think they're kings of the world, a characteristic not merely confined to middle managers in the illegal narcotics business as I'm sure you know.' Chris gave a momentary chuckle, remembering examples from his own career in the National Health Service.

'Maybe he was indeed king of his own small world, which comprised one inelegant block of an estate in Peckham. Either way, he had been responsible for tempting dozens of the estate's young people into heroin addiction and, as such, if he were a king, Darren Lake was certainly a malign one deserving of regicide.

'Anyway, to curtail what could become a depressingly lengthy story, a plan was devised to lure the miscreant Lake to a disused building on some wasteland in Dulwich. The land had recently been bought by developers so it was in the process of being cleared for new housing. Do please take another cookie to behead at your leisure, dear.'

Chris reached forward into the Tupperware box and decided to nibble this second cookie by the toes first. Mrs Mendoza used the opportunity to drain her teacup and pour herself another. Faint smells of spices cooking began to circulate indicating that the Bengali restaurant next door was starting to prepare for their lunch service. Mrs Mendoza lit an incense stick in an olfactory counter-attack.

'Once in the building, an old garage with bars on the window, three members of The Twelve overpowered Lake and injected him with enough lorazepam to knock him out for a couple of hours. Once sedated, they set fire to the garage, locked the door and retreated to a safe distance. However, they were only a few metres away when the younger member of the group heard screaming. They turned back to see Lake's hands frantically clawing at the bars on the window.' Chris stared at Mrs Mendoza, wide-eyed, his half-eaten cookie momentarily forgotten. One of the more recent unwritten rules of The Twelve, instigated during the 1970s, was that regardless of their crimes, the group's targets should not have to suffer unnecessarily.

'There wasn't a doctor in The Twelve at the time so clearly a mistake had been made with the dosage. It was too late to save Lake – and it would have been difficult to explain if he had somehow managed to stay alive. The other two members of The Twelve that night simply dismissed it as merely unfortunate. Lake was dead and the manner of his death was immaterial. However, the subject of our tale could not dismiss what had happened so easily. He began to be tormented both when he was asleep and when he was awake. He would see faces melting before him as if his mind had been taken over by some powerful psychotropic substance. He considered leaving The Twelve after only two cases.

'After two weeks of anguish, he decided to talk to someone. He chose the two members of The Twelve to whom he felt closest; a man and a woman, Christina and Basil. Basil was a former army man who went on to open a small bookshop in his later years. Both had welcomed him warmly into the group just a few months before and, although they were perhaps not yet friends, certainly he felt he could trust them.

'The three of them met for drinks, not far from here in fact, in Shoreditch, and the very fact of being able to share the burden began to ease it. They started meeting every few days and soon all feelings of leaving The Twelve were forgotten. He began to laugh again. In time, the terrible images which had plagued his thoughts began to diminish and eventually disappear completely. Ultimately, that man went on to become one of the most celebrated and long-lasting members of The Twelve that we have ever had.'

'Lexington,' breathed Chris with a sense of astonishment.

'Exactly,' replied Mrs Mendoza, smiling. 'He trusted his friends and now I am trusting you with this story. He won't mind me telling you but it must go no further.' Chris nodded that he understood. 'You must now trust your friends to help you through the next crucial stage of your recovery. It may take a little time or you may already be nearing a return to normal. All that can be certain is that they will always be there for you, whether you believe it or not.'

Chris popped the remains of the cookie squirrel into his mouth and swallowed loudly. He was feeling unusually emotional but in a more positive way than he had felt in a long time. 'What happened to Basil and Christina?'

Mrs Mendoza lowered her eyes. For a long time, she didn't speak and Chris was afraid he had somehow offended her. 'Basil died in 2014 after a short illness. He had been replaced a couple of years earlier by Owen, in case you're interested.' She raised her face to the window and lost herself in the cloudless sky. Chris noticed that Mrs Mendoza's eyes were brimming with tears. 'I loved him more than I've ever loved anyone before,' she whispered.

Chris's eyes widened in sudden realisation. 'Christina,' he said quietly, and knelt to hug the old lady as gently as he could.

'Another of my secrets which I must ask you to please keep,' said Mrs Mendoza, her feeble frame embracing him in response.

13

Owen frowned as the figure moved unsteadily from the upstairs bedroom to the bathroom. The former surveillance officer had asked whether it would be possible to install infra-red technology into the cameras observing the house inhabited by Paul and Tiffany Storey. As a result, he could track their every movement as opposed to just when they walked past a window or, in the case of Tiffany, on the sporadic occasions she left the building. Moreover, he could do it from a laptop.

During his first eight-hour shift – he'd decided to share the duty with Graham and the two of them could alternate the surveillance distantly from their house in Finsbury Park – Paul Storey had moved only once. This might be normal behaviour at night but not between midday and early evening. Graham had reported a similar lack of activity. Now, at just before 9am, Paul appeared to be making his solitary journey of the morning.

Tiffany, by comparison, was in a state of almost perpetual motion, navigating the stairs over twenty times a day, constantly moving between rooms including Paul's where their interactions always appeared brief and formal as opposed to maternal. She would bring her son food on what looked like a tray twice a day and then remove the tray around an hour later, sometimes with what appeared to be a momentary conversation but often with no more than a glance. The two never touched. To Owen, the relationship seemed more like prisoner and jailer than son and mother.

'Anything unusual?' asked Graham, shuffling closer in the bed and planting a kiss on Owen's temple. 'Oh, look, he's on the toilet. How delightful.' The brightly coloured thermal image of Paul could be seen sitting patiently for about ten minutes before rising to his feet, cleaning himself and then returning to his room. 'Dirty little bastard didn't wash his hands.' Graham made a face of disgust. 'And clearly he needs to eat more fruit and veg.'

'There's something really not right about that house,' said Owen, placing the laptop carefully on the floor and then turning to cuddle his partner. 'I suspect the only way we're going to find out what's going on would be to get inside. Whether that means we have to find a way to get in while the inhabitants are unconscious somehow, I'm not sure at this point. I doubt we can simply knock on the door and ask to pop in for a brew.'

Since becoming lovers and moving in together a few years earlier, it was not uncommon for Graham and Owen to discuss Twelve cases in bed. Owen often commented to other members of the group that the proximity of another warm body tended to get his investigative brain functioning better. The fact that the two of them occasionally shared their bed with Catherine Daniels as well, presumably meant that, on certain days and nights, Owen's deductive abilities could be elevated to even greater heights.

He had already figured out that perhaps the best way to assassinate Paul, if that's what was required, would be to pump carbon monoxide through an air vent. Owen felt sure that David's plumbing skills would come to the fore during the planning and that if the poisoning were done at night then Tiffany, whose room was on the other side of the house, could be largely unaffected. So long as a doctor was on standby with oxygen, the plan might work.

'In the same way,' said Owen, gently caressing Graham's grey hair, 'if we simply wanted to make them unconscious so we can get in, I'm sure Monica could get some nitrous oxide or something. We pump that into the house and wait for them to pass out and then we go in. I'm not the expert, of course. It's just ideas.'

Graham leaned in for a kiss. 'And what then, clever clogs?'

Owen admitted that he hadn't got that far yet but that he would work on it. 'Perhaps some closer contact would help fire my synapses,' he said innocently while at the same time moving his hand down Graham's back until it was nestled inside the elastic of his partner's pyjama bottoms squeezing a buttock.

An hour later and across the north of the city, Thomas was just arriving in Primrose Hill for his own morning of surveillance. Monica had told him that she needed to spend the day getting her hair cut and nails done in advance of the evening's joint birthday party so he may as well use the time wisely.

The day was hot, as it had been for three weeks, but the air seemed more humid now and there was a threat of thunderstorms later in the day so Thomas had decided to observe the Wisby house between ten and three in the afternoon before heading home. He'd brought a hat for shade and a book to pass the time and also made himself a chicken sandwich in case he got peckish. Finding an empty bench suitably placed to watch the house, Thomas settled down amidst the passing joggers and dog walkers and began to read, keeping half an eye on the house for signs of the ex-cardiologist.

Around eleven, a woman whom Thomas estimated looked about forty years old walked up the stone steps to the Wisby house and let herself in. She was carrying a medium-sized bag from the top of which protruded the nozzles of plastic bottles of various colours. *Cleaner*, thought Thomas and returned to his book, first making a mental note to tell Monica that Dr Wisby was the sort of man to employ domestic help.

Half an hour later, Thomas's chapter was distracted by the arrival of an ambulance outside the doctor's house. He watched as the cleaning lady, apparently in a state of distress, opened the door to the two paramedics and pointed toward the back of the house. Twenty minutes later, the paramedics returned to their ambulance and carried an empty stretcher into the house. Ten minutes after that, they returned the stretcher, still unoccupied, back to the ambulance and drove off leaving the cleaning lady weeping softly on the doorstep.

Thomas breathed a sigh of relief. Clearly it wasn't serious as Dr Wisby hadn't needed to go to hospital. He went back to his book, only to be disturbed again when a police car turned up just before midday quickly followed by a silver Mercedes van with blacked-out windows from which two men emerged with their own stretcher. At around 12.30pm, the two policemen left the house followed almost immediately by the Mercedes men who were carrying a body bag on their stretcher.

'Poor Dr Wisby,' Thomas whispered to himself and removed his hat as a mark of respect as the occupied stretcher was placed into the back of the Mercedes before being driven away. *He was younger than me*, thought the former sports coach as the silver van disappeared out of sight. 'Although his diet left a lot to be desired.'

Then a second, arguably more terrifying thought entered his head. Monica would not be happy.

14

'How was Dr Wisby?' asked Monica as the two of them were getting ready for the evening celebrations. Thomas had taken a matter of minutes to change into a pair of smart jeans and a thin, light-blue cotton shirt and was now waiting patiently while Monica finished her make-up.

He had decided to withhold the bad news until after the party in case it affected his lover's enjoyment of the festivities. You're only seventy once, he argued to himself. Best not tarnish the occasion with news of unfortunate events. 'Oh, you know,' he muttered casually. 'Quiet.'

'Did you actually see him?'

Thomas attempted to think of a way not to lie exactly but also to shut down this line of questioning as swiftly as possible. 'Briefly,' he said. 'But he was getting a lift somewhere so...' He allowed the sentence to evaporate into the air which was now thick with palpable pre-storm energy. The heat of the previous weeks was now breaking down and dark thunder clouds had replaced the blue sky of earlier in the day.

'Hmm,' said Monica nonchalantly as she applied her

lipstick. 'I wonder where. Never mind. Our car will be here in a minute. I'll just spend a penny and we can be on our way.'

The party location was La Stella, the Italian restaurant where Thomas had first met Lexington some nine months before and where he had been introduced into the secretive but extraordinary world of The Twelve. Although he hadn't been back to La Stella since that autumn afternoon, the owner, Simone, greeted him like an old friend with kisses and a warm embrace. He held out both hands in front of himself in admiration of Monica, then leaned back to look her up and down and then embraced her too. 'I cannot believe that you are old enough to be in this crazy group of people,' he said, half-feigning amazement. 'They are too ancient for you, Señora Monica. You should be hanging with the youngsters like me. We go to a nightclub later and dance all night. Si?'

Monica blushed and took Thomas's arm. 'Simone, we'd better be careful,' she winked, 'my boyfriend's watching.' Now it was the turn of Thomas's cheeks to redden.

Simone had moved all of the restaurant's tables to the side of the room so that the guests could mingle while food was made available to them during the evening. The place was already comfortably full with various members of The Twelve and Commissioner Green as well as a number of people Thomas didn't recognise but assumed they were old friends of Chris and Monica from their non-Twelve lives. He could see neither Chris nor Anna, nor Lexington for that matter, but he imagined they were all on their way.

Just then, the restaurant door opened and Lexington arrived accompanied by a dramatic flash of lightning followed almost immediately by an angry growl of thunder. The octogenarian, now walking with a cane and seeming to have aged more rapidly in the months since retirement, jumped slightly at the sudden noise then, looking around, realised that everyone had turned in shock and were now applauding his spectacular entrance. 'I suppose I couldn't have timed that much better,' he announced, rebalancing, before being engulfed by Simone as cherry-plump drops of rain began exploding violently onto the pavement outside.

Simone wedged the door open so that slightly cooler air could eventually move in. This also allowed those nearest the door to watch as the drops turned to a deluge and soon the gutters outside were flowing with water and small bits of refuse. 'It's about time,' said David, joining Thomas and handing him a glass of red wine. 'This humidity has been a challenge, even for me.'

Thomas enquired whether the plumber had been to see the Morrises lately and David explained that he was keeping them updated with the situation regarding Paul Storey but that he didn't want to mention quite yet that there may be doubts about his guilt. 'I'd rather go to them with something concrete rather than just guesswork. I know that Owen has been observing their movements inside the house and he also has some ideas about how to get to Paul if we need to. I've been over there to have a look myself and in terms of pipework into the house, there are a few options. I've analysed the structural survey from when the Storeys bought the place. I doubt they've done any major work on the internal plumbing so we should be in a decent position when the time comes.'

Another lightning flash seemed to intensify the rain even more and Thomas worried that the gutter might overflow into the restaurant. He looked over towards Monica who was chatting away to a couple of women he didn't know. A friendly pat on the shoulder alerted him to Lexington's presence. 'Oscar Wilde once said,' he began, '"never commit murder. A gentleman should never do anything he cannot talk about at dinner". Unless of course one is in the exquisite company of assassins. How are you both?'

Thomas was still slightly distracted by the lack of either Anna or Chris but he shuffled it to the back of his mind while he and David gave Lexington an update on their lives and, naturally, the Morris case. 'And how's Monica getting on with being in charge? I've tried to be as hands off as possible just to give her a chance to find her feet if you'll excuse the mixed extremities.'

'She's okay,' said Thomas as convincingly as he could. 'If I'm honest, I think she's been fairly surprised by the amount of admin.'

The older man smiled knowingly. 'I suspect it may be time to reveal a secret,' he said. 'Because I may have a trick or two to assist with the mundane elements of the role. It's important that the leader focuses as much of her attention as possible on each case in hand. Speaking of which, may I enquire what the next step might be with regards to this nasty Morris business? Oh, good evening, Suzanne. You smell divine as usual.' The commissioner had wandered over and kissed them all on the cheek. Thomas felt he would almost certainly never be able to get used to being kissed by the commissioner of the Metropolitan Police.

'Anna's going into the office later this week to spend some time with DI Black and the piece of burned jacket,' she revealed. 'Hopefully together they'll be able to make some headway and then I expect there will be another of our delightful gatherings to figure out what happens next. Incidentally,' she said, undertaking a quick survey of the room, 'Anna's late. And Chris for that matter.'

At that moment, Monica dashed past with her phone to her ear. 'Wait a second,' she was shouting. 'I'm just going outside where it's quieter.' *And wetter*, thought Thomas. He grabbed an umbrella from the stand by the restaurant door and hurried after her, just managing to open the shelter in time before another downpour. 'He's what? Where? Okay, we're on our way. I'll bring Suzanne.'

'Everything all right?' asked Thomas, sensing from Monica's anguished face that it almost certainly wasn't.

'It's Chris.' She sighed in exasperation. 'He's been arrested.'

15

'I'm wracking my brains but I'm not sure I've even seen a desk sergeant look quite so terrified,' said Suzanne Green a couple of hours later as she huddled with Monica, Thomas, Anna and Chris in a corner of La Stella having rescued the latter two from Bethnal Green police station. 'Although, to be fair to him, it's not every day the boss comes and drags a dangerous criminal out of custody.'

'And not merely his immediate boss,' added Thomas. 'But *the* boss.'

Following Anna's phone call, Monica had grabbed Martin, whose cab was parked in a bay round the corner from the restaurant, and she, Thomas and the commissioner had weaved across London through driving rain and hail to the East End where Chris was incarcerated on a charge of obstructing a police officer.

He had been to visit Dimo, the young Bulgarian whose basic knowledge of martial arts Chris had been taught prior to the conclusion of the last case in the early spring. One of the deflection moves Dimo had passed on had almost certainly saved Chris's life and the retired doctor had stayed in touch with the young man, helping him with job applications and references.

Partly thanks to Chris, the Bulgarian now had a sales job with a stationery business in east London and was progressing well. After a quick coffee at a Turkish place in Hackney, Dimo had offered Chris a lift back to Anna's in his company car so he could get ready for the evening's party. The two of them were just passing Dalston Junction station when they were pulled over by a police van under suspicion of "driving without a licence". After Dimo had produced his licence, the officer told Dimo that he "didn't look the sort to be driving such a nice car" and it was at this point that Chris intervened and was arrested.

'I was perfectly polite,' he pleaded unconvincingly, nursing a restorative glass of Chianti, 'but I wasn't going to have a young man who is doing a great job putting his life back together, treated in such a way. He's not a criminal, after all. He *was* a criminal, admittedly, but that's not the point. The police officer was out of order and I gave him a piece of my mind. Actually, come to think of it, I may have used a few less polite words as things got a bit heated.'

'The police officer in question will be spoken to,' said the commissioner wearily. 'I might request his presence in person at Scotland Yard purely to put the fear of God into him. And naturally no charges will be brought against either you or Dimo. Just try not to make a habit of this, though, please.' She gave Chris a friendly squeeze and wandered off to talk to Graham and Owen who were loitering under a black-and-white photograph of Alan Rickman, one of many portraits of famous La Stella patrons dotted throughout the restaurant's dining room.

'You gave us a scare,' said Monica. Chris apologised but admitted that, in a weird way, the whole experience was quite exhilarating. During his discussion with Mrs Mendoza, she had suggested that his trauma may have the additional consequence of making him a bit more reckless, if only temporarily. Being in a cell, albeit only for a matter of hours, had been quite the adrenaline boost.

'It'll be interesting to see if I have any bad dreams tonight,' he pondered. 'Anyway, I'd better mingle. There are people here I haven't seen since before Christmas because of everything we've been doing. I won't mention the arrest. I'll just blame Anna for taking too long getting ready.' The ex-pathologist wrinkled her nose and gave him a gentle shoulder push.

Once Chris had wandered out of earshot, Monica took the opportunity to quiz Anna on the state of his mental health. 'He's definitely been improving,' she explained, sounding relieved. 'The dreams are less frequent and his quality of sleep seems better too. The visits to Mrs Mendoza have been transformational, in fact, a couple of days ago he came back from seeing her with a real spring in his step. He wouldn't say why.' Thomas silently echoed Anna's sense of relief. Maybe they wouldn't need to discuss the now redundant Wisby option after all.

'Everything okay?' asked Lexington, joining them after a lengthy discussion about opera with Simone. 'I didn't get the chance to wish you a happy forthcoming milestone birthday before you had to dash off. I've heard all about the prison break excitement so you don't need to fill me in on that front.'

Monica embraced the old man tightly as if he were a human lifebuoy and she was far from shore. 'I think it's going all right so far,' she faltered, 'although there's so much bloody paperwork. All the properties and the art and the finances. Plus I'm being plagued by a couple of estate agents who simply won't understand that I'm not in a position to sell anywhere despite them apparently having buyers without chains queuing up to purchase. I honestly don't know how you did it on your own for so long. It's exhausting.'

Lexington smiled mischievously and looked towards the door. 'The rain is abating,' he mused. 'Anyway, I think it's about time I introduced you to someone. You may think this was a little cruel on my part but, put simply, I didn't do it all by myself. I had help. Are you by chance at home tomorrow, Monica? Shaking off the after-effects of this evening, perhaps?' The ex-chemistry professor confirmed that she would be. 'At twelve noon on the dot, you will receive a visit from Bobby City and your life will be transformed.'

'Bobby City?' Monica had never heard this name before. 'Who or what is Bobby City?'

'I must say no more,' said Lexington mysteriously. 'But you will thank me. Bobby City. Your place. Noon tomorrow. Bobby is never late.'

16

The following day at noon precisely, and with Monica's and Thomas's mild hangovers still chipping away at various parts of their heads, the door buzzer in St John's Wood rang. 'That'll be him,' said Thomas, aware that the sound of the buzzer had slightly invigorated the hangover pixies going about their evil work. 'Hello?' he mumbled into the intercom.

A rasping female voice with perfect received pronunciation which would have made even Veronica proud, barked back and caught Thomas by surprise. 'Bobby City to see Monica Lodhia.' Thomas pressed the entry button as an unexpected shiver of fear made its way uncomfortably down his spine.

'Is that him?' asked Monica, emerging from the bedroom. She had earlier lit an expensive candle which Thomas had bought after his recent Wisby experience, hoping it would in some way distract Monica from his failure to communicate the cardiologist's fate. As a result, the apartment smelled of peonies, one of Monica's favourite scents.

'Her,' replied Thomas with uncertainty. 'I think. She's on the way up.' A minute later, there was a powerful knock on the door which once again gave the pixies licence to redouble their activities. He opened the door to find a small, thin and shaven-headed black woman dressed from head to foot in tight leather. Thomas estimated she was in her seventies, although she could easily have been a decade younger or older.

'You must be Thomas,' she beamed, thrusting out a bejeweled hand, 'Bobby City at your service.' Although she was at least a foot shorter than Thomas, Bobby's handshake reminded him of something similar to strangulation and he wondered, not without trepidation, what this intriguing person was going to do to them. 'Lexington has told me all about you and it's my pleasure to be of assistance.'

Lexington has told us precisely nothing about you, thought Thomas as Bobby City strode confidently into the apartment to greet Monica with a brief hug only slightly less terrifying than her handshake. 'Has Lexington told you what I do?' she growled, still beaming. Bobby reminded Thomas of a cross between an owl and a wildcat. They both shook their heads like guilty children being interrogated by a teacher over some schoolyard graffiti. 'I organise,' said the owl/wildcat slowly, elongating every syllable. 'I was Lexington's PA for ten years before he joined The Twelve in 2002. He gave me the nickname as my real name is Roberta Urban. Bobby City stuck. I quite like it. If I didn't then it would not have stuck. Please open your computer and show me how far you have got with the Excel spreadsheets.'

Monica whimpered. She went to her corner desk which faced the window, opened her laptop, somehow got through the security checks although her hands were trembling slightly, and turned the screen so that Bobby could view it. 'I see no spreadsheets,' said the visitor, calmly. 'How are you organising everything, Miss Lodhia? Are you a stranger to PowerPoint?'

Sheepishly, Monica reached into a drawer and retrieved an A4 pad of paper. She turned to the first page which was covered in dates, scribbled notes and numbers. 'Hmmmmm,' said Bobby without malice but with a faint note of disappointment. 'I believe I have identified the source of your struggles. That didn't take long.' Monica let out a noise which Thomas had never heard before and which resembled the sound of a woodland creature in imminent peril.

'I never really had to use spreadsheets at the university,' she admitted in almost a whisper. 'I managed to avoid them.'

Bobby City straightened her back, rolled her shoulders and cracked the bones in her fingers. Some of her rings clanked against each other. 'This is not a problem,' she said. 'Well, it *is* a problem, but it can be easily solved. May I have your phone, please, Monica? I shall need to download a couple of apps and then you may have it back. Is your passcode 4228 by any chance?'

Monica was aghast. 'How did you know that?' she whispered. 'Not even Thomas knows my passcode.'

'Simple deduction. You are a chemist. Your name is Monica. The atomic numbers of the elements Molybdenum – Mo in the Periodic Table – and Nickel – Ni – are 42 and 28 respectively. It doesn't take a genius.' Monica blushed with embarrassment. 'Oh, and Thomas does now know, by the way. In case you wish to change it.'

'It's okay,' squeaked Monica. 'Thomas and I have no secrets.' Thomas gulped as quietly as he could under the circumstances.

Once into Monica's phone, Bobby tapped away for a couple of minutes, occasionally asking for Monica's thumbprint to confirm purchases, and then returned the device to its owner. 'I shall be about an hour at this laptop,' she said. 'I suggest you both go and do something else and I'll call you if I need you. Don't go far.'

Thomas offered the visitor a coffee which she declined in favour of a cup of English Breakfast tea, 'made in a china teapot if possible, please, and served in a teacup and absolutely not a mug. No sugar. Thank you.'

'I wonder if she wore that leather during the heatwave,' Thomas mused as the two of them settled into the bedroom where he had decided to read his book while Monica studied the new apps on her phone before giving up and diverting her attention to pictures of cats on social media. The sound of furious tapping of keys interspersed with slurping of tea emanated from the distant side of the apartment. After a while, and with the excitement of the previous evening catching up with him, Thomas drifted into a doze.

He was awoken by Monica gently squeezing his earlobe. 'Thomas,' she was whispering, 'when did you last see Dr Wisby again? Yesterday morning, didn't you say?'

At the mention of the unfortunate doctor's name, Thomas was suddenly wide awake and alert to his ongoing mild deception concerning Wisby. 'That's right,' he said. 'It was just a brief glimpse. He was going somewhere. A vehicle picked him up.'

'What sort of vehicle?' delved Monica. Thomas sensed trouble.

'I don't know, a silver one.'

'And did he walk to this vehicle, Thomas?' He wasn't entirely sure he liked Monica's tone. And if he wasn't mistaken, the pressure of her finger and thumb on his earlobe was ever so slightly intensifying. 'I only ask because his sister has posted on Facebook that he died in his sleep a couple of nights ago following a heart attack. Ironic for a cardiologist. So if he did manage to walk to a silver vehicle after death, then The Twelve could probably use a man with such unusual post mortem abilities.' She smiled sarcastically at Thomas. 'Don't you think?'

'I'm ready for you,' shouted Bobby down the corridor. Thomas breathed out.

'This conversation is not finished,' said Monica in a disconcertingly steely purr as she finally released Thomas's ear and wandered in the direction of the apartment's living space.

Bobby had created a fairly easy-to-understand spreadsheet with all the financial outgoings and income as well as the dates when certain expenses needed to be paid like cleaning bills, council tax and insurance. 'I've synced everything to your phone,' she announced proudly, 'but you won't actually need to do anything as it'll happen automatically. The phone notifications are just so you know what's happening and when. If you decide to make any charity donations as Lexington did, just let me know and I'll put you in touch with James Wheeler at the bank. Such expenditure needs to go through an offshore account so it can't be traced back. James is an expert at such matters. He also ensures that the required tax is paid. Any investigation of The Twelve by HMRC would be... unwelcome.

'I've also created a separate spreadsheet with all of The Twelve's birthdays and relevant dates in case that's helpful. Don't forget that Lexington's eighty-second birthday comes at the end of the month after yours. On December 25th, it naturally signals both Christmas Day and the anniversary of your,' Bobby City paused, considering her terminology, 'intimate connection.'

Monica clicked on this second spreadsheet and noted that, as Bobby had suggested, Christmas Day also contained the initials, M and T with a heart symbol. This made her smile. 'You're amazing,' she told Bobby. 'May I hug you?'

The leather-clad PA bristled. 'I'd much rather you didn't,' she said definitively. 'No offence. Tactile people generally make me uncomfortable. With the odd exception. But here's my card. Call me with any questions.' Monica studied the card which was matt black with gold lettering and read simply, *Bobby City. Gets Shit Done*, along with a mobile number.

'I'm amazed that Lexington never mentioned you before,' said Monica, clasping the card to her chest. 'I suppose he wanted to see how I got on without you.'

'Exactly,' Bobby said, smiling. 'He's naughty like that. Brilliant but naughty. Thank you for the tea. I'll see myself out.' She turned towards the door of the apartment and moved to leave. 'Oh, one more thing.' She winked at Monica and nodded towards the bedroom where Thomas was tentatively awaiting his punishment for the Wisby debacle. 'Don't be too hard on Thomas. He's doing his best in what is still unfamiliar territory.'

The door clicked shut and Monica stared in wonder at the spreadsheet on her laptop. It was a thing of beauty. Then she glanced at her cello, dormant in the corner, and considered her next move.

Thomas stared at her, wide-eyed and suppliant, as she returned to the bedroom. 'I was trying to find the right moment to tell you,' he pleaded. 'We just hadn't got there yet, what with the party and the hangovers and the Bobby stuff and everything.'

Monica remembered the Christmas Day notation on the spreadsheet and clambered onto the bed beside him. She stroked his hair in a way that suggested to Thomas that either she was going to strangle him momentarily or, just possibly, that everything was going to be all right.

'Let's just hope Chris gets his mojo back soon, shall we?' she purred. 'Maybe getting arrested will somehow help that process.' She kissed Thomas on the lips and collapsed back into the pile of pillows at the head of the bed. 'You're forgiven, by the way. Although I'm currently not sure how. I guess the Bobby visit has taken a weight off my mind. Who knew spreadsheets could lift my mood!'

17

nna Hopley and David Latham waited patiently on curved seating in the reception area of New Scotland Yard, waiting for DI Ted Black. As usual, the place was a hubbub of activity with uniformed officers ebbing and flowing through the brightly lit space while friendly arrivals staff checked people in and directed their onward travel as required. Anna usually preferred to work alone in such circumstances but, during the joint birthday party, David had politely asked whether he might tag along, his reasoning being firstly that he had a personal interest in the case and secondly that he was always keen to learn new disciplines. 'I've admired what you do since we first met,' he'd admitted. 'It would be a privilege to finally watch you at work.'

Since the meeting at the crescent in King's Cross, like Owen and Graham, David had also been keeping a close eye on the home of the Storeys. Unlike the couple in north London, David's observations had been closer to the action. He'd quickly located various spots in the cemetery from where he could watch both the side and the front of the house and had spent the occasional hour or two hidden from view, monitoring son and mother. He'd rarely seen Paul but had often seen Tiffany wandering around the ground floor, mundanely going about her daily chores.

A few days previously, David had seen her leave the house via the side door and walk towards the high street, most likely to go shopping. Not long after Tiffany had left, the plumber observed a slim figure moving uneasily behind a first-floor net-curtained window. The figure stopped briefly, waved weakly to nobody in particular and then returned in the direction he had come. 'What are you doing in that room, Paul Storey?' muttered David to himself.

'Welcome to you both,' said Ted Black as he shook hands with first Anna and then David. 'So good to see you again. I'll take you to the lab downstairs where we've set up the piece of evidence under a microscope for you.' He led them to a lift from where they descended to a basement laboratory which, to Anna's eyes, was kitted out with most of the new technology she had requested. 'The original forensic report is here too for your reference as well as some case notes typed up by McMullan and a couple of bits of evidence from the Storey house. If there's anything else, please just call me,' said Black, excitedly. 'I'll text you my mobile number and I'm here all day so I'm only two floors up. I can be with you in less than a minute.'

Once the door had closed behind them, the two members of The Twelve put on disposable lab coats, masks and gloves and Anna studied the charred piece of sleeve under the microscope for a couple of minutes, moving it gently to get a fuller picture, before inviting David to take a look. It was larger than she had anticipated with most of the upper arm salvaged plus part of the back of the jacket. 'There are specks of blood,' she warned him. 'Are you sure it won't upset you?' The plumber solemnly replied that he would be okay.

'So what we see here are tiny flecks of Justin's blood which would have made their way onto the jacket during the attack,' she indicated. 'The direction of the flecks suggest that the blood was moving at speed which is why they fade at one end. You could only see this with the microscope. To the naked eye, they would just look like tiny dots. I'm now going to check the blackened edges of the material to see whether there is anything that was missed in the original investigation.'

Anna carefully moved the slide under which the piece of jacket was secured so that she could focus on the borders of the material. Around most of the perimeter, the blue was replaced abruptly by burned cloth. 'Hmm, this is interesting,' mused Anna suddenly. David was deep in thought, meanwhile, and Anna assumed the sight of his friends' son's blood had shaken him. 'There's a tiny piece of black material here on the very edge of this piece. To the untrained eye, it would look like charring but it's not. It looks like part of a pattern on the jacket.'

'It's the right sleeve, isn't it?' said David suddenly. 'So the pattern would be on the back.'

Anna confirmed that it was indeed a right sleeve. The stitching and the creases would be consistent with that. 'Would that mean that the person who stabbed Justin and got blood speckles on the sleeve would have been right-handed?'

'Yes, that's probably right,' said Anna with a smile. 'Unless the blood came from one of the wounds inflicted by one of the other attackers, which is a possibility. But looking at the distribution and knowing the geography of the wounds on Justin's body, my considered assessment would be that whoever was wearing this jacket used their right hand to cause the injuries.'

David thought back to his observations from the cemetery. He admitted to Anna that he had been secretly observing the house and had briefly seen Paul Storey. 'He was waving with his left hand,' he said, quietly.

Anna rose from the microscope and walked over to the table on which DI Black had left the paperwork relevant to the case. 'This is also interesting,' she said. 'There's a letter here which Paul wrote to his mum while in prison awaiting the court case. I'd need to look at it more closely but the left to right blurring on some of the letters would suggest a left-handed person. Often the heel of the left hand lightly runs over the text causing slight smudging which you don't get with a right-handed person.' She took off her right glove and reached for her mobile phone to call Ted Black. 'Hi, Ted. It's the people in the basement. Do you have any footage of Paul Storey being interviewed, please? And also some carbon dot powder if you have some? Thank you.'

She explained to David that carbon dot powder wouldn't have been available to the original forensic team but that it may come in handy now. Around twenty minutes later, Black returned to the room with a laptop and the required powder. 'There's an hour or so of footage from the interrogation,' he said. 'Hopefully it'll be enough. I'll leave you to it.'

Hesitantly, David pressed play and the two of them watched as Paul Storey fidgeted and squirmed under what seemed to be intense questioning by McMullan. He was a broad-shouldered, shaven-headed young man, very different, David thought, to the waif-like figure he'd seen at the window. Storey's "no comments" were spat out first confrontationally and later almost lethargically but, more importantly, he was occasionally drinking from a glass of water which he would always pick up with his left hand. 'It's not proof of innocence,' said Anna, 'but it certainly begins to lift the burden of guilt marginally, especially as there's no mention of him being left-handed in the 2013 court evidence. Have you ever thought of becoming a detective, David?'

The plumber blushed. Somehow, he had created an unexpected scenario where Paul Storey would be innocent of the murder of Justin Morris which would mean disappointment and anguish for Henry and Diana as well as more complexity to the current case. The last thing they needed.

'There's just one more thing I'd like to do while we're here,' said Anna and she returned to the microscope with the powder.

'What does the powder do?' asked David. The retired pathologist explained that it showed up fingerprints that couldn't previously be seen. She flipped through the original case paperwork until she found an enlarged printout of Paul's fingerprints.

'It's a new weapon in the forensics armoury,' she said. 'I thought it was worth a try because if they missed the tiny piece of pattern on the back of the jacket as well as the left hand business, who knows what else got missed.' Anna delicately moved the microscope slide to show the back of the jacket. 'David, could you please carefully take off one of your gloves and open my phone. The passcode is 2943. Then I need you to open up an app called UVView and very carefully hold the light over the material at an angle so you don't contaminate it. Thank you.'

David did as he was told. In a weird way, this was the most fun he'd had in ages.

Anna hummed. 'That's also interesting,' she said, scrutinising the fragment with intense concentration. 'There's part of a fingerprint here on the back with a double loop whorl. Paul's fingerprints don't possess such a pattern, which means that whoever's fingerprint this is, it's definitely not Paul Storey.'

18

That night as they lay in bed together, the midsummer light finally dwindling to something approaching darkness, Anna, as usual, discussed the day's events with Chris; he was eager to remain in touch with the case, especially as he had begun to get the nagging feeling that his expertise may soon be required following the untimely death of Dr Wisby. Anna explained about the fingerprint and how David had identified a discrepancy in the evidence regarding Storey's left-handedness. 'Furthermore, from what David says,' she suggested, 'Paul Storey is not at all well.'

'I wonder,' contemplated Chris, as Anna traced his collarbone with her fingers, careful not to put pressure on his scar. 'I've learned quite a bit about PTSD over the last month or so, both from Mrs Mendoza and my own research. My case is relatively mild, thank goodness, but I wonder whether Paul is suffering from a much more complex and severe version. Why else would someone not leave their own house for years?'

'Unless he's scared of something outside,' said Anna, absentmindedly. 'Much of this doesn't make sense at the moment. It's becoming critical that we pay Paul a visit. We can discuss with the group at yoga tomorrow. Why don't you come along? It may help with your reintegration?' She ran her hand over his ear, tickling the hairs which sprouted from it. Chris turned his head so they could kiss.

'That's probably not a bad idea,' he said. 'But, do you know what's an even better idea?' Anna giggled as he began to kiss her neck at the same time as his hands reached for her hips.

With the weather now settled back to the combination of warm sunshine and occasional showers more typical of a British summer, weekly yoga classes were reinstated. Anna taught the classes, which took place on the ground floor of a house on Chalton Street near the British Library which The Twelve had bought in the 1950s specifically for the purpose. The yoga itself had been instigated in the 1930s by a member of the group named Hilda Graham whose belief, gleaned from travelling in India in her early life, was that their ageing bodies would benefit from low-impact stretching exercises. Moreover, The Twelve of the 1930s had also found that weekly classes strengthened not only their muscles but also the bonds within the group. Yoga had therefore become a key element of Twelve life and something that they all enjoyed.

Even Lexington, in his eighties, found benefit in the less taxing poses and so he had continued to attend sporadically, often, as today, giving up halfway through and sitting the remainder of the class out in a comfortable chair, massaging his knee.

'I'm so relieved the heatwave is over,' said Monica, arriving slightly late with Thomas as they had decided to take the bus. 'Ooh, look who's here!' She immediately made a beeline for Chris who scooped her up, wincing momentarily on account of his injury. Thomas joined in the group hug and soon everyone had piled in like a team of senior football players celebrating a goal. 'You didn't tell me you were coming!'

'I decided last night,' said the retired surgeon. 'Anna persuaded me.' He winked quickly in the direction of the pathologist who growled seductively in response. 'We thought it would be a pleasant surprise.'

'It's more than pleasant,' Monica grinned, 'it's delightful in every way. Does this mean you're back?'

Chris suggested that although he wasn't fully recovered, a gradual return to full Twelve operational duties would probably be suitable, particularly in view of the fact that, with Dr Wisby no longer a viable option on account of being dead, the next available medical possibility for The Twelve was at least a couple of years away from being ready.

'Which means you're stuck with me for a bit.' Chris grinned. 'And vice versa.'

Martin groaned theatrically.

An hour later, with everyone exhilarated from the class as well as being slightly sweaty – although the temperature had fallen by around ten degrees, it remained in the low twenties – the group convened a quick meeting to bring everyone up to speed with the Morris case. Martin and David had gathered chairs from an adjacent room for some of the older participants while others leaned against walls, rehydrating with water. Terry put the kettle on in case anyone fancied a tea. He had also made banana and nut protein bars as a post-exercise snack in case anyone wished to indulge. Veronica ate two, justifying this by revealing that she had only had a bowl of strawberries for breakfast and was therefore ravenous.

Anna and David explained their findings from the afternoon at New Scotland Yard, the plumber almost bursting with excitement as he relayed their discoveries. 'We'll need to tell Suzanne about the fingerprint,' said Anna, 'but it definitely doesn't match Paul's.'

'Could it be Tiffany's?' asked Belinda. 'Maybe his mum took it to be burned. To protect him.' Anna agreed that it was worth checking but that everything now suggested that Paul wasn't wearing the jacket when Justin Morris was murdered and that he wasn't the one who tried to dispose of it.

Catherine had also met with Amanda Harker, the junior reporter who had covered the case ten years earlier. Unfortunately, Amanda hadn't been able to remember much of the detail as she had since left journalism to study design; however, she had kept some of her notebooks from the time, 'in case they ever came in handy, I suppose,' and managed to locate the relevant one for Catherine. 'In amongst the mundane court stuff, Amanda had written the words "coercion?" and "blackmail?" in the margins. Apparently she asked the editor at the time whether she could investigate further and was told that the paper's proprietor had ruled that it was a waste of time. Nothing more came of it. The editor died a couple of years ago so I can't check it, and he certainly never mentioned anything to me at the time.'

'So many questions.' Monica was deep in thought. 'If Paul didn't kill Justin then who did? If he knew who did it then why didn't he say anything when the case came to court? And why has he been virtually imprisoned in his own house for years? I suppose there's only one way to find out. We need to talk to Paul and Tiffany. And that's not going to be easy. I'll let Suzanne know what we've uncovered and, in the meantime, could I please ask David, Terry, Graham and Catherine to figure out the best way to get to both of them. I strongly suspect it won't be as easy as simply ringing on the doorbell.'

Veronica asked whether she could also help as 'it's my first one and I really want to get my hands dirty. Plus, I guess there isn't going to be an assassination now.'

'I wouldn't put money on that,' muttered Chris, darkly. 'Someone will have to pay a price.' From his corner seat, Lexington nodded sombrely and stared out of the window at a pigeon which had landed on a nearby wheelie bin.

Before the group separated, and as they were tidying away the chairs, Monica asked whether Martin had remembered where he'd seen the face in the photograph of DI McMullan's leaving do before. 'I've been wracking my brains,' said the cabbie, 'but it's not coming. I might be mistaken anyway and it's probably not that important.'

It was on the bus home to St John's Wood that Monica's phone rang. 'It's Lexington,' she whispered to Thomas. 'I hope he hasn't forgotten anything. I don't really want to have to go all the way back.'

'I couldn't help overhearing your conversation with Martin,' said the old man. 'I don't suppose with everything that's been going on, that you've managed to get very far with the archive in Baker Street, have you?' Monica had almost forgotten. On the day of their handover back in May, Lexington had taken her into a locked room to which only she now had the key. Inside the room were books dating back to the 1830s in which details of every Twelve case had been recorded: victims, locations, faded newspaper clippings, all relevant minutiae which may help future Twelve members. Lexington had suggested that, during quieter moments, she examine some of the cases partly for pleasure and partly for ideas. In addition, she would need to keep records of all the cases during the course of her tenure and place them in the archive.

'I've...' She hesitated, trying to think of a polite way to say that she hadn't had the time. 'No, Lexington, I'm sorry. It's been a bit frantic. Keeping on top of everything. It'll be easier now I know Bobby.'

At the other end of the line, Lexington hummed. 'Quite understandable,' he said. 'Perhaps you might meet me there tomorrow at 6pm. Bring Thomas if you like. We can have a drink and I can show you something which might or might not help but should intrigue you nonetheless. Don't forget the key to the archive. I no longer have one, of course. Cheerio.'

19

At the other end of the line, Suzanne Green shared Monica's amazement that the original investigation into Justin Morris's murder had been even more amateur than she'd imagined. 'I'm also more than a little concerned that Ted didn't pick up on the left hand, right hand business during the second investigation but then if his work resulted in four racists behind bars then maybe some things slipped through the net even then. The forensics I can understand. I doubt that fingerprint piece would have been visible without the carbon dot powder.'

'I don't suppose there's a record of Tiffany's fingerprints?' asked Monica. The commissioner replied that she doubted it as Paul's mother had never been accused or even suspected of committing an offence but would check the police database anyway.

Monica put her phone on speaker, rolled her shoulders and grimaced as she stood looking across the rooftops of St John's Wood. The morning's yoga had felt slightly tougher than usual, doubtless because of the four-week heat-enforced hiatus since the last one. The muscles required had grown familiar with inactivity as if they had descended into an enforced midsummer hibernation. She was delighted to have Chris back, though, as was Thomas who had virtually skipped kitten-like all the way from the bus stop. 'The next thing we would like to do is to somehow talk to Paul and Tiffany. We appreciate it won't be easy but...'

'Sorry to interrupt, Monica,' said Suzanne with some urgency. 'It's important to know one additional thing about the Storeys. We've had them under surveillance, as you know. They've also been regularly visited by social services over the years and none of those visitors have ever gained access. What tends to happen is that Tiffany comes to the door, very politely answers questions but refuses to let anyone in. On the odd occasion that someone from social services asks to see Paul, she apparently shouts up the stairs to ask if he's all right, he shouts back that he's fine and that's that. They aren't permitted to force access and equally they can't easily obtain a warrant to enter the building because, on the face of it, there's no obvious danger to anyone inside. So, what I'm saying is, if you want to talk to them, you'll need to be much cleverer than simply turning up, however kindly and well-meaning you may look.'

Monica thanked the commissioner and, once the call had finished, made herself a coffee and typed a long text to the group outlining the situation with regards visits to the Storey house. David texted back almost immediately. He was, at that moment, observing the house from his favoured spot in the cemetery but had noticed no activity over the preceding two hours. Owen then texted to say that, using the infra-red camera, he could see Paul in his room as usual while Tiffany was in the downstairs living room. From the position of her posture, head in hands, it looked like she was crying.

The following day at six, Monica and Thomas arrived at the Baker Street house armed with the requisite key in Monica's case, and a state of extreme anticipation in Thomas's. On the day back in late spring that Monica had taken over from Lexington as The Twelve's leader, she had been the only one permitted to venture into the locked room towards the rear of the extensive Georgian house. Today, maybe he too would be allowed to see what was inside.

'Don't get too excited,' warned Monica in a friendly yet downbeat tone. 'Lexington might simply want you there to pour the drinks and for moral support.' To Thomas, even a supporting role was tantamount to ecstasy.

It transpired that Lexington was already in position as the two of them wandered down the hallway, past the Van Gogh sketches which Thomas had admired on his first visit a few weeks previously, and into the large living room. Lexington had settled into a brown leather armchair having poured himself a large brandy, and was reading a Marian Keyes novel.

'Oh good evening,' he said, rising unsteadily to embrace first Monica and then Thomas. 'I thought I'd be early. Get things ready. Plus, I was in the vicinity and I needed a wee so it was either here or the Underground station. Frankly, the facilities here are so much more pleasurable. Can I offer you a drink?'

Monica decided on a vodka and lime while Thomas agreed to join the old man in a brandy. 'I hear Bobby City's visit was a resounding success,' Lexington proposed, with as innocent an expression as he could muster. 'I'm sorry I didn't tell you about her before but I suppose I didn't want to bombard you with info all at once. Plus, if I'm honest, the mischievous part of my character wanted to see how you got on without her. I had always assumed that you were a whizz with a spreadsheet, unlike myself.'

'I simply cannot tell you,' Monica enthused, 'how much of

an angel that woman is. She transformed my life in the space of an hour.'

'She transformed mine too.' Lexington smiled. 'In more ways than one.' Monica shared a look with Thomas who raised an impish eyebrow.

'Do you wish to elaborate?' enquired Monica, desperately attempting not to sound too interrogative but equally aware that she may be on the verge of uncovering some gossip.

'Another time, perhaps. Let's just say that my relationship with Bobby has, over the years, taken a variety of forms. She is a highly talented woman.' Lexington took a swig of brandy, closed his eyes and seemed to drift momentarily into a haze of blissful reminiscence. 'One of the curious things about getting very old,' he sighed, 'is that some of one's memories fade with the light while others sharpen into even more vivid focus. I suppose that if one is lucky enough, it's the more enjoyable memories that take the latter route.' He placed his near-empty glass back on its side table and gave himself a shake. 'Anyway, to business. Now, should we allow Thomas into the room or shall we leave him here? It's your choice. You're in charge now.'

Monica balanced the options. 'We tend not to have secrets from each other,' she said. 'Apart from not telling me that Dr Wisby had died.' She shot Thomas a look of benign fury which caused him to shrink slightly and tighten his grip on the stem of his brandy glass. 'But on reflection, I don't see why not.' Thomas brightened. 'As long as he behaves himself in there.'

The three of them walked slowly down the short corridor where Monica retrieved a key from her zipped pocket and opened the door. Behind it were a couple of short steps down into a small, windowless library filled with books and files of myriad colours and types, like the distant corner of a well-organised but ancient bookshop. Lexington flicked a light switch and the room's treasures became more visible. 'Welcome to the history of The Twelve,' he said. 'Everything that anyone could possibly wish to know about the group is here. Oh, look at this.'

He reached up to a shelf just around his shoulder height and picked out a small notebook with a gold leather cover. '1890. The fiftieth case that The Twelve were involved with. A fairly junior but effective member of one of the many criminal gangs operating in Victorian London. Edward Blunt known, unimaginatively, as Sharp Eddie, both on account of his surname and his proclivity for removing the fingers of shopkeepers who refused to pay a levy to the gang.' Lexington leafed carefully through the pages, turning each one as if it were made from the most fragile tissue. 'Ended up drowning in one of Bazalgette's sewers, which, by the sounds of this account, was a suitable end for a particularly unpleasant fellow.'

He handed the notebook to Thomas who caressed it in a state of awe before gently closing the cover and placing it back in its home. 'This is amazing,' he said, gazing around the room wide-eyed. Monica smiled at his childlike wonder. She had felt the same sensation back in May when Lexington had inducted her into this amongst the many other secrets of The Twelve. She felt regret that she hadn't managed to spend more time in this hallowed place since late spring and silently vowed to correct that over the coming months.

'But we're not here to worry about 1890,' said Lexington. 'We need to find something a little more recent.' He stepped carefully round to a corner of the room where he ran his finger diligently along the various spines of the books until he found what was required. 'Here we are,' he announced triumphantly, extracting a thin black exercise book from which he blew a light cloud of dust. '1963. The Slaven case. I trust you shall find it most enlightening.'

20

Beryl Edwards peered out from her first-floor window overlooking the crossroads in Wanstead on London's north-east side. Across to her left was the wasteland and the remains of the bomb crater from over twenty years before; Beryl remembered hearing it explode as she sheltered in her cellar on an otherwise unexceptional day in April 1941. Apparently the land had been bought by developers but so far there was no sign of any rebuilding, certainly not in that direction. To her right was the usual evening scene. Those teenage boys loitering around the lamp-post on the corner on their bikes.

Beryl remembered seeing something on that new news programme on BBC2 about groups of youngsters being unruly and causing a commotion, many of them smoking underage, but these particular youths were no trouble. They were polite young men, aged, she estimated, between about fourteen and twenty, and Beryl wasn't the kind of woman to get the police involved unless it was absolutely necessary. She smiled, lit an Embassy filter and inhaled, closing her eyes in pleasure as the nicotine rush hit her lungs. One of the boys, the youngest one, looked up, saw her and waved. 'Hello, Aunty,' he shouted, just loud enough to be heard through the single pane of glass. Instinctively she waved back, tapped her ash into a practically empty teacup and moved away from the window. It was getting dark now and Beryl had some organising to do.

As leader of The Twelve since the beginning of 1961, Beryl, a former headteacher who had also volunteered during the latter part of the war to assist with naval operations planning, had overseen two reasonably straightforward assassinations, low-level criminals foolish enough to be enticed onto riverside wasteland and dispatched efficiently with the minimum of fuss.

The current case, Beryl's third, was more challenging. Jerry Slaven was woven into the fabric of London's criminal underworld and this meant that the strategy to get rid of him would be more complex and detailed than simply an invite to a disused warehouse down by the docks. Slaven was smarter than that and much better connected. The Twelve would be required to use all of their combined expertise and ingenuity.

Beryl had decided to use a variation on a tried and tested method to get close to Slaven; befriend not one but two of his associates and patiently forge a connection over time. Two of The Twelve were designated one Slaven associate each. Ray Flynn, a recently retired car mechanic, had volunteered to get close to the best man at Jerry's wedding, Charlie Garfield, a petty thief with a tendency to spend the odd three-month spell in prison before being released to reoffend with tedious predictability; meanwhile Roger Scott, an ex-army captain who had fought his way across north Africa in '43 and had suffered a minor shrapnel wound to his left leg for his trouble, was assigned to a relatively junior member of the Slaven gang named Frank Burnett.

After several weeks of frequenting the same pubs and gently initiating conversations – the train robbery in August provided ample material for a while – Ray and Roger each made a breakthrough in the space of a few days in early September. Ray managed to infiltrate Charlie's team of darts regulars having practised for up to six hours a day at home and then challenging the least capable of the regulars to a friendly match, wagering a half-crown on the result. Ray had won, used his winnings to buy a round of drinks for the entire team including his vanquished opponent, and was formally invited to join the group whenever he happened to be in the pub, The Blue Posts in Deptford.

Roger, meanwhile, had got lucky one day when he entered The Five Bells in Camberwell, wearing one of his medals, the Military Cross. The Twelve's research had uncovered that Burnett had also won the Military Cross and the two men naturally got chatting and soon were traversing common ground together. Within weeks, a fragile friendship of sorts had formed and Roger began to subtly introduce into their conversations the fact that he was looking for a bit of extra work in security or protection – even at the age of sixty-five, Roger Scott could hold his own in a fight which he happily demonstrated on two occasions when drunken brawls broke out in the streets outside the pub.

By the first days of October, Roger had met with Jerry Slaven and the two men had quickly developed a rapport. Slaven was steadily building a protection racket across south-east London and felt that a man like Roger, with his respectable army background, could help persuade reluctant shopkeepers. 'You can go in there,' he growled, 'and because you're an old fella, they won't expect any trouble. You can explain the delicate situation to them and then, if they won't agree to our terms, that's when you get heavy.'

Roger said that that sounded acceptable and that he would look forward to the first target, a corner betting shop off the Old Kent Road on the outskirts of Walworth. 'I'll do it alone,' he told Slaven, knowing that if this plan was to work, he would need to be unobserved by any of Slaven's cronies. 'Trust me, it's better that way. How much do you want in payment?' Slaven said that fifty pounds a month should do it, otherwise the place would be smashed up and robbed on a regular basis. A pay off to the local police would keep their noses out of it.

When Roger returned from the betting shop with one hundred pounds – 'I decided fifty was too little. He's doing good business around here. I hope you don't mind.' – Slaven was delighted. Of course, the money didn't belong to the betting shop; it was a gift from The Twelve's expansive coffers and the betting shop owner had been fully briefed on the situation in case another of Slaven's gang paid a visit to ask questions. On each subsequent occasion where Roger was asked to draw another small business into Slaven's web, he would return with more money than expected. 'You're better at this than I am,' said the gangster, laughing and pointing a thick, threatening finger. 'But don't you try taking over or I'll finish you.' Roger confirmed that his sense of loyalty to Slaven was unshakeable and the two men embraced, one of them eagerly anticipating the day when he could eliminate the other.

Just over a mile away in Deptford, and after a few drinks, Charlie Garfield was always happy to share tales about his best mate, Jerry Slaven. 'One of the cleverest men you'll ever meet, and one of the most dangerous.' Ray listened attentively as Garfield kept him and the rest of the darts fraternity updated with various titbits about the Slaven business empire and its successes. Soon Ray heard word about a new member of Slaven's inner circle, an 'old fella but really strong. Surprisingly good with his fists. Apparently he beat up a whole platoon of Germans on his own twenty years back.' Ray kept as near to the margins of these conversations as possible, careful not to give any indication that he knew Garfield was talking about Roger. He nodded in admiration when Garfield spoke about how

Roger had doubled the gang's income from a certain postcode within a fortnight and how Jerry Slaven was so delighted at this progress that he was thinking of moving in on another postcode controlled by a rival gang, the Tylers.

All of this time, Beryl and the rest of The Twelve were working on a strategy to get Roger alone with Slaven in order that the assassination could take place.

'Were they lovers?' asked Monica, raising her head momentarily from the notebook. 'Beryl and Roger. I sense there's something going on. A woman's intuition.' Lexington explained that he wasn't aware of anything in the archive to suggest such a dalliance; however, this being the early 1960s, and after the Lady Chatterley obscenity trial, it would be unwise to rule anything out. Monica gave a nod of curiosity and continued reading.

A date was set for early December. Roger would arrange to meet Slaven at an ironmonger's shop in Southwark under the pretence of wanting to interest the gangster in buying the shop which happened to be owned by another member of The Twelve, Stanley Jacobs. Roger had been subtly suggesting to Slaven that if he had ambitions to move into other gangs' territories, he would need somewhere to build and repair weapons instead of buying them which was proving increasingly costly. The shop could also serve as a permanent location, which could also be used as a base from where to launch attacks south into Peckham and beyond. On luring the crime boss to the shop, four other members of The Twelve, watching and waiting from a distance, would overpower Slaven, knock him out and then transport him in Stanley's van to the river. With the tide going out, Slaven's body would be far into the Thames estuary within the hour.

In the record, Beryl had written that at around 5pm on the

evening of the planned assassination, Roger dropped by to see her on his way to Southwark.

I knew it, thought Monica, but decided not to mention anything so simply smiled to herself instead.

'I'm going to pop in to see my sister on the way,' he said. 'Her phone's been on the blink so I haven't heard from her in a week. I should be in Southwark by seven and Slaven isn't due until eight so there's plenty of time.' Beryl asked whether Roger's sister was still in Catford at the house she herself had visited while monitoring Roger before inviting him to join The Twelve. Roger confirmed that she was. 'I'll take the bus,' he said. 'It's probably easiest.' Beryl told him to take care and he left around 5.30pm.

Plenty of time for a kiss and a cuddle, imagined Monica, by now fully confident in her assessment of this romantic entanglement.

Around a half hour later, Beryl's phone rang. 'Wanstead 2030,' she greeted the caller. There were some mechanical noises while someone, who seemed to be in a telephone box, frantically put change into the relevant slot. It was Ray Flynn.

'You have to call off the job tonight, Beryl,' he gasped. 'Slaven knows it's a trap.'

21

Ray had been playing darts with Charlie Garfield since mid-afternoon and the younger man had become steadily more drunk and, as a result, progressively more loquacious. During a break between games, Ray had politely asked about Slaven and his favourite old collaborator, Roger. 'I hear that's going to end badly,' slurred Garfield. Ray immediately registered alarm bells.

Word had somehow got back to Slaven that all was not as it seemed with his new accomplice and a few discreet enquiries led him to become suspicious. Slaven decided to get to the truth and that meant overpowering Roger with a group of associates and interrogating him until he talked. One theory was that Roger was in league with the Tylers. They'd beat him until they found out.

'Do you think it would be possible to get to Southwark to warn him?' asked Beryl, not panicking but merely weighing her options. Ray replied that he couldn't be certain and also pointed out, sensibly, that if he were caught then the entire operation would fail. It would be better, surely, for him to maintain his cover, a suggestion with which The Twelve's leader reluctantly agreed.

Beryl thanked Ray, replaced the receiver and walked as briskly as she could to her desk, a large mahogany affair with four drawers on each side. 'Thank goodness for efficient filing,' she muttered to herself as she reached down to one of the lower drawers and pulled out the entire contents which comprised around a hundred sheets of paper, letters, notes and receipts. Beryl rifled through the papers until she found what she was looking for; the address and phone number for Roger's sister in Catford.

She wandered back to her telephone, simultaneously lighting a cigarette, and dialled the number. The permanent engaged tone reminded her that Roger had mentioned a fault with his sister's line. Beryl swore. She replaced the receiver calmly and then went back to her window, dropping ash on the carpet on the way. 'Bugger.' She'd have to get the Bissell out later but right now there were more pressing matters. She phoned Stanley's shop but there was no answer, the ironmonger had most likely gone to a pub for a couple of hours before returning to the shop ready for the evening's activities. 'Bugger,' she muttered under her breath for the second time in as many minutes.

There was the bus, of course, but she couldn't guarantee getting to Southwark in time. She could try to flag down a taxi but, at this time of night, it wouldn't be easy to find one that was keen to venture south of the river. Cabbies were such a capricious breed. Beryl couldn't imagine one ever being allowed into The Twelve. She stared out into the darkness, wracking her brains for a burst of inspiration which could save Roger from a beating or worse.

Her anxiety increasing by the second, Beryl glanced down at the lamp-post on the corner. Just one boy remained. The youngest one. He was probably only thirteen or fourteen. *I wonder*, she thought. She went back to her desk, retrieved a black-and-white photograph of Roger from the top drawer, and went downstairs to her front door, collecting a shawl from her coat hook to protect her neck against the winter chill.

'Evening, Aunty,' said the boy cheerfully, grateful for some company.

'On your own?' asked Beryl kindly. The boy explained how his friends had gone to see a pop group at one of the pubs over in west London.

'The Detours, they're called, Aunty,' he said. 'But they're not really my thing. A bit loud for my liking. And the drummer is a bit madcap if you ask me. I prefer musicals myself. Have you seen *Half a Sixpence*, Aunty? I'd give my right arm to see *Half a Sixpence*.'

Beryl frowned. 'I wonder whether you might do me a favour,' she began. 'It's quite a big favour but it's an important one. If you can do it, I'll take you to see *Half a Sixpence* if your parents agree to it. How does that sound?'

The boy's eyes suddenly became huge and sparkled in the yellow lamplight. 'Really, Aunty? You're not pulling me leg, are ya?' Beryl confirmed that she was deadly serious and what's more she would throw in a programme and some bon-bons.

'Are you familiar with this gentleman?' she asked, showing the photograph of Roger. 'He visits me from time to time.'

Monica's grin widened.

'Captain Scott?' said the boy. 'Of course, Aunty. He often brings us butter mints when he comes by. I'd know him anywhere. I'd even know him by his walk. Slight limp on the left.' Beryl breathed a sigh of relief. Perhaps this highly unorthodox plan could work after all. Without going into specifics, she explained how Roger was in danger and outlined the route he'd be taking to Southwark via Catford on the buses.

'What I need you to do, please, is to intercept him before he gets to the ironmongers and then ask him to call me from a safe telephone box so I can explain all. Do you think you can do that on your bicycle?' Beryl could feel her hands shaking with worry now, her cigarette ash tumbling onto her slippers.

'Easy-peasy,' said the boy. 'I know all the short cuts, Aunty. Give me half an hour.' He sped off in the direction of the river and disappeared into the night. Beryl shouted to the boy to be careful, took a last long drag of her cigarette down to the filter and walked back into her house in search of another.

Five cigarettes and two strong cups of tea later, Beryl's phone rang. She picked it up within one ring, hoping for the best yet anticipating an alternative.

'Did you send me a boy on a bike?' asked Roger with a mixture of confusion and slight irritation. Beryl was so relieved that she decided to ignore the latter. She explained how Ray had found out that he was in danger and how she had had to improvise a way to alert him before he reached the ironmongers. 'I'm impressed,' said Roger. 'The young chap you sent must have worked out that the bus from Catford terminates at Waterloo which is where I am at this moment. I was just about to walk to the ironmongers but I won't now. I've asked him to go and warn the others. I hope that's all right. I've given him a couple of shillings for his trouble. I was flabbergasted to see him so far from home.'

Beryl slumped back in her telephone chair in relief and exhaustion. 'I'm at rather a loose end now,' said Roger. 'Shall I pop over for a brandy?' Sixty years apart, both Beryl and Monica beamed in anticipation.

Around half an hour later there was a knock on Beryl's door. *That was quick*, she thought, imagining that Roger had queued at the station for a taxi but she was mistaken. Beryl opened the door to the boy, slightly out of breath but with an aura of quiet satisfaction.

'All fine and dandy,' said the boy. 'Captain Scott is safe and the old blokes in the shop opposite the ironmongers are going to wait until the coast is clear and then they'll be in touch.' He grinned proudly. 'I might have also caught a glimpse of them fellas that were going to duff up the captain, just in case you need anyone to identify them. And the captain gave me a couple of bob so it's been a good night all round, Aunty.'

Beryl was so thankful that she almost gave the boy a hug but decided, on balance, that a handshake was more proper. 'I'm Beryl Edwards, by the way.'

'Pleased to be of service, Aunty Beryl,' said the boy. 'My name's Martin. Martin Francis. Now we're friends, we can go to the theatre together.'

'I look forward to that enormously,' said Beryl. 'I'll let you know some dates so you can ask your parents. And thank you again.'

Martin turned his bike in the direction of home. 'You shouldn't smoke, by the way, Aunty. My mum says it's unhealthy.'

Beryl Edwards thanked Martin Francis for his spontaneous health advice, waved him goodbye and went in out of the cold to light another cigarette and await Roger's arrival.

22

'That's officially amazing,' said Monica. 'So we kept tabs on Martin right from the early sixties until he was ready? That's some crazy forward planning.'

Lexington explained that for most of the sixties, seventies, eighties, nineties and the early part of the 2000s, The Twelve wasn't so much keeping an eye on Martin but simply making sure they were aware of his whereabouts, his marriage to Pauline, his career, his general well-being. It was only around 2010 after Pauline's death that they started monitoring Martin with a view to his induction into the group. It was Lexington himself, a few years from becoming leader of The Twelve, who was tasked with monitoring and assessing Martin's suitability.

'A long but fruitful apprenticeship, you might say,' the old man mused, carefully placing the notebook back in its position. 'And I know what you're thinking, Thomas. Surely I told you at our first meeting that The Twelve had never failed to complete a case successfully, am I right?' Thomas agreed that the question had tentatively crossed his mind. 'If you read the next notebook at some point, you'll learn that Ray remained undercover for the next seven months while an alternative plan was hatched. This new strategy involved persuading Jerry Slaven to purchase a new car, a beige Vauxhall Viva, I believe, which was then adapted by Ray so that the brakes would fail on the journey away from Ray's temporary garage under some railway arches in Hackney. For good measure, Ray filled the car boot with petrol and added small propane canisters to the inside of the front bumper, rigged with carefully positioned Swan Vesta matches – Beryl's idea. To ensure that no innocent bystander was harmed, and surmising correctly that Jerry would drive at speed away from the garage, The Twelve bought an old Bedford van which Roger parked directly around the first corner, and spread oil on the road so it would be impossible for Jerry to stop. The bang, early one morning in August 1964, could apparently be heard as far away as Liverpool Street. There's an article from the *Evening News* in the file too.' He made an explosive gesture with his hands, spreading his fingers wide while mouthing the word 'Boom!'

The Twelve always get their target, thought Thomas, *as long as they know who their target is*. The current case hadn't yet revealed him. However, the revelation about Martin had reminded Thomas of another question he had been meaning to ask for some time. 'Lexington,' he began tentatively, 'just out of interest, when did you start monitoring me? It wasn't the sixties, was it?'

Lexington led the way out of the archive room followed closely by Thomas as Monica turned out the light and locked up behind them. 'Not at all, my dear fellow.' He smiled reassuringly. 'You came to our attention during the 2012 Olympics. One of your athletes, a four-hundred-metre gold medallist as I recall, did a television interview afterwards where she praised you for your belief in her but also mentioned that you were thinking of retiring – you were approaching sixty, I believe. Margaret Wilmot, the leader before me, was watching the interview and her ears pricked up. We had been struggling to find someone with a sporting background for a couple of years and had just recruited a former footballer who was an outstanding addition to The Twelve but who only lasted five years, sadly. Margaret felt we needed to think more long term so that we could always have a number of members with good fitness for their age.

'Initially, a couple of us kept an eye on you every few months until poor Alice died, after which we slowly intensified observation until the time was right for all of us. Which is when I invited you to our delightful late lunch. I trust that is sufficient detail for the time being.'

Thomas nodded. Monica had wrapped an arm around his waist admiringly.

'Anyway,' said Lexington, settling back into his chair, 'I hope this has been an interesting diversion for you. If you don't mind, I'll just sit here for half an hour before I leave. I've got a bit of brandy left in the glass and I've reached a rather juicy point in my book. I can't easily read on the bus with all the distractions.'

Monica expressed surprise at his choice of reading but Lexington was adamant. 'This Rachel Walsh woman is addictive,' he said. 'Such a complex and vibrant character. She reminds me of a friend I had in the sixties. A wonderful Irish woman named Colleen. I'll never forget the exquisite times we had together.' A wistful look clambered over the octogenarian's face as his mind redrew distant memories.

'You never married, did you, Lexington?' asked Thomas warmly.

The old man was clearly still reminiscing. 'I was too busy having fun for most of my long and wonderful life to think about glorious institutions like marriage,' he said. 'By the time I was finally ready to settle down, the opportunities had passed.'

'When was that?' asked Monica, momentarily thinking of her own mortality.

Lexington glanced at his watch. 'About four hours ago.' He grinned mischievously, settled back in his chair and opened his book. 'I'll see you at yoga next week. Cheerio.'

It was still light and not too chilly as the two of them walked hand in hand the short distance back to St John's Wood. Armed with this new information about Martin, Monica felt they might be nearing a breakthrough, although exactly how a case from 1963 was relevant, she couldn't fathom. 'I'll call Suzanne in the morning,' she said as they ambled across the canal halfway to home. 'I'll see if she can send us a text of that photograph of McMullan with the face Martin thinks he recognises.'

The two of them reached Monica's apartment just after 9pm after taking a back-street detour to buy some milk at a twenty-four-hour grocery store. 'Your big birthday is fast approaching,' said Thomas, as they collapsed on Monica's sofa. 'You seem to be taking it in your stride.'

Monica feigned a look of surprise. 'Is it? I'd almost forgotten.' In truth, she hadn't forgotten at all. Yet, unlike forty, fifty and sixty, Monica felt mildly troubled by this particular landmark birthday although she couldn't put her finger on why. Emotionally she was in a happier place than she'd been for years; mentally Mrs Mendoza had commented at their last meeting that she had never seen Monica so balanced; and physically the yoga and the additional exercise with Thomas was making her feel stronger and more confident than ever. And yet, there was trepidation as the occasion loomed closer.

'We'll do something special on the day,' said Thomas. 'Just the two of us.'

Monica said that sounded perfect. 'It's still a few days away,' she added, running a hand through his hair as a means to distract herself from birthday thoughts. 'How about we do something special, just the two of us, right now?'

The following morning, Monica texted the commissioner to ask for the photograph which Martin had identified. 'Are you aware of a criminal family called Slaven,' she asked, 'just out of interest?'

The name rang a distant bell in Suzanne's mind but they certainly weren't among the major gangs taking up space in her mental and physical inboxes along with everything else. The summer had, as usual, unleashed a plague of marches and counter-marches in central London, each with their own highly political risks for the officers policing them. Every weekend seemed to bring another media storm fuelled by carefully edited smartphone footage which apparently showed heavy-handedness on the part of policemen and women.

'There are so many new gangs these days, it's a challenge to keep up, if I'm honest. I'll do some digging and talk to the commander in charge of gang violence but I can't personally recall anything revolving around the Slavens for a while. I know they used to be a big deal a few decades back but they've been quiet as far as I know for quite some time. It's entirely possible they became tax-paying, law-abiding citizens. It does happen. Rarely. Anyway, I'll get that photograph over to you as soon as possible.'

After the call, Monica opened her computer and did a search for Beryl Edwards. As expected, there were a number of them including a psychotherapist working in Phoenix, Arizona and a woman who ran a knitting circle in Cumbria. Narrowing her search, Monica finally discovered an obituary from 1983 in a local Kent newspaper. It outlined Beryl's long career in teaching, her work in the Second World War and even had a black-and-white picture of Beryl in her later years. She was wearing a cardigan and sitting in a chair, holding hands with a distinguished-looking gentleman of around the same age sitting beside her.

The final line of the obituary mentioned that '*in her final years at Ash View Care Home, Beryl enjoyed constant companionship from Roger Scott whose death at the age of 82 was reported in last week's newspaper.*'

23

When Thomas found her a few minutes later, Monica was in floods of tears. He'd never seen her like this. It was the reverse of the usual scenario with Thomas in tears and her affectionately providing the comfort. He enveloped her in his arms, oblivious as to what had caused this sudden emotional overflow. 'Beryl,' she whimpered, pointing weakly at the computer screen, where the image of the sweet but deadly old lady and her late-life love was still visible.

Thomas helped Monica to stand and together they walked gingerly to the sofa where he held her while she sobbed. A year ago, thought Thomas, he wouldn't have known what to do with a crying woman but now, with the closeness of his relationship with Monica, it came as second nature to him to hold her while the waves crashed around her. 'This isn't just about Beryl, is it?' he suggested.

Monica raised her eyes to him. 'I must look a complete state,' she said, rummaging in a pocket for a tissue that she knew wasn't there. Luckily, Thomas was rarely without a clean handkerchief, even in July. 'I'm sorry.' She sniffed, wiping her nose.

'Don't be daft,' Thomas comforted. 'What is it you always tell me? It's good to get it all out. It makes a change for you to be the one in tears. You're the strong one in this partnership. I'll make us a cup of tea and we can talk about it.'

Ten minutes later, the two of them had settled back onto the sofa with mugs of Earl Grey, entwined in each other even though Monica's turmoil had temporarily subsided. 'I think Beryl was the catalyst,' Monica began. 'I've never been bothered by the approach of a big birthday before but this feels different. When I was nearing thirty, I'd already had one failed marriage but my career was taking off so I didn't really give it a thought. Forty and fifty, I'd spent years with Patrick and I was happier than I'd ever been up to that point. We spent my fortieth in a beautiful, tiny, perfect hotel in Siena and my fiftieth in an even more perfect but somewhat larger hotel in Berlin. He was gone two months later, of course, but I couldn't know that then.'

Thomas swept a stray strand of Monica's hair behind her ear and kissed her head, aware that losing her second husband in the World Trade Center attacks in September 2001 had had a profound effect on Monica and was one of the reasons for her strength as well as her vulnerability, both things he loved about her.

'Sixty, I suppose I was still wrapped up in work and pondering retirement. I think I'd cut back my hours at the university by then. I don't really remember. It just didn't feel like a big deal. Seventy, on the other hand. It feels colder. Darker.' She twisted her head to look at Thomas and stroked his cheek. 'I think that if I didn't have you, it might be intolerable.' Her brown eyes filled with tears again.

'You and The Twelve,' she gulped, 'it keeps me going. I mean, it's been challenging these last few months with Chris and everything but I wouldn't change it for the world. You saw Lexington earlier. He's only been away from it a few months but already there's something about him that just feels... I don't know, like he's lost a major part of himself. Is that going to happen to us?' Monica dissolved into sobs again and Thomas decided the best course of action was simply to hold her while she stumbled her way through the turbulence or until he could think of something to distract her.

Eventually, when the sobs had receded into pitiful sniffles, Thomas recognised his moment. 'Why don't we go away,' he announced. 'A holiday. You and me. After the school holidays have finished and the resorts are less crowded. We have money; we can go anywhere. A cruise, maybe. Or just a couple of weeks exploring somewhere. What do you think?'

Monica managed a feeble smile. 'That sounds fabulous,' she said. 'As long as this case is done and dusted. I'd love to pack a bag right now but we can't just leave it in limbo.' She reached up and kissed him gently. 'I love it as an idea, though. Thank you, Thomas. You are just the sweetest man.' She retrieved his tear-damp handkerchief from under her bottom and dabbed her eyes again. 'Oh, and you know I said I was happier than I'd ever been when I was with Patrick?' Thomas nodded. 'I think I'm even happier now. Despite current evidence suggesting the opposite. I trust you more than anyone I've known in the last twenty years and that's huge for me.'

Thomas kissed her again, this time lightly on the cheek. 'Life is short,' he said quietly. 'And the years go by faster the older you get. When you get to our age, it's like being on one of those bobsleighs in the Winter Olympics, hurtling around the curves and praying that you don't crash into something.' Monica turned to look him in the eyes, hers still glistening. 'You're doing great,' he continued. 'And, on the days when you think you're not, I've got you.'

Monica's phone pinged. Suzanne had sent through the photograph of McMullan with the group of friends as well as a grainy blow-up of the man whom Martin had seemed to recognise. Thomas cuddled her lightly as Monica read the commissioner's brief attached message. 'I think your seventies are going to be your best decade,' he said. 'Beryl would be proud of you.'

She eased herself off the sofa and walked back to her computer where Beryl and Roger were still immortalised in monochrome harmony. 'I've just remembered what I was going to do next,' she said, tapping away at the keys. 'Before my mini meltdown. I was interested to see whether there are any pictures of Jerry Slaven. I know how to narrow the search now so if there is anything then it shouldn't take too long. Oh look, here we are. Jerry Slaven. Good God!' Monica's shout of shock was enough to divert Thomas from taking the drained tea mugs into the kitchen. 'That's not possible.'

Thomas placed the mugs on the nearest surface, a corner of Monica's kitchen island, and walked over to her, placing his hands gently on her shoulders. On her computer screen was one photograph of Jerry Slaven taken in 1962 while on her mobile was another photograph taken fifty years later featuring the same man.

24

'It can't be Jerry,' Monica gasped. 'He died in a beige Vauxhall Viva in 1964. But it looks exactly like him. Must be a son. We need to do some investigation.' *At least this seems to have partially taken her mind off being seventy*, thought Thomas in a state of relief. 'We need to talk to Martin.'

She scrolled through her contacts until she found the ex-cabbie's name. 'Shows how rarely I call him as an individual,' she mused. 'He's generally part of the WhatsApp group.'

After about half a dozen rings, Martin picked up. 'Wait a moment,' he shouted. 'I'll go somewhere quieter.' In the background, Monica could hear what sounded like 'Another Suitcase In Another Hall' from the musical *Evita*, fading away as he moved location. 'Ah, that's better,' said Martin, breathlessly.

'Where are you, Martin?'

'Gym.'

'There's a gym that plays *Evita*?'

Martin laughed and then coughed as he was still slightly out of breath from whatever exercise he had been doing. 'Yes, I discovered it about five months ago. It's in Hackney. It's popular with people who work in the theatre. Understandably. They're all younger and more flamboyant than me, plus a lot of the men are very muscular, but they're extremely friendly. They treat me like a celebrity because I know all the words to "Defying Gravity" and I can reach the high note if I start low enough.'

'He's joined a gym,' Monica mouthed to Thomas, her thumb over the microphone. 'It plays Elaine Paige.' Thomas gave her a look of bemusement and wandered into the kitchen area retrieving the dirty mugs on the way. 'Any particular reason for joining a musicals gym at your age, Martin? I mean, I'm all for encouraging everyone to stay fit but I suppose I'm just intrigued.'

There was a slight hesitation at the other end of the line. Monica wondered momentarily whether the physical exertion had been too much for poor Martin. 'I've met someone,' he said, finally. Monica took a moment to fully register what she was hearing.

'You've what?' she asked, slightly more hysterically than even she was expecting. Thomas looked up from the dishwasher, wondering what fresh disaster had been sent to dampen the pre-birthday mood. 'Sorry,' said Monica, recalibrating, 'I meant to say, goodness, that's exciting news, Martin. Anyone we know?' Thomas returned to the housework matter in hand.

It was something of a relief to hear that Martin hadn't suddenly entered into a relationship with any other members of The Twelve. Apparently her name was Joanne, she was sixty-eight, a retired librarian, and they had met online just after the end of the Burrows case in March. Martin had felt that enough time had elapsed since the death of his wife, Pauline, in 2009, and 'besides, everybody else seemed to be coupling up so I thought, why not? She loves musicals as much as I do so we have lots in common. We both joined the gym so we can be more, um, active together.'

A disturbing and unerotic image floated uninvited through Monica's mind and she had to glance at Thomas to shake it. 'Coffee?' he mouthed, lifting an imaginary cup to his lips. Monica nodded in relief. The image had vanished.

'I'm delighted for you,' said Monica, her equilibrium now at least partially restored. 'Now, why did I call you? Oh yes. I'm going to text you two photographs. One is an enlargement of the picture with DI McMullan showing the face you vaguely recognised and the other is a picture of someone you might remember from your youth. Is that okay?' Martin agreed that it would be fine. Fascinating, even. 'I'll do it as soon as we finish the call. Can you look at them before you go back to Joanne in the gym, please?'

Martin said that he would look at the photographs immediately. Besides, Joanne wasn't in the gym that morning as she was volunteering at a nearby school for children with special needs. 'She goes and reads with them twice a week,' he explained. 'She's a bit of an angel.'

Everyone has something to keep them busy, thought Monica. Helping disadvantaged kids, knitting circles, book clubs, exterminating criminals. Whatever floats one's particular boat. 'Of course she is, Martin,' she said. 'Stand by.' She finished the call and went over to her computer to copy the photograph of Jerry Slaven onto her phone ready to send to Martin. 'He's got a girlfriend,' she said to Thomas who had carefully placed a fresh cappuccino on her desk. 'She sounds virtuous beyond reason.'

'Oh well,' replied Thomas casually, settling back on the sofa, 'I suppose we can't all be murderous masterminds.' Monica shot him a look halfway between admiration and bashfulness. She texted Martin the two photographs accompanied by a quizzical emoji face and waited. A notification from Bobby City flashed on her computer. *Your annual home contents insurance on The Twelve's properties has today been paid. I've managed to reduce the premium by £40,000.*

Another virtuous one, thought Monica enviously.

A minute later, Martin's succinct one-word response pinged into her phone.

Fuck.

25

Two days before Monica's seventieth birthday, in the early afternoon, The Twelve gathered at a hastily arranged meeting to discuss the status of the Morris case. The venue, an imposing Victorian house overlooking a small green in east London, had been chosen by Monica for selfish reasons – she wanted to treat herself to some blooms from the nearby flower market for her birthday. This suited most of The Twelve anyway as the majority lived east of central London and in fact Terry had been quietly but persistently lobbying for a while for the group to use more properties nearer to his place in Whitechapel. Martin could visit his nearby gym straight after the meeting, which delighted him as it meant he could meet Joanne for "Sondheim Saturday" although neither of them would be taking part in the associated spin class. Chris could have walked from his own house five minutes away, had he not been still cohabiting at Anna's.

Monica had messaged Lexington the previous day to see whether he wanted to attend but the former leader had politely declined owing to a hospital appointment. *Nothing to worry about unduly,* he had texted. *Just old person stuff.* He had also suggested that Monica contact Bobby City to make her aware of the meeting in order that she could arrange for the venue to be cleaned. *We haven't used it for a while so...* This text ended with a series of cobweb emojis and a waving ghost.

Sure enough, the house was sparkling with the distinct aroma of furniture polish and air freshener when Monica and Thomas arrived an hour earlier than the others to refamiliarise, or in Thomas's case, familiarise themselves with the amenities. Whoever had cleaned the place had conveniently left a scented candle and some long matches so that the smell of cleaning could be countered by pomegranate noir. While Monica searched out the kitchen and found fresh milk in the fridge, a selection of herbal and non-herbal teas and a coffee machine with an abundance of pods, Thomas studied the sketches of trees which were dotted through the hallway and main meeting area. 'Mondrian,' shouted Monica confidently from the kitchen. 'Early stuff. Before he went abstract. Do you like them?' Thomas confirmed that he did while secretly searching for "Mondrian abstract" on his smartphone. Spending time in The Twelve was a constant education in a variety of disciplines.

Over text, Monica had explained to Martin and the rest of the group that one of the photographs, the one featuring Jerry Slaven, had been taken in the early 1960s while the other, with DI Brian McMullan, had been taken around fifty years later.

She had also found out through Suzanne Green that the man in the second photograph was almost certainly Tony Slaven, Jerry's son, and a relatively minor criminal during the nineties who, according to a superintendent former colleague of McMullan, was believed to be an informant on equally minor drug dealers in the Acton and Ealing areas of west London. According to the super, who also happened to be in the photograph from around 2011, McMullan would have a knack of knowing where and when certain drug dealers would be peddling heroin and cocaine and would organise officers in a pincer movement to arrest them. The rumour at the time was that McMullan was secretly meeting with Slaven who didn't trust the mobile phone network and preferred to communicate anything important in person.

Terry and Martin arrived slightly late but with butter and sultana cookies still warm from the locksmith's oven in Whitechapel and driven the short distance by the cabbie so nobody felt like complaining. Martin was, unusually, wearing a tight purple T-shirt with the slogan *Mad 4 Musicals* emblazoned on it in swirly yellow lettering, a one-month anniversary gift from Joanne. This prompted Graham to suggest the cabbie wear more bright colours as 'it's a counterpoint to the dour grey of your crew cut, dear.' Martin glowered in response but perked up when Belinda gave him a cuddle and told him she thought it was very fetching. 'It's fashion, innit?' He grinned proudly.

'Anything else we need to know about Tony Slaven at this stage?' asked David as the meeting formally began. 'Bearing in mind we don't currently have a connection between him and Paul or Tiffany Storey.'

Monica sensed the former plumber's frustration at the lack of information although she had her suspicions. The very fact that a detective inspector investigating the Justin Morris case appeared to be friends with a criminal based around the same area as the killing was enough to ring a distant yet persistent alarm bell. 'He's sixty-one. Married to Janine who is eleven years younger. Two kids, both boys, now in their thirties – Janine had them young, when she was still a teenager. No criminal record although he was known to be involved in some bank fraud in the nineties and early 2000s. Suzanne has suspicions that McMullan leant on witnesses and nothing ever came to court. Apparently he's been quiet since about 2010, to all intents and purposes living peacefully in a big house in Chiswick.'

'Quiet since the Morris murder,' said Catherine, quietly. She was sitting with Belinda on a burgundy sofa by the window and the summer sunlight streaming through gave the two of them a seraphic aura. The correlation between the Morris murder and the decline in activity by Tony Slaven was not lost on anyone.

'I will do some more digging into Tony Slaven,' said Monica. 'Interestingly, his father was assassinated by The Twelve in 1964.' She glanced at Martin who responded with a conspiratorial smirk. 'Now, how far have we got with plans for talking with the Storeys?'

The group of five who had been working together looked around at each other to decide which of them was going to take the lead. 'Shall I...?' asked Catherine tentatively. David indicated she should go ahead. He had spent hours every day watching the Storey house from his vantage point in the cemetery, desperate to glean any knowledge which might help to either prove that Paul Storey was guilty or, if he wasn't, to suggest who might be. 'Okay, we have two options,' began Catherine.

The first option was to win Tiffany's trust. This would naturally take some time, if indeed it could be achieved at all but the plan would be to station Veronica and Catherine nearby – 'I have a friend with a guest room in Ealing so we can base ourselves there for a while,' said the ex-journalist. She explained that when Owen or Graham spotted Tiffany leaving the house for her occasional coffee, the two of them would dash to the café, sit as close to Tiffany and her friend as possible and attempt to open up some dialogue. Catherine had timed the journey from her friend's house to the café at just over two minutes if they walked briskly.

'There's a slight possibility she might recognise me from the television,' said Veronica, 'which might be helpful in initiating a conversation. Although I'm not banking on it. I'm not that big-headed.'

David explained that he was reticent about this option as he preferred the immediacy of option two. 'Which is?' asked Monica.

'Carbon monoxide into their air vents until they pass out,' said David, grimly.

Silence filled the room momentarily before being replaced by unconvinced, low-level muttering. A couple of the elder members of the group, Owen and Martin, had used this gas once before in 2013, but on that occasion to kill, not to cause loss of consciousness. 'Risky,' growled Martin darkly. Owen nodded with solemnity at the memory.

'We appreciate precautions will need to be taken,' said Terry, 'and they will be. We'll require pure oxygen to treat them both afterwards, although our hope is that we won't need to wait until they fully lose consciousness before we move in. With any luck they'll be woozy and vomiting while we pick the lock and gain entry to the house.'

Monica had several thoughts swirling but the key question involved Chris. She turned to look at the former surgeon with an expression which took the form of a plea. 'You're going to need me for medical checks and, unusually, making sure people don't die.' He sighed. 'Oh well. I guess it's time to vacate the back seat.'

26

'Will that be okay?' asked Anna, squeezing Chris's hand. The two of them were squished tightly onto a two-seater sofa under a Mondrian tree having deliberately created less space for themselves with cushions in varying hues. 'If you're not ready then I can probably cover it, as long as you tell me what I'm basically doing. I appreciate I'm more at home with the dead who rarely require oxygen but, hey, what's the difference at the end of the day? Apart from the heartbeat. And the breathing.'

'I think I should be all right,' said the former surgeon wearily. Chris still wasn't completely back to his usual self. He had certainly improved since his impromptu arrest; it had crossed his mind to return to the police station to thank the desk sergeant involved but, on reflection, he had decided that the poor man had probably been through enough for one summer, what with the Metropolitan Police commissioner turning up unannounced in a party dress and giving him a right earful. However, on advice from Mrs Mendoza, and caution from Anna, he was trying hard to pace himself when it came to active Twelve service.

Nonetheless, he was the only member of the group to have actually dealt with carbon monoxide poisoning during his career, from a recovery perspective at least, and despite the fact that he trusted Anna to be able to administer the correct treatment if he gave her some basic guidelines, Chris felt a sense of responsibility both to the Storeys and The Twelve to do his best. His duty of care was paramount, regardless of the patient and how they became unwell.

Monica thanked him and balanced the options. Although she now had the responsibility for each case, the new leader couldn't help wondering what Lexington would do. 'I think we try both,' she said. 'At least for a month to six weeks. We'll review it at the end of August to see how much progress has been made with Tiffany – that's unless there's a breakthrough before that. In the meantime, Terry and David, perhaps you could work on plan B in terms of locks, air vents and the like. I'll acquire the carbon monoxide if someone else could please get hold of the oxygen.' Chris and Anna both raised hands containing a cookie. 'And Graham and Owen, in the course of your observation of the house and its surroundings, could you please undertake a risk assessment as far as possible, please. We need to ensure that only the potentially guilty are put in danger.'

Before they left the house, Belinda tentatively asked whether she could help Team Veronica on Tiffany-watch. 'I need something to occupy my time at the moment,' she explained quietly. The linguist drew Monica into a huddle with Veronica and Catherine and explained that her husband, Malcolm, had entered the final stages of his dementia and had become less aggressive and more childlike. As a result, Belinda had resumed visits to him in the care home but seeing his deterioration was taking its toll. 'I just think that if I can be more useful in this case, it'll take my mind off that a bit,' she explained. Veronica gave her a hug and said that not only would she be welcome to help but that the three of them should organise some fun outings as well. Belinda noticeably rallied, albeit tearfully.

'Are you sure *you're* okay?' Monica asked, also giving her a friendly squeeze.

'I will be,' said Belinda. 'It's the end bit now. They aren't sure whether it'll be days or weeks or maybe a few months but I feel I should be there for him when the time comes.'

'It's not the easiest of cases,' said Thomas as they squeezed carefully through the crowds of locals and tourists to escape the flower market.

'It never is,' replied Monica who had fallen in love with some long-stemmed roses with white petals fringed with vibrant pink. Thomas, in another burst of romance, had bought the entire remaining stock of them amounting to thirty-eight blooms and was now almost constantly blushing at the admiring looks of others as he carried the huge bunch through the throng with Monica holding on to the back pocket of his jeans with one hand and a Saturday newspaper in the other.

They surfaced from the main ocean of people into slightly calmer waters, flagged a passing cab and set off for St John's Wood.

'Someone's got the love bug,' said the grey-haired taxi driver with a chuckle. 'If I came home to my missus with them roses, she'd be flabbergasted. She might even give me a kiss.'

Monica smiled. 'I'm sure a lovely man like you doesn't need roses to get a kiss from his wife.' The cabbie laughed, a loud, throaty chortle which reminded both passengers of their friend. 'It's a bit of a long shot but do you happen to know a taxi driver named Martin Francis? He's a friend of ours. Retired now although he still drives his cab around the place.'

The driver's face brightened as if illuminated by footlights. 'Martin? Of course I do. Such a beautiful, beautiful man. Always so helpful, especially when I was starting out. I've only been doing this twenty years. Since I left the army aged forty. Martin was a godsend. Always looked out for me in those early years. I ain't seen him for a while though. Friend of yours, you say? What a small world. What he's up to these days? Keeping out of trouble, I hope.'

Monica was already making calculations in her head so Thomas explained, within the parameters of what was sensible, that the cabbie was indeed keeping fit and keeping busy and had recently joined a gym. 'What's your name, if I may ask?' said Monica. 'I'll tell him we've met you.' They had stopped at a traffic light by the hotel at King's Cross which inspired her to reach for Thomas's hand and give it an affectionate squeeze.

'John Bailey, at your service,' he said. 'Captain John Bailey if we're being precise. Royal Regiment of Fusiliers.'

'I'm Monica Lodhia and this is Thomas Quinn. We're pleased to meet you, Captain Bailey.' She paused and looked out of the window as the hotel sailed by. 'Purely out of interest, any plans to retire?'

Ten minutes later, Monica was standing on the pavement outside St John's Wood while Thomas paid the taxi fare. 'What time do you finish today, John?' The cabbie said that she and Thomas would be his last passengers of the day as he had started work at four in the morning and he had to get home to Cricklewood for his late Saturday lunch. His wife, Sandra, was a fantastic cook, especially her roasts. 'Well, I think you and Sandra deserve an evening to remember.'

She extracted six of the roses and carefully wrapped them in the superfluous business pages of the newspaper. 'These are for you and Sandra.' She grinned. 'And we hope we see you again some day. I personally also hope you get that kiss.'

John Bailey, after a brief attempt at polite refusal, took Monica's floral gift and placed it carefully on his passenger seat. 'I can't thank you enough.' He winked. 'You never know, I might even get more than a kiss. Send my best to Martin.' He switched off his orange light and drove off towards the north as Thomas and Monica waved from the bottom of their steps.

'I know what you're thinking.' Thomas beamed as he watched John Bailey's taxi disappear out of view.

Monica retrieved her door key from her shoulder bag and turned it in the lock. 'Always best to think ahead,' she purred.

27

'Are you admiring my seventy-year-old arse, Thomas Quinn?'

Monica had pulled on and half-buttoned one of Thomas's shirts after some blissful and leisurely birthday morning sex and was on her way out of the bedroom to make coffee. Thomas had offered to do so but she was already en route before he'd managed to gather the required energy. She half-turned with a radiant smile, expectant of an answer. 'I am,' he replied. 'And I can categorically state after careful analysis that, in a subtle yet definitive way, it is an improvement on your sixty-nine-year-old arse from yesterday.' Monica's grin widened further and she blew him a kiss which he pretended to catch, reaching to his right and almost toppling out of bed.

'I shall return with coffee,' she announced, 'and also an idea I'd like to run past you. Something I've been thinking about for a couple of days.'

Thomas watched as she vanished down the short corridor to the open-plan kitchen-living area. He rearranged himself puppylike into the plump, white pillows in readiness for her return as the sounds and then smells of fresh coffee permeated the apartment. What idea could Monica be considering? Could it be something involving the two of them or The Twelve or something else entirely? He couldn't suppress the nagging feeling that Monica might ask him to marry her. It was just the kind of thing she would consider doing and, if he was honest, although they'd only been together since Christmas, the thought had also crossed his mind once or twice. Neither of them were getting any younger and the thought of a close companion in later life was immensely appealing. Maybe the image of Beryl and Roger together in their final days had given Monica some inspiration.

Thomas tried to dismiss the thought from his mind, not because it was troubling but because he felt sure that it was more likely that Monica's idea was Twelve-related. He reached over to a bedside table to retrieve his phone and find something to distract himself. He scrolled through social media, a whirlwind catalogue of news stories, vintage sports clips and pictures of cats. A distant, all-powerful algorithm had clearly decided where Thomas's interests lay. Maybe Monica was thinking of getting a cat, he pondered, although this only succeeded in resurrecting the idea of marriage in his musings.

Monica returned barefoot with a mug in each hand. She set one down beside Thomas and then paced round the bed and placed her own on the opposite bedside table before climbing back into bed for a cuddle. 'Do you want to hear my idea?' she whispered excitedly. 'It's about the future.'

Thomas braced himself. Whether cats or wedding bells or something else entirely, he was ready.

'I've been thinking,' she began. 'As leader of The Twelve, I want to do something useful. Something that helps society.' Thomas unbraced incrementally. He felt an overwhelming sense of relief although, at the edges of this, he also detected the faintest feeling of disappointment.

'Don't we already help society? You know, with all the death and the charity donations and that.'

Monica giggled and pulled him closer. 'Yes, of course, but I'm thinking of something bigger. I'd like to leave a legacy. Not just a financial one, although of course I've made my will accordingly. I'd like future members of The Twelve to look back at Monica Lodhia's tenure and say, "My goodness, she achieved so much". And I'm thinking specifically about the properties we own.'

Thomas extracted himself slightly from her embrace and reached for his coffee. He sipped it, realised it was still too hot and returned to his original position. 'Go on.'

Monica explained that The Twelve currently owned eighteen properties outright, dotted around London. Most had been bequeathed to them by former members dating back as far as 1885 when the east London house at which they had gathered earlier in the week was gifted by Charles Stafford, leader of the group from 1874 to 1883 and a former explorer specialising in the Middle East and western Asia. With no dependents, Stafford had stated that The Twelve could use his house for meetings after his death and his example had led to a flurry of similar property acquisitions throughout the late nineteenth and early twentieth centuries. 'There are no mortgages,' Monica continued, 'and of course most of them are empty most of the time. I checked and the last time we actually used Quilter Street was just under two years ago. That's crazy, especially at a time when I'm constantly hearing about housing shortages and people like nurses and junior doctors unable to afford their rents and having to commute for hours to get to work.'

Thomas made another attempt at his coffee, this time with more success. 'I think I know where this might be going,' he said with a slurp.

'So what I propose is that we rent some of them out, maybe three to start with, to see how we go. We rent them to people who are most in need, like the nurses, and we charge hardly anything. We could charge nothing, of course, allowing people to live rent free but I don't want to arouse suspicion. We wouldn't advertise in local papers because we'd just be inundated. Instead we would have to be more subtle about it. Listen out for people who are in need; friends of friends or children of friends. Do you see?' Thomas agreed that it sounded like common sense.

'We'd have to move the art out, naturally,' she continued, 'but there are plenty of other places for it to go. And, of course, there are certain properties where we couldn't make it work. Beckton, for example, because of the gold-plated bath in the garage. That would definitely arouse suspicion and, realistically, there's nowhere else it could go. Its proximity to the main sewer and the river is vital.' Thomas was reminded of his first evening as a member of The Twelve when he had been mildly disturbed by a WhatsApp conversation between the other eleven. The excited chatter had centred around the case of a paedophile rapist named Raymond Hunt whose body had been dissolved in an acid bath at a Twelve house in Beckton before having the plug pulled on his liquid remains.

'It's a great idea, Monica. I love it. And I love you.'

Monica grinned. 'I love you too,' she said. 'I'll run it by the group later on. I'm thinking the house we were just in, the one in Belgravia maybe and there's another down in Clapham that we haven't used for yonks, largely because of Martin's allergic reaction to most things south of the river. Is the coffee okay, darling?' Thomas confirmed that it was now the perfect temperature to drink. 'I'm excited about my birthday dinner tonight,' she said, reaching for her mug.

She had just put it to her lips when both phones pinged. A message from Graham to the group. Tiffany Storey was on the move.

28

Within a couple of minutes, Catherine had messaged to say that she, Veronica and Belinda had pulled on their trainers and were scampering towards the café where Tiffany always met her friend. They had briefly stopped to allow Belinda to retie an errant shoelace, conveniently providing the opportunity to text. With any luck they should beat her there by about three minutes. According to Graham, Tiffany was wearing blue jeans and a pink T-shirt; she should be fairly identifiable.

David Latham was already on his way to the Storey house having flagged down a taxi on Willesden High Road. He texted that he should be outside within ten minutes. Graham would keep a close eye on Paul Storey, currently in his room as usual, and inform everyone of any unusual movements. Terry texted to ask if David could please take close-up photographs of any locks on the Storeys' front door. The flurry of WhatsApp activity on his and Monica's phones curiously reminded Thomas of wedding bells. He attempted to put the thought to the back of his mind, without success. 'I was about to suggest a birthday shower together,' said Monica through a sigh, waving her phone at him, 'but I suppose we'd better see how this pans out, at least for the next hour or so.'

Veronica's group arrived at the café slightly out of breath and looked around to see whether there was anyone wearing a pink T-shirt. There were around a dozen tables in the main part of the café, most of them occupied. Catherine also noticed a short corridor leading past some toilets into a smaller alcove. She ventured down the corridor and found three more tables at the back of the café, two of which were occupied. At one sat a middle-aged woman with peroxide-blonde hair and a harsh expression who looked up at Catherine and gave the visual equivalent of a canine warning growl. At the other table sat a pair of college students each silently working on their laptops with headphones through which Catherine could faintly hear the staccato beats of hip-hop music.

The ex-journalist dashed back to the front of the café where Belinda had taken a table by the door while Veronica was ordering cortados for each of them. 'I'll sit at the back,' she said. 'So we've got every base covered. There are three tables back there.' Catherine took her coffee and carefully walked to the rear space where she settled into the one vacant position, ignoring the silent aggression from the lone woman and smiling at the students. She rummaged in her bag and found her headphones, plugged them into her phone and scrolled to find a podcast, ostentatiously directing the screen at the woman to indicate that, for the next half hour, the podcast would be receiving her full attention.

At the front of the café, Belinda and Veronica watched as Tiffany arrived. She was a thin, tired-looking woman in her fifties, worn and lined from the pressure of existence. Belinda estimated she could be nearer to sixty than fifty but Tiffany's was one of those deceptive faces which forbade an accurate age assessment. The new arrival did a quick scan of the room like a hunted animal checking the coast is clear before making a dash for safety, and then headed down the corridor towards Catherine. On seeing Veronica, Tiffany registered a momentary glimmer of bemusement before moving away. 'Do you think she recognises me?' the former TV presenter whispered. Belinda agreed that it was possible.

'Busy in here today,' said Tiffany angrily as she sat opposite her friend and glanced cautiously at the three other customers in close proximity.

'You wanna get yourself a coffee?' asked the friend, looking at Catherine who appeared deep in concentration with her podcast although, in reality, she had turned the sound down to almost silence. 'These won't bother us. They're lost in their own little worlds.'

Tiffany shuffled in her seat. 'I won't, if you don't mind,' she said. 'I can't stay. He's not having his best day today so I need to get back. I'll just take what we need if it's all the same to you.'

'Fair enough,' said the friend, emotionlessly. She reached into her bag and pulled out a regular-sized envelope which she passed to Tiffany under the table. 'Same as usual. Tony sends his best.' Tiffany took the envelope, folded it and pushed it uneasily into her jeans pocket before standing up which allowed her to push it further down.

'Thanks,' she said, turning back towards the front of the café. 'See you in two weeks.'

'I'll be here. Take care.'

Tiffany walked at speed back down the corridor towards Belinda and Veronica who both looked up at the same time. Veronica hoped that the woman would say something, just to be able to begin some sort of conversation, but she was disappointed. Tiffany, in her pink T-shirt, hurried out of the café as if scared by something. 'Flying visit,' said Belinda with a frown.

Just under a mile away, David had arrived at the door to the Storey house. *I'm here*, he texted. *Can I get an update of the positions of Paul and Tiffany please.* Graham responded to confirm that Paul remained in his room. Veronica texted to alert him that Tiffany had left the café. *And she's walking fast. Assuming she's headed straight back, you've got about seven or eight minutes to be safe.*

Okay, this won't take long, thought the plumber. He texted to ask Terry whether he was ready and the locksmith confirmed that he was indeed awaiting photographs to assist with the next part of the case. He'd been baking a ginger cake but it didn't need to come out of the oven for a while. It was, nonetheless, making his entire house smell delicious.

David brought his phone up to the Storeys' single lock and took three pictures plus a video for good measure. Then he walked round the side of the house, photographing the various air vents and any other structural anomalies which might prove useful, before retreating to his usual observation point in the cemetery.

Tiffany's back, texted Graham from his bedroom a couple of minutes later as he watched the woman quickly open her door and then saw her infra-red ghost speed upstairs to where the image of Paul was still horizontal on his bed.

David sat in the graveyard altering the filter on his photos to make them clearer for Terry's expert eyes before sending to the group. *It's a Banham M2002 deadlock*, texted the locksmith. *An expensive lock and a very good one. Unusual for a house like that.*

Can you pick it? texted Monica. Terry confirmed that it would be more of a challenge than the common Yale locks but, all things being equal, it shouldn't take him any longer than about five minutes. He'd spend some time practising over the next few days.

Arguably the more important question, he suggested, was why the Storeys felt they needed such a lock. Who or what were they trying to keep out?

29

Catherine was unable to respond to any of these texts. She had needed to place her phone upside down on the café table in case the woman next to her caught sight of anything which might jeopardise the case. Eventually, after about ten minutes, the woman finished her coffee and left, allowing Catherine to reconvene with the other two members of The Twelve at their window table. 'Tony sends his best. That's what she said. And she handed over an envelope. Could it be this Tony Slaven, do you think?'

Hurriedly, Catherine texted The Twelve an overview of what had happened in the café. Monica asked whether any of them got a photograph of Tiffany's friend to see if they could identify her. The group of three looked at each other sheepishly. *They're back in two weeks,* texted Catherine. *We can plan to get a snap then. We'll be more prepared.*

In St John's Wood, Monica emitted an exasperated sigh but decided to let it pass. She knew a retired Turkish police detective who would have meticulously planned to get photographic evidence without being asked. *No problem,* she texted back with an additional blue heart emoji. *Well done, everyone.*

Thomas was avidly receiving and digesting all of these texts while relaxing on Monica's sofa in one of her dressing gowns. 'Can I still interest you in that shower?' he cautiously enquired, unsure whether or not her mood had changed owing to events a few miles to the west.

Monica placed her phone carefully on her desk and realised that even though it was nearly 10.30am, she was still only wearing Thomas's shirt. 'Okay, let's get clean,' she said, pulling the shirt over her head. 'Unless of course you want to get dirty again first.'

Over the next few days, the various members of The Twelve busied themselves in preparation for the next stage of their plan. David paid a visit to Diana and Henry Morris as he'd promised to keep them appraised of all the elements of the case. This also gave him the opportunity to see how Henry's treatment was progressing. After David had explained to the couple the case's developments including those relating to the jacket, Henry had needed some time alone. He hugged his friend, thanked him for the update and ambled to the opposite end of his garden where he extracted some garden tools from a small shed and began deadheading some early flowering perennials.

'The doctors are very happy with him,' said Diana, pouring David another cup of tea as the two of them sat under a garden parasol at a small table near the house. 'He was wise to get checked out when he did. If he'd left it another six months then we would almost certainly be looking at a very different prognosis. All being well, he should finish the radiotherapy in

October and then it's just a question of keeping an eye on things every few months just to make sure nothing's coming back.'

She smiled towards her husband who, although weaker than usual a couple of days after his most recent treatment, was remaining busy and who waved a pair of secateurs in response. 'If Paul Storey isn't guilty,' Diana added regretfully, turning back to face David, 'then I suppose we've troubled you for no reason. Your group could have been getting on with something else. I am sorry.' The former plumber explained that, actually, they were rather intrigued by the case and even though it wasn't as straightforward as their usual activities, it had certainly given everyone something to get their teeth into. Veronica in particular was finding the whole business fascinating.

'Somebody was the fifth killer of Justin,' he said. 'With any luck, we'll find out who he is and then we can deal with him.'

Monica had meanwhile asked the group about her idea of renting out a selection of Twelve properties and this had been met with universal approval. She had furthermore sought the advice of both Lexington and of Bobby City who, after some mild grumbling about having to change the insurance details, had agreed that it was entirely sensible and a forward-thinking move for The Twelve in the twenty-first century.

Monica had also sourced some carbon monoxide canisters as well as some fixed flow regulators and tubing which David had requested. With Martin's help, she had stored everything in the downstairs toilet of a Twelve house in Shepherd's Bush. 'This is another one of the places I'm thinking of renting out, in case you hear of anyone who could benefit,' she told the cabbie. 'After we've removed these canisters, of course.' Martin said he could ask around a few of his old mates to see whether they knew anyone suitable. He'd be selective about it so as not to arouse suspicion.

In Kensal Green, Chris was teaching Anna the rudiments of

administering pure oxygen after carbon monoxide poisoning. Her spare room had been transformed into a domestic approximation of a hyperbaric chamber in which to practise. 'All being well,' said Chris, 'the two of them won't be too badly affected and as long as they breathe the pure stuff through masks for an hour or so, they should be broadly fine.'

'And if they aren't?' asked the forensic pathologist with a tone of concern.

Chris gently kissed her forehead. 'Then we seamlessly drift from my area of expertise, i.e. the living, to yours. The non-living.'

Catherine's group, meanwhile, saw no need to stay with her friend Celia in Ealing until closer to the date of Tiffany's next visit to the café. This allowed Belinda to have daily visits to her husband in his final days, often accompanied by Veronica who had quickly become a good friend to the quietly spoken linguist. Catherine split her days between her home in Barnes and occasional visits to Owen and Graham in Finsbury Park, partly to keep an eye on the goings-on in the Storey house and partly because the three of them often shared a bed. The former journalist enjoyed being single in her sixties but sometimes, more so during a case she had noticed, she craved male attention. This arrangement also suited Owen and Graham who had both been married to women before first becoming widowed and, after joining The Twelve, becoming lovers. 'Anything that adds spice to one's advanced years is surely to be embraced,' announced Owen one balmy morning as he surveyed his lovers' bodies on their king-size bed in the bright July sunlight.

Almost two weeks later, on a warm evening before Tiffany's next scheduled meeting, Catherine arrived at her friend, Celia's house in Ealing to find Veronica already in the garden with a glass of white wine and a magazine. The former TV presenter had kicked off her sandals and was wiggling her toes in the fading sunlight, enjoying the herby, garlicky smells emanating from the kitchen. 'No Belinda today,' she said, sadly. 'Last few hours or days for Malcolm apparently. But on the plus side, Celia's opened some delicious Viognier.' *Poor Belinda*, thought Catherine, although Malcolm's illness had been dragging on for so many years that it must feel like a relief when the time finally came.

Celia emerged from the kitchen with a spare glass for the new arrival and the chilled bottle of white wine, kissed Catherine on the cheek and disappeared back inside to finish preparing dinner. 'What are you reading, V?' the journalist asked, topping up her friend and then pouring for herself.

'It's just one of these local rags,' said Veronica. 'Came through the door about an hour ago. It's mostly adverts for estate agents but I thought I'd catch up on local news while I'm here. Look, they have a whole section at the front where they photograph people at local events.' She passed the magazine to Catherine who scanned the relevant page, entitled *Out On The Town*, with growing interest.

'Celia!' she called out. 'Have you got any more of these magazines? The...' she turned to the front cover which carried a close-up photograph of some dark-pink summer flowers in Gunnersbury Park and the imaginative headline *Blooming Summer* in white type, 'the *West London Enterprise*.'

'Good Lord, no,' said Celia, poking her head out of the back door with one hand in an oven glove patterned with oranges. 'I generally throw them out as soon as they drop through the box.'

Damn, thought Catherine.

'But I know the editor,' Celia continued brightly. 'She lives a few doors down the street. Rachel Robins. She's probably got a stash.'

30

There was a two-hour wait for a reply after Celia had texted Rachel Robins but eventually the editor responded with apologies for her tardiness but also a decent excuse. 'She's out tonight,' said Celia, reading the message which she revealed had been sent from a toilet cubicle at a nearby hotel. 'Rotary Club Summer Ball, apparently. One of those tedious evenings of the year but one she feels obliged to attend, she says, owing to the large number of older ladies who use the occasion as an opportunity to get as drunk and indiscreet as possible. But she says we can pop over tomorrow evening around seven if that's convenient.'

'Busy day tomorrow.' Veronica beamed, almost bouncing in her garden chair. 'I'm so excited.' Catherine gave her friend a look of mild concern but chalked it down to first case nerves.

The following morning, the two of them arrived at the café extra early to get the necessary seats. Veronica took the alcove to avoid suspicion, while Catherine sat by the window. When, by 10am, there had been no sign of the mystery woman and no text from Owen or Graham to say that Tiffany was on her way, the ex-journalist and the former TV presenter began texting each other.

She did say two weeks, didn't she? Xx

Yes. But of course they may not always meet at the same time of day. Xx

We might have missed her. We could be here for hours. Xx

Don't worry. Graham or Owen would have let us know yesterday if there had been any movement. If there's nothing by 12, we'll call it a day. Xx

I need a wee. Shouldn't have had that tall latte after all the tea at breakfast. Xx

At that moment, Graham texted to say that Tiffany was leaving the house. Almost simultaneously, the mystery woman entered the café, ordered a cappuccino and, with an impatient exhalation and a roll of the eyes, went to sit in the alcove next to Veronica who ostentatiously inserted earphones and started nodding rhythmically to music that wasn't playing while simultaneously checking her texts from Catherine.

Can you hold it? Xx

Probably not. But I've got a few minutes until T gets here so I'll go now. Xxx

Veronica rose from her seat, removed an earphone and turned to the new arrival with the friendliest smile she could muster. 'I'm just going to the ladies. Could you please make sure nobody takes away my coffee?' The woman nodded with as much reluctance as it was possible to squeeze into a simple head movement. 'Thank you,' replied Veronica, still smiling.

As it was such a small café, there was only the one toilet. It was engaged. Veronica hovered outside for a minute before texting Catherine. *Someone's in there and I'm about to burst. Xx.* This text was accompanied by an emoji of a face looking as embarrassed as possible.

I think I saw a woman with a baby go in there just now. Maybe knock and check they're all right. Xx

Don't worry. I'll go back to the alcove and use what remains of my pelvic floor muscles. Can you let me know when she comes out please? I can't see the door from where I'm sitting. Xxx

Catherine texted a thumbs up emoji and a pink heart and Veronica returned to her coffee. 'Busy,' she said to the woman, who ignored her. Veronica replaced her earphones and pretended to listen to the non-existent music while she concentrated on thinking of anything non-liquid. A minute later, Tiffany arrived, slightly flustered. Catherine wondered whether this poor woman ever experienced moments of tranquillity and calm.

Unlike the previous meeting, on this occasion Tiffany bought herself an espresso before sitting down opposite her friend. 'Staying longer than last time then?' asked the woman, dismissively.

Tiffany yawned. 'A little bit longer,' she said. 'Just long enough to down this.' She gulped half of her coffee. 'He wasn't good in the night so I haven't slept much. Again.'

'Do you want us to send one of our doctors round?' asked the woman with a scowl.

Suddenly a look of paralysing fear crossed Tiffany's face. '*No!*' she shouted, wide-eyed. 'No visitors. You know he doesn't react well to visitors. I'll take care of him. I've always taken care of him. I'll just take my payment and get back.'

Veronica's phone vibrated. *Toilet is free. Xx.* Faced with the choice of staying to listen to the end of the conversation and risking an embarrassing accident or a much more comfortable alternative, Veronica plumped for the latter. By the time she returned to the alcove, Tiffany had vanished.

At the front of the café, Catherine was pretending to apply make-up using her phone as a mirror while actually using her camera setting so she was ready for Tiffany's companion to leave the café, which she did a few moments later. *I got a couple of good shots,* she texted Veronica. *Come see. Xx.*

Veronica joined her friend and relayed what she'd heard of the conversation. Catherine then texted the group with an update and the best of the two photos of the woman. *We may have some more info later,* she texted. *Seeing a local contact on a journalistic hunch. X.*

At seven that evening, Celia walked them both round to Rachel Robins's house which was about a hundred yards down the same road on the opposite side. Rachel, a petite woman with a shock of curly blonde hair, greeted them all with air kisses and invited everyone into her spacious kitchen which, like Celia's house, looked out onto an even more spacious garden, 'although,' Rachel pointed out, 'Celia's points south-west so she gets more sun; lucky thing. I only really get the morning.'

The local magazine editor opened a bottle of fruity red wine and poured three glasses. 'It's a bit of a long shot,' began Catherine, 'but I was reading the current issue and I wondered whether you might have back copies. We're particularly interested in the *Out On The Town* pages with photographs from local events. We're trying to identify someone and I thought she might have attended something in the area over the years. Veronica here saw her in a café and thought she might have gone to school with her but she can't recall her name.'

'I seem to remember that we were friends about fifty years ago,' added Veronica, keen to extend her role in the pretence, 'but my memory isn't what it was.'

Rachel took a swig of wine. 'I do have all the back issues,' she said, 'but it would probably be easier to go to my computer in the first instance and look at all the flatplans of each issue. We can narrow down the search to the relevant pages to save time.' Rachel Robins's computer, which was of the widescreen variety, was in her front room which looked out onto the road. 'Okay,' she said, 'let's start with last month and work backwards. Shout if you see her.'

Forty minutes later and the two members of The Twelve were beginning to lose hope. They had studied photographs from seemingly every local west London business event of the previous three years and scanned hundreds of pictures of smiling entrepreneurs, executives and management types, all holding glasses of warm wine and revelling in their own networking prowess. 'How far back does this go?' asked Veronica, her enthusiasm slowly beginning to wear off.

'I think I've got everything back to 2015,' said Rachel, 'so we're halfway through.'

Suddenly Catherine shouted, '*There!*' and pointed to a picture of the woman from the café standing between two men at an event apparently called Arboreal Action for Acton which aimed to encourage local businesses to pay for the planting of more trees on the streets of the borough. All were smiling and one of the men and the woman were holding glasses of wine; the third man had a bottle of beer. 'Can you focus in on the caption please, Rachel.'

The editor magnified the image. Catherine and Veronica had to stifle a gasp.

AAA Chairman Reg Lewis shares a drink with local businessman Tony Slaven and his wife Janine.

31

'I don't suppose you know Reg Lewis, do you?' asked Catherine. The magazine editor didn't but thought that her husband who ran a landscape gardening business might have come across him. Despite the fact that he was only upstairs, Rachel Robins texted her husband, Will, and asked him if he could spare a minute. The three women immediately heard movement from above, the rattle of heavy boots on wooden flooring, and soon a tall, bright-eyed man with a bushy grey-brown beard appeared in the doorway. He looked around the room and gave a polite but shy wave to Veronica and Catherine who reciprocated in kind.

'Darling,' said Rachel, 'I'm just helping these lovely ladies with a bit of local research. Did I imagine it or do you know Reg Lewis from that tree campaign group a few years back?'

Will Robins was distracted by the photograph on his wife's computer screen. 'Yeah, I've bumped into Reg a few times over the years, including at this event as it happens.' He pointed towards the computer screen. 'I managed to avoid being photographed but then Rach knows I'm not one for the limelight, as it were. Dear old Reg. He's a bit bonkers but his heart's in the right place which is more than can be said for these two.' He pointed at Tony and Janine Slaven and a look of distaste spread across his face as if he'd just bitten into a juicy apple and encountered half a maggot. 'If I never see them again as long as I live, I'll be a happy man.'

Veronica and Catherine exchanged a glance and gently pressed Will to expand on his knowledge of the Slavens. According to Will, the Slavens had attended the AAA event not because they had any particular interest in local trees but instead because they wanted to get investors in one of their own businesses, which was apparently importing rare plants from Asia. 'They seemed nice enough and I'm always in the market to see some new plants for our clients. The wealthy ones in Berkshire with the big gardens are always on the lookout for anything a bit exotic that they can show off to their friends. Anyway, I gave them my email and phone number and asked them to send through some information. I think I got a message from them the next morning asking for an initial sum of thirty thousand pounds. Of course, I don't have that sort of money to simply give to a couple of people I've only met once so I said I'd think about it and asked whether they could put me in touch with some others who were already investing. Needless to say they didn't. Instead they just sent daily emails, even at weekends, asking whether I'd reconsider. When I stopped responding to their emails, I started getting phone calls from Janine and she would get progressively more aggressive. In the end I blocked her calls.

'But I know someone who gave them a down payment of twenty thousand pounds on the promise of hundreds of plants when the business was fully up and running. Predictably, nothing arrived after a few months and when he tried to contact the Slavens, they told him that the company had gone into liquidation and the money was gone. He wasn't happy but luckily he had good insurance so he didn't lose out. I don't know if that's helpful. I'll make a cuppa while I'm down here. Can I interest anyone?' All three women declined politely and Will ambled off towards the kitchen.

'They sound delightful,' said Veronica. 'No wonder Tiffany isn't a fan.' They thanked Rachel, who printed out a copy of the photograph for them to take away, and walked slowly back to Celia's house where Catherine called Monica to update her on everything they had learned. The ex-chemistry professor was in St John's Wood with Thomas entertaining Chris and Anna so Catherine was put on loudspeaker for everyone to hear while Monica put the finishing touches to a spiced aubergine dish she was on the verge of serving.

'Sounds like we need to get into the Storey house,' said Anna, 'not only to find out what's actually going on but also to check on Paul. It doesn't seem like he's in the best of health.' Chris added that it was mildly ironic that a month ago they were plotting to assassinate Paul Storey and now they were planning to potentially save him. Monica thanked Catherine for the update and said that she would arrange a meeting of the whole group along with Suzanne Green 'probably not tomorrow because we'll be whiffy after yoga but maybe the day after, depending on her schedule which seems a bit manic this week.'

'She always makes time for you,' said Anna, smiling. 'I have a sneaking suspicion that dealing with us is actually one of the most fun parts of her job. Certainly a hell of a lot jollier than doing the media rounds as she was doing earlier.' The four of them had already discussed the commissioner's delicate handling, on that morning's TV and radio networks, of the news regarding a uniformed officer filmed using racist language towards a Bengali shopkeeper in Kilburn.

'Her job doesn't get any easier,' said Thomas. 'She's doing

her best to weed out the undesirables in the Met but there just seem to be so many of them.'

Chris, meanwhile, was staring towards the window at the mid-evening light, deep in thought. Since his recent regular meetings with Mrs Mendoza, he had been doing a fair bit of reading about post-traumatic stress disorder and, although it was too early to be sure, something about Paul Storey was ringing a persistent and increasingly worrying bell.

32

It was not until after the weekend that Suzanne Green had finally managed to find some spare diary time and the commissioner was full of apologies on arrival at The Twelve house in Minera Mews, a short hop from Sloane Square. Thomas was particularly delighted to be able to revisit this Twelve house as he hadn't had the time earlier in the year to investigate its art, a selection of Rossetti sketches from the 1860s which, according to Terry, were given to a member of The Twelve by the artist in 1871. 'It was a chap named Fawley, if memory serves,' said the locksmith. 'Used to drink with old Dante Gabriel when he lived in Cheyne Walk not far from here. Apparently there's one of his handwritten poems somewhere too.' Thomas suspected this literary treasure might well be locked away in Baker Street along with any number of other priceless items.

Only eleven members were in attendance at the meeting as Belinda was still spending time with her husband in his final days. 'I'm so sorry about the delay in gathering,' said the commissioner, settling into a comfortable armchair and gratefully accepting an espresso from Owen. 'It would have been sooner, of course it would, but for this bloody Kilburn idiot and the media storm that he's wrought upon the Met. God knows I've done my best to expel these morons but it's like painting the Forth Bridge. You think you're finished and another one pops out of the woodwork. Plus, at this time of year with less going on politically, the media drag things like this out for as long as possible. The recruitment policy before I took over left a lot to be desired. I'd retire tomorrow if I could. The more time I spend with you guys, the more appealing retirement becomes.'

Over the weekend, as usual, the various members of The Twelve had busied themselves with different tasks, some related to the group and some not. Owen and Martin had been continuing to monitor their allocation of potential new recruits. One of Owen's was a charity CEO on whom The Twelve had been keeping a close eye for a couple of years. 'I attended a fundraising event and won a dinner with the chap at the auction. It cost £11,500 but I thought it was worth it as it's an opportunity to really get to know him. The charity was delighted as the same prize only made four grand last year.'

Martin, meanwhile, had been tracking a recently widowed watchmaker who also had an interest in bomb disposal. Everyone secretly hoped that this hobby, should the watchmaker ever make it into The Twelve, would never actually be required but nonetheless it was a useful talent to possess.

Terry made individual Bakewell tarts which he proudly presented at the meeting. 'I make the frangipane myself,' he had revealed. 'So much better than shop-bought. I like to think it's the free-range eggs which make the difference.'

Monica intimated that the commissioner would almost certainly have a place within The Twelve when she did eventually retire, but since she was only in her late forties, such thoughts seemed a little premature. 'Would you still consider me if I went and did the public speaking circuit for the next fifteen years?' she asked.

Monica confirmed that, assuming both that there was a vacancy and also that the public speaking business didn't transform Suzanne into a complete megalomaniac, she would still be a shoo-in for a role 'although, if I'm being selfish, I'd rather you didn't retire quite yet. The Twelve have become fans of yours and we'd rather not have to go through the rigmarole of introducing ourselves to another new commissioner any time soon if it can be avoided.'

The plan regarding the Storeys had developed rapidly following the latest encounter with Tiffany and Janine in the café. David had carefully worked out the best inlet for carbon monoxide to be pumped into the house, an air brick at the rear of the building which would allow a constant flow of gas under cover of darkness. Monica would be on hand to monitor the safety levels while Graham and Owen would maintain a constant watch on movement inside the house. Once the Storeys were immobile, Terry would pick the lock and six of them would enter the house; Terry, David and Monica as well as Anna and Thomas with oxygen canisters as well as Veronica for support. The former TV presenter fist-pumped the air in excitement.

Martin would be positioned on the street outside the house in case anyone needed transport. His cab would also be used to store canisters. By Monica's assessment, having worked out the internal area of the house, if they started the gas infusion around midnight at a certain rate, it should be safe to move to the next stage around two in the morning.

Once inside, the group would open all the windows to prevent anyone else from succumbing to gas poisoning; Anna would treat the Storeys with oxygen and then, once they were lucid, hopefully by dawn, conversations could begin. 'We're aware that we may need to tie them up,' said Monica. 'Initially at least. Until there's hopefully a degree of trust. Would that be okay, Suzanne?' The commissioner confirmed that they should do whatever they felt necessary to move the case forwards.

'I'll be in Kensal Green at Anna's,' said Chris. 'It's only a mile or so away if you need backup.'

'In the meantime,' said Graham, 'I've been delving into Tony and Janine Slaven and their various business interests over the last decade or so. They appear to have a history of registering companies and then leaving them dormant, sometimes for years. I managed to get banking records for two of the businesses and in both cases there are long periods with no activity and then a sudden deposit of funds, hundreds of thousands of pounds in one day, which then all gets withdrawn and disappears into an offshore account. The businesses claim to specialise in random areas like importing dentistry equipment or international property cleaning but I suspect all of them are a cover for something else. Arms or drugs, most likely.'

'Neither of them have criminal records,' said Suzanne, 'although one of the sons does. Leo. He did three months in 2015 for beating up a taxi driver.' Martin growled and bit violently into a Bakewell, dribbling a viscous stream of jam down his chin.

'We'll set a date, then,' said Monica, decisively. 'Next Thursday? It's due to be a warm night with no rain so that makes perfect conditions.'

'Sorry,' said Martin, mid-wipe, 'taking Joanne to see *Six*. You know, the one about the wives of Henry the Eighth. I've bought us a box right near the stage.'

'Friday, then?' Monica said with a sigh. Everyone agreed that Friday night into Saturday morning was entirely acceptable.

Anna's phone pinged; a message from Belinda asking

whether she was with Chris and, if so, could he please call her urgently. 'Excuse me for just a second,' he said, turning on his phone and wandering into the quiet of the kitchen at the back of the house. He returned a couple of moments later looking deep in thought. 'It's her husband, Malcolm. She's asked me if I can help speed things along.'

'Are you okay to do that?' asked Monica, conscious that he was still easing himself back into the often turbulent waves of The Twelve.

The ex-surgeon nodded solemnly and reached for Monica's hand which he kissed gently. 'In a weird way, I suspect it will be a part of my own complex healing process.'

33

The hospice was at the brow of a leafy hill on a side road just outside of Windsor to the west of London, a slightly imposing Georgian house which had been converted in the 1980s. As Chris drew up to the entrance, he noticed a white wisteria which covered the front of the building was bravely attempting a second blooming of the summer, doubtless encouraged or confused by the warm spell. The whine of aircraft making final approaches into Heathrow filled the air every few minutes as they descended over the nearby castle.

According to one of the kind-faced nurses, Sir Elton John was a neighbour and, if you went to the far end of the long, flower-filled garden to the rear of the building, you could just make out a corner of his extensive mansion. The nurse, whose name was Wilhemina, delighted in telling everyone that a few years ago a bowel cancer patient was convinced she had seen the rocket man himself, peering cautiously from an upstairs window. Chris and Belinda suspected that the sheer distance made this unlikely but decided, on balance, that the story was best kept unquestioned as it seemed to give both Wilhemina and her patients such joy, an emotion which was sometimes in short supply in such a building.

Chris had informed Belinda, and the group, that he would need to pop home to get the necessary supplies but then he would jump in his car and be there within a couple of hours, traffic permitting. East London to Windsor would always be a challenging journey but he'd be as quick as he could. Thomas had expressed surprise that he'd known Chris for almost a year and didn't know he owned a car. 'I'm a surgeon. It's part of our specific Hippocratic oath to own a sports car. Mine's an Alfa Romeo 4c. She's red. Stupid car to have in London so I rarely drive the thing. If you ever want to borrow it, let me know.' Monica glanced at Thomas and made a low purring sound, thoughts of a romantic drive into the countryside filtering into her mind.

Chris had excused himself and taken a taxi back to Victoria Park. He had been spending so much time at Anna's that his own house had acquired an aroma of stale emptiness, of air that hadn't had an excuse to circulate and had grown lethargic. An impressive pile of mostly purposeless post had accumulated. Chris flipped quickly through the envelopes, rescued the half dozen which looked important and put them in his case to peruse later. Then he strode into his study and opened the cabinet where he kept various medicines in case of emergency. It was always cool in the study and there was a small refrigerator for any medicines which required it, although his prize today did not. He located a bottle of morphine and a couple of syringes and placed them in the case before opening the top drawer of his desk and finding his car keys as well as those to the small garage round the corner where the Alfa was kept. 'I hope the bloody thing starts,' he muttered to himself as he opened the garage doors a few minutes later, trying to remember the last time he drove it and realising it was probably about six weeks ago to visit his eldest daughter in Surrey.

He didn't have to worry. One turn of the ignition key and the Alfa, the colour of arterial blood, roared gratefully into life, as if delighted to be roused from slumber. Chris quickly texted Belinda to say that he was on his way and to ask her to carefully consider whether she was sure this was what she wanted.

It transpired that the journey west wasn't as tricky as Chris had imagined apart from a slight delay due to roadworks outside Hammersmith. 'You made good time,' said Belinda as she hugged him in welcome at the entrance to the hospice. 'And thank you again for this.' She introduced him to Wilhemina whose luminescent smile, Chris thought, could light up any room, however potentially sad that room might be.

'Don't sign in, Dr Tinker,' she said, beaming. 'It would be better for your presence to be as private as possible.' Chris expressed surprise that the nurse apparently knew what was about to happen but Wilhemina was quick to reassure him. 'This happens much more often than you might expect,' she said softly. 'And even if the law doesn't currently recognise this need, we do.' She placed a hand on his upper arm and gave it a gentle squeeze. 'Come and meet Malcolm. He's been looking forward to your visit.'

When she had joined The Twelve in 2017, just under a year after Chris's own arrival, Belinda had spoken of her husband with great affection, showing the group photographs from their lives together, travelling the world, imagining future adventures. With no children by choice, and with cash to spare through their successful careers – hers in linguistics, his in pharmaceuticals – they had seemingly had everything needed for an idyllic retirement. Then came Malcolm's diagnosis, a few days after his sixty-third birthday.

The man in the hospice bed bore no resemblance to the Malcolm of those earlier photographs. The vibrant, bon-vivant husband had vanished and in his place a pale, gaunt, immobile apparition barely existed, almost translucent but with the merest shadow of a frown as if frustrated with the shrinking world it inhabited. 'He's been like this for five days,' said Belinda. 'He wouldn't want this. We discussed it many times over the years, even before his illness. The true Malcolm would hate being here. He would want peace.' Belinda picked up Malcolm's left hand as she had done consistently over the previous weeks. As usual, there was not even the barest sense of a grip from Malcolm.

'I'll leave you,' whispered Wilhemina, closing the door behind her. 'Let me know when you're ready.'

Chris opened his bag and carefully extracted a vial of morphine, a pair of surgical gloves and the two syringes, explaining to Belinda that the spare was simply there in case the first one was in some way faulty. 'It's never happened to me before,' he said, 'but doctors are a superstitious lot.' He pulled on the gloves, opened the vial and observed methodically as the syringe barrel filled with liquid. 'You're absolutely sure?' he asked.

Belinda nodded. 'One more thing,' she said. 'Can I help?'

Chris was unsurprised. He had known Belinda long enough to be aware of both her emotional strength and her sense of duty. 'A final act of devotion for the love of your life.' He smiled. 'Of course.' He found a vein with ease, a slow-moving purple tributary on a barren, parched landscape, and gently inserted the needle. 'Push together?'

Belinda reached forward and placed her thumb over Chris's. She watched with fascination as the pain relief surged into the blood vessel. After a minute or so, Malcolm's breathing changed, the shallow breaths replaced by more rapid, short bursts. 'Normal,' assured Chris. Belinda moved to the opposite side of the bed to stroke her husband's head. Malcolm's frown appeared to dissolve, replaced by the faintest flicker of a smile. 'Sleep now,' whispered Belinda. 'I love you.' She kissed him on his forehead as Malcolm took a last shallow breath.

The two of them stood silently for around ten minutes, Chris noting the occasional tear trickling slowly down Belinda's nose. Finally, the linguist took a deep breath, gave herself a shake and walked over to Chris for a hug. 'Thank you,' she said softly. 'And by the way, how are *you* feeling? I know it's been difficult these last few weeks, since your injury.'

Chris maintained the hug. It felt therapeutic for both of them. 'I'm good,' he said. 'I'm almost back to normal, I think. There was a moment back there when I was close to calling it a day but then I realised that I need The Twelve. I'd be lost without everyone's friendship and love. I think we all would.' To his surprise, Chris now felt tears swell in his own eyes and he drew Belinda back into the safety of their embrace.

After another few minutes of silence, Chris asked whether she required a lift home. 'Oh, don't worry. I've got my own car,' she said, a sense of relief replacing feelings of sadness. 'I'll stay for a bit and sort out all the necessary paperwork with Wilhemina. You should get back.' She grasped Chris's hands and squeezed. 'Thank you again for this. You're a treasure.'

'Well, it's not my first rodeo.' He grinned, packing away all of his kit. 'And I just hope that when my time comes, there will be someone to provide me with the same dignified end.' Belinda concurred.

Driving back into London and with John Coltrane as his soundtrack as he swept over the Westway, Chris's thoughts returned to Paul Storey whose home was barely a quarter of a mile away from the flyover. The surgeon felt that his own recovery from post-traumatic stress was almost complete. Hopefully enough to fully immerse himself back into the world of The Twelve. Yet he had the nagging suspicion that the next few days would test this resolve and he would need to somehow be fully ready.

34

Most of the lights had gone out in the Storey house, all except the yellowish night light in Paul's bedroom which was constantly on during the hours of darkness. As expected, the night was warm but, equally as expected, the windows in the house were closed. They were always closed as if the occupants were afraid of someone getting in while they were sleeping. This possibility was not lost on the six members of the team who were currently surrounding the building. Monica, Thomas and David were at the back, ready to begin pumping odourless, poisonous gas into the property, while Terry, Anna and Veronica were in Martin's cab at the front of the house listening at low volume to the original 1979 Broadway cast recording of *Sweeney Todd* with Len Cariou and Angela Lansbury. Their roles in the night's activities weren't scheduled for a couple of hours but everyone felt it best for them to be in position in case matters moved faster than anticipated.

Terry had baked a large quantity of particularly fine flapjacks. Anna regularly photographed herself and Veronica chomping on them and texted the pictures to Chris in a friendly attempt to make him envious. Chris responded by popping to a nearby twenty-four-hour newsagents and stocking up on snacks of his own.

Just before midnight, Graham texted from across town creating vibrations in seven pockets. The Storeys had gone to bed. *Let's begin.* David had acquired an air-brick adaptor which could cover all the small holes and allow minimal carbon monoxide to escape into the surrounding atmosphere. Monica had checked the Land Registry to work out the internal area of the house and, from that information, had calculated the amount of gas required.

'With any luck they'll just stay asleep and we can get in and do what's necessary without too much trouble,' she had explained earlier that evening. David, his equipment in a small bag on his shoulder, crept carefully towards the house, located the air brick and then attached the adaptor to the wall using heavy duty brick tape. Next, he connected a ten-metre pipe to the adaptor and eased himself back to where Monica was waiting with a hundred-litre canister of poisonous gas.

Graham had already assessed, through careful observation of the various rooms during daylight hours, that the Storeys were unlikely to possess a CO detector or indeed any alarm system anywhere in the house. David had brought two alarms – one for carbon monoxide, the other for smoke – to fit at a later point. 'We don't want them coming to any harm, do we?' he muttered in what was, for him, a slightly sinister fashion. The plumber remained still not entirely convinced that Paul hadn't had at least something to do with the attack on Justin Morris.

Monica attached the other end of the pipe to the gas canister and opened the valve to commence a steady flow into the Storey house. 'We'll do ten minutes just to double-check there aren't any alarms,' whispered Monica, 'and then, assuming all's well, we'll keep going for another hour and a bit and hopefully that should be enough.'

Around an hour later, Terry arrived at the back of the house with supplies of flapjacks as Thomas had complained of a rumbling stomach. The locksmith also used the opportunity to 'spend a penny in that graveyard' as Martin had told him it was too late to find a nearby pub with a toilet. 'Nice balmy night,' he said to Thomas on his return. 'Beats a shed on a golf course in bleedin' March.'

At around 1.40am, Graham texted. Tiffany was on the move. *Looks like she's a bit unsteady. On her way to bathroom.* A few minutes later, another text arrived. *Looks like she's being sick.* This text was accompanied with a green face emoji.

Any movement from Paul? texted Monica. Graham replied that Paul remained in bed.

Just before 2am, Graham texted again. *Tiffany collapsed and motionless in bathroom. Paul status the same as before.* Terry and Veronica took this as their cue to begin the second phase of the operation. Monica closed the valve on the canister and she and Thomas went to help Anna manoeuvre the oxygen tanks out of the taxi before joining the team at the front door. Meanwhile, David tidied away the equipment at the back of the house and transferred it back to the cab.

'This is all so clever,' squeaked Veronica admiringly as Terry worked meticulously to pick the Storeys' high-quality lock. The locksmith explained that due to the complexity of dealing with such a piece of equipment, he had ended up fitting one to his own back door to allow him to practise more regularly. His first attempt had taken twenty minutes but, after considerable tweaking of technique and purchasing of a few extra bits of kit including an electric lock gun, he had whittled his personal best down to forty seconds.

'Got it,' said Terry, pushing the door gently. It didn't move.

'Bugger,' said Terry. 'Must be something else. Hang on.' He rattled the door as lightly as he could in case Tiffany was in any state to react. 'Internal deadbolt halfway down,' he announced. 'Not a major problem. Merely an inconvenience.' He reached into his bag and extracted a drill. 'This is where we find out if Tiffany is truly conscious or not.' He grinned. 'I'll be as quiet as possible and I'll fit them a new door when we're done here.'

'Do we need to worry about explosions?' asked Veronica. 'Is it safe to switch the lights on?'

Monica explained that the levels of carbon monoxide would be far too low to cause anything to ignite. 'It would need to be about twelve per cent of the atmosphere in the house,' she pointed out, pulling a portable carbon monoxide monitor from a small shoulder bag, 'which would mean Tiffany and Paul would have been dead long ago. I'll take a reading as soon as we gain access. If my calculations are more or less correct, we should be looking at around zero point two-five per cent.'

It took around five minutes for Terry to drill a hole large enough for him to insert a small electric wood saw blade. 'Good job I charged this baby,' he said with satisfaction. Graham texted to reassure them that Tiffany remained on the bathroom floor. Monica silently hoped that she had calibrated the gas quantities correctly.

Eventually, Terry had created a hole large enough for Veronica to squeeze her hand through and, with instruction from the locksmith, she was able to reach in and unbolt the door which swung open to reveal a short hallway filled with supermarket carrier bags which appeared to be stuffed with clothes and children's toys. Monica switched on the monitor and took an initial reading. 'Zero point two-nine per cent,' she said, frowning. 'Slightly higher than I was expecting.' She decided to keep to herself the thought that this level was nudging towards dangerous for anyone who had been exposed to it for any length of time.

Apart from the carrier bags, the other most obvious element to the inside of the Storey house was the smell of ammonia which Monica realised was probably urine. Terry switched on the hallway light and the five of them edged through to the bottom of the stairs from where they heard a low moaning sound above them. 'Open all the windows down here,' said Monica, directing her request towards Veronica and Terry, 'while we check upstairs.'

With Anna and Thomas carrying the oxygen, they and Monica climbed the scuffed and worn carpeted stairs which were festooned on one side by more overflowing plastic bags. Monica reached the top first just as the moaning sound ceased.

There were four doors off of the landing. Two were closed. In the room which was clearly Tiffany's bedroom, the bed was in disarray as if its occupant had needed to abandon it quickly. In the other open room, a windowless bathroom, Tiffany lay slumped against the bath next to a pool of vomit. She was wearing a light oversized pale-blue T-shirt with no underwear. A puddle of urine had gathered on the floor between her legs.

Despite being apparently unable to move, Tiffany's eyes were wide open and, despite the warmth of the summer night, Thomas shivered. He had never seen a look of such concentrated fear.

35

'We're here to help you, Tiffany,' reassured Monica, equally alarmed at the dramatic effect their arrival had apparently had on Tiffany Storey. The woman tried and failed to lift herself off the bathroom floor. Even an attempt to pull herself up using the rim of the bath failed. 'She needs oxygen.' Anna squeezed into the bathroom, slipping momentarily on the wet floor, and tried to place a mask over Tiffany's face through which to administer oxygen. Tiffany, assuming this was another bid to murder her, fought with all her remaining strength and, at one point, managed to scratch Anna's cheek with her blue-painted fingernails until she finally collapsed exhausted into the puddle of vomit.

'All windows downstairs are now open,' reported Veronica from the doorway. 'Oh my God,' she spluttered, seeing Thomas and Monica now lifting Tiffany's head gently off the floor.

'Can you dampen that flannel,' requested Monica, pointing to a tattered red piece of cloth crumpled and dried by the Storey sink, 'and pass it over please, V. Smell it first just in case it's used for cleaning products.' Veronica confirmed that it smelled of nothing more sinister than soap and Monica cleaned Tiffany's face and neck with no resistance. Whether that was because the carbon monoxide poisoning had finally sapped all her strength or because Tiffany had come to a realisation that these elderly strangers weren't in fact there to kill her, Monica couldn't be sure. She handed the flannel back to Veronica who rinsed it before wiping Tiffany's legs as best she could. 'Let's lift her into her bedroom where there's an open window.'

Thomas and Terry did the lifting while Anna followed with the oxygen cylinder and mask. They placed Tiffany carefully on her bed, an untidy double which had been somehow squeezed into a room designed for smaller furniture. There was just enough space for a small chest of drawers although this had been positioned at right angles to the base of the bed otherwise the drawers wouldn't have opened. Most of Tiffany's clothes appeared to live either on the floor in piles or hanging precariously from the curtain rail like bedraggled sails of a colourful yet becalmed ship. 'It's good there's a slight breeze,' said Anna, placing the oxygen mask over Tiffany's mouth with greater success this time. 'Can you hold this in place please, Terry, while I take a quick measurement with the pulse oximeter.' She rummaged in her shoulder bag and extracted the small digital instrument before applying it to the least varnished of Tiffany's fingers, conveniently her middle one. 'Oh, and let's protect her modesty and find this poor woman a pair of knickers, please.'

Monica, meanwhile, after cleaning up the bathroom floor with toilet paper, had taken Veronica's hand and the two of them had taken the half dozen steps down the landing to Paul's room, unsure of what they might find. Paul's door was closed. Monica thought about knocking but quickly decided that was absurd and, with great caution, opened the door.

Paul's bed was empty. In fact, Paul's room appeared empty. It was a larger space than Tiffany's, again with a double bed in the centre with a small gap between it and the wall, and this time there was the luxury of a wardrobe as well as drawers. The room also boasted a widescreen TV and a variety of games consoles and remote controls. In contrast to Tiffany's room, Paul's was relatively tidy although what struck Monica was that the sheets and pillowcases, with their themes of superheroes, were more appropriate for a primary school boy than for a man in his thirties.

'Paul?' whispered Monica. There was no reply. 'Can you open the window please, V?'

Veronica moved towards the window and had just opened it marginally when she heard a faint crack underfoot as if tiptoeing through dry bracken. She had accidentally trodden on something. Looking down Veronica let out a stifled scream. She had stepped on Paul's skeletal hand.

Monica rushed over to the side of the bed from which Veronica was backing away. She pushed the window fully open and looked down. The picture in her mind of Paul Storey, derived from images of him after the trial in 2013, was of a cocky, healthy young man with the build of a bantam-weight boxer. The Paul Storey who looked like he had been unceremoniously half-shoved under his bed like a discarded toy, was a fraction of that size.

Monica gently pushed the bed towards the door so that she could see Paul in his entirety. He was face-up on the carpet with his eyes closed and he was wearing a pair of Spiderman pyjama bottoms stained with urine which had also created a small pond under what remained of Paul's emaciated bottom, really just a thin veneer of atrophied muscle over his pelvic bone.

'Is he dead?' asked Veronica in a slight panic. *God, I hope not*, thought Monica remembering the slightly high reading on her CO monitor. She knelt down, taking care not to lean on any of Paul's all too visible bones for fear they might snap, and gently raised his wrist, itself little more than a joint shrouded in skin.

'No, there's a pulse,' Monica said with obvious relief, 'but it's very weak. Go fetch Anna urgently but don't mention anything about this in case Tiffany can hear. And ask her to bring the second oxygen cylinder.' Veronica dashed from the room and returned moments later with the former forensics expert.

'Jesus Christ!' half-screamed Anna. 'Is he...?'

'There's a pulse,' said Monica, 'but it's barely there. I suspect that considering the state he's in, the carbon monoxide would act quicker. It looks like he's fallen out of bed and possibly hit his head.'

'Oh,' said Veronica with contrition, 'and I might have stood on his fingers. Sorry.'

With great delicacy, Anna placed her ear to Paul's chest, his ribs pressing into her cheek. 'Very shallow breathing,' she said. 'In any other circumstance, I'd say we need to get him to a hospital quickly. However, I appreciate that could be a challenge.'

'What do we do?' asked Veronica, mildly agitated. Monica sympathised. For a first case, this one wasn't perhaps proving the most straightforward.

Anna pulled her phone out of her pocket and accessed her recent calls to quickly find Chris's mobile. 'Luckily,' she smiled, 'we have an alternative.'

36

Ordinarily, at 2.15am on a Saturday morning, Chris would be dozing peacefully in Anna's bed, recently untroubled by the dreams which had plagued him earlier in the summer. On this occasion, he was awake, partially surrounded by sweet wrappers, and watching cricket highlights, having napped for an hour earlier in the evening. He had had the suspicion that his skills might be required at some point before dawn and therefore a snooze might be wise. He had been right.

'Is he okay to travel?' asked the former surgeon after Anna had explained the situation.

'He's going to have to be. We'll lay him on the back seat of Martin's cab and three of us can cushion him from falling. I don't think the hand is broken. Probably just bruised tendons but I'll give it extra protection. There won't be much traffic at this time of night so we'll just have to forgo seat belts. Suzanne can tell me off if we get stopped.'

'Have you got a pulse oximeter reading?' Anna admitted that she hadn't yet got that far. She dashed back to Tiffany's room, swerving round various bags of what appeared to be jumble, and retrieved the instrument from the woman's finger, noting a reading of ninety-one; not great but equally not disastrous. Paul's reading, however, was more concerning.

'He's eighty-eight,' she told Chris with obvious concern. 'The other one is ninety-one. What do you suggest?'

At the other end of the line, the ex-surgeon was mentally working through the various options and rejecting all those which would either endanger Paul or risk both the failure of the operation and a flurry of awkward questions. 'Bring him here,' he said. 'For now at least. I'll treat him in the spare room. Tiffany will have to stay there. You should probably stay with her but be careful and let me know when she's in recovery please.' Anna agreed. 'One more thing.'

'Yep?'

'I love you.'

Anna was momentarily thrown. Chris had shied away from saying those words even though she herself had used them reasonably liberally since the birthday party at the end of June. She had simply assumed that he was typical of men of his generation and didn't open up as easily as her female friends. 'I love you too,' she replied, failing to stifle a spreading grin. Monica looked up and couldn't help beaming too.

'Oh, one more thing, and this really is the last thing.'

'Yes, darling?' Anna virtually purred this word mellifluously.

'If there are any left, can you ask someone to bring me one of Terry's flapjacks, please.'

———

Monica rapidly divided the team into two. She, David and Anna would stay with Tiffany in the house while the others carefully transferred Paul to Kensal Green in Martin's taxi. Veronica scouted through the house for towels and cushions to make the short journey as comfortable as possible. Martin had also made it abundantly clear that, emergency though this might be, he would rather not have a cab 'smelling of piss for the next three weeks,' especially as he planned to take Joanne down to Southend before the end of summer. 'Piss is not an aphrodisiac,' he had stated. 'Not for me anyway. I know some people are into that, I've seen the videos, but not Martin Francis.'

Monica did her best to wash the cold urine from Paul and managed to change him into a pair of clean pyjama bottoms patterned with robots. Paul's legs were, much like the rest of him, just skin and bone and reminded Monica of starvation victims she'd seen on the news. 'There's nothing of him,' she whispered to Thomas. 'I can't imagine how he got this way.'

With extreme care, Thomas and Terry carried Paul Storey across the landing, down the stairs and out into the night. Paul emitted a faint gurgling sound as they transferred him outside and Terry was worried that he was going to be sick. Instead, a gobbet of bubbly saliva emerged from the left side of his mouth. 'I'm not sure if that's good or bad?' murmured Terry with concern.

They placed Paul softly on the back seat of Martin's cab which Veronica had somehow converted into a reasonable approximation of a luxury bed using what sparse raw materials were available in the Storey house. 'Take this,' Anna said, handing Thomas a spare pulse oximeter. 'I'm sure Chris has one but just in case. And also make sure he's taking in the oxygen as best you can.' Terry took the gas canister and Veronica placed the mask with care over Paul's mouth, cradling his head apologetically while the two men sat on the floor to prevent him falling off the seat if Martin had to brake suddenly.

'I'll have stiff knees after this,' grumbled Terry but Martin reassured him that it wouldn't be a long journey and he knew a route that avoided speedbumps. Besides the speed limit was twenty so they wouldn't exactly be flying around west London corners.

Monica gave Thomas a squeeze. 'Keep in touch,' she said as he got into the back of the cab and crouched down as a barrier between Paul and the hard floor. 'I'll let you know how his mum's doing.' She stood on the pavement and watched as the taxi eased away slowly before it turned a corner and was gone. She took a moment for herself and looked up at the summer night sky. There were only a handful of stars visible on account of the street lighting with one in particular shining brighter than the others. 'I wished on a star a few years ago,' she whispered to herself, thinking of Thomas, 'and that one came true. Maybe I'll try it again.' She closed her eyes and wished that somehow the Storeys would both be okay and that she had done the right thing in splitting them up, probably for the first time in years.

Monica breathed in deeply, preparing herself emotionally for the next stage of the operation. She was just exhaling as David Latham hurried towards her from the house in a state of urgency. 'We need you,' he said in a hushed voice. 'Tiffany's kicking off.'

37

Monica scampered up the stairs to a curious sight. Tiffany had been tied to her bed using various items of clothing including what looked like a rubber skirt. She also had a pink hoodie with a picture of a unicorn pulled over her head and then the oxygen mask stuck to her face with David's masking tape which was tightly wrapped around the hood. Her eyes had retained their look of fear but it was now conflated by one of incandescent fury. To Monica's eyes, she resembled a collision between an alien and a Care Bear. In a sex dungeon.

'Just to explain,' said Anna with a tinge of embarrassment, 'we thought a gag would be advisable, just until we've had a chance to explain what's actually happening. But equally we needed to keep the oxygen mask in place in addition to which we didn't want to use masking tape on Tiffany's hair because that would be a bugger to get off and it would be painful and so... voila!' Monica gazed upon the stricken woman with a mixture of pity and disgust. Tiffany scowled as best she could within the parameters of her unusual situation. The fact that these strange old people didn't seem to want to cause her harm was slowly beginning to register. What they did seem to want to cause her was extreme embarrassment.

Monica adopted a pensive expression. 'Given the circumstances,' she said, 'I think you've done a decent job. The unicorn is a nice touch.' Tiffany attempted to speak but she was still weak and the noise that emanated from the layers of oxygen mask and tape was indistinct. Monica took another reading on the oximeter. 'Ninety-two now. Excellent progress. Once we get to ninety-five or ninety-six to be safe, you can come off the oxygen.'

Tiffany made another attempt at speech and this time, perhaps because Anna's ears were becoming attuned to the muffled rumbling, the noise was mildly comprehensible. 'I think she's asking why she needs the oxygen in the first place,' she said. Tiffany nodded, wide-eyed with both residual fear but also excitement at being able to communicate. If this was some sort of weird kidnap, she thought, at least she was making progress.

'Okay.' Monica sighed. 'There are things I need to explain to you, Tiffany, but then when we remove the mask from you, there are also things we need to ask you. Is that okay?' Tiffany remained impassive, saving her energy for possible struggles ahead. 'The first thing to make clear to you is that we are not the police.' Tiffany raised an eyebrow suspiciously. 'The second thing, and possibly even more important, is that we're not here to hurt you or Paul.'

Tiffany struggled to form a sentence which Anna translated as 'Where's my fucking son?'

'We'll come to that,' continued Monica, 'but basically he's being cared for. You've both suffered carbon monoxide poisoning and so you both need medical help to recover. You're doing really well so you should be feeling more or less normal in a couple of hours. Paul seems to have other medical issues so his recovery will take longer but he's in good hands.' At this moment, Monica said an internal prayer to whoever might be listening, in the hope that Paul was almost with Chris and could actually be saved.

Again, Tiffany's gurgle required translation. 'She asks who poisoned them,' said Anna. Monica deflected the question and decided to press on.

'Without going into too much detail, we are a group which has a keen interest in justice.' Tiffany rolled her eyes and pretended to fall asleep. Monica persevered. 'As you'll know, many years ago, Paul was in court for his part in a murder. However, the jury couldn't agree on his guilt and, unlike the other defendants, he was set free. We have done our own investigations and we have come to the conclusion that it is unlikely that Paul was directly involved at all.'

David, who was standing in a corner of Tiffany's bedroom looking out at the edge of the cemetery, exhaled noisily. Tiffany, meanwhile, opened her eyes with something approaching a sense of interest. She mumbled six syllables which Anna translated as 'I have the worst headache.'

'However,' said Monica, 'there are a number of factors which don't make sense and that's why we'd like to talk with you. As soon as we can get you off the oxygen, we'll get you some painkillers.' She glanced towards Anna. 'We have painkillers, right?'

Anna nodded. 'Three different types. Including the strong stuff.'

Tiffany murmured again. 'She says you could have just invited her for a coffee,' said Anna. 'I think she's joking.' Tiffany gave an impression of someone falling about laughing which, in her current predicament, was challenging.

Monica persevered. 'There are so many questions but I suppose the main two would be, what's happened to Paul over the last few years, and why are you meeting with Janine Slaven?

Are either or both of these things linked to the Justin Morris murder?'

This time, Tiffany was silent. She slowly closed her eyes and appeared to be focusing on her breathing, either in an attempt to rapidly hasten her recovery or simply to avoid Monica's questions. After about five minutes, she opened her eyes again and, with renewed strength, uttered a sentence which even Monica could now understand.

'It's not safe here.'

38

'Most importantly,' said Chris, quietly so as not to wake the neighbours, 'who's got the flapjacks?' He was waiting outside Anna's house for the arrival of the taxi. The short journey through west London's leafy side streets had taken no more than seven minutes and had been largely uneventful except for a brief moment on Scrubs Lane when everyone apart from Veronica and Martin had had to duck down as a precaution to avoid being seen by a police car.

Thomas and Terry unfolded themselves from the floor of Martin's cab and the locksmith performed a couple of yoga stretches just to loosen up some joints before the trek into the house where they lay the patient on Anna's widest sofa. 'He's in a very bad way.' Chris frowned, giving the patient a quick initial examination. He took another oximeter reading and, despite Veronica's heroics with the oxygen tank during the drive, Paul's reading had remained stubbornly at eighty-eight. 'Far from ideal,' said the former surgeon. 'And yet, now he's here, he's got a better chance than he did. And,' he smiled at Veronica, 'Anna was right about the lack of broken finger bones.' The former TV presenter exhaled audibly and handed over the remaining flapjack wrapped in kitchen roll liberated from the Storey house.

Thomas felt that, if anything, Paul's condition had worsened but then he appreciated that his medical knowledge stretched only really to sports injuries like a torn Achilles, something he was fairly certain that Paul hadn't suffered any time in the recent past.

Chris directed everyone upstairs to Anna's spare room which had been rapidly converted into something approaching a field hospital, Thomas and Terry once more carrying the slender body of Paul Storey while Veronica managed the oxygen tank. Martin took up the rear as Chris had asked him to stick around on the basis that the young man's treatment was more likely to require external supplies than Tiffany's. They laid Paul face-up on the bed. Veronica sat next to Paul and repositioned the oxygen mask over his face. Chris asked how many more oxygen cylinders Monica had managed to acquire and Martin replied that there were two more in the boot of the taxi. 'We may need more,' said Chris uneasily, 'but we'll see how we go.'

He pressed Paul's fingernail and noted that the blood took far too long to return it from white to a healthy pink. 'He's severely malnourished,' said the former surgeon, 'but we can't hospitalise him for obvious reasons. This could be interesting.'

Suddenly Paul's right arm spasmed, shocking Veronica and making Terry jump. 'Okay, I'm going to have to get some more equipment,' said Chris, looking at his watch. It was just after three in the morning. Probably too early to call his youngest daughter without worrying her unduly. He made a quick calculation and decided that he could risk waiting until six to make the call unless Paul's condition worsened. 'I'm going to take a calculated gamble,' he added to nobody in particular. 'To be honest with you all, there's always a risk to any treatment of any kind but equally there's a risk to non-treatment. The magic trick of every doctor worth their salt is to weigh up the various options and follow the path that seems the least precarious. Battered old rope bridge to cross the raging river or slippery rocks. That kind of scenario.'

Veronica enquired about the immediate plan and Chris explained that they would treat the carbon monoxide poisoning over the next three hours and hope for an improvement on the oximeter reading of eighty-eight and then at six he would text his daughter, Lucinda, who was working as a junior doctor at St Mary's Hospital just over a mile away, to see whether she could help with some equipment to at least begin to tackle the malnutrition. 'She's taking some time getting her hands dirty on the wards while applying for cardiology consultant jobs,' he explained.

'Do you think it's wise to ask a junior doctor to get involved?' asked Thomas. 'She might get struck off.'

'It'll depend largely on the identity of her senior on duty,' said Chris. 'Cross all your fingers; we might get lucky.' At that moment, Paul spasmed again, his right leg this time erupting uncontrollably. 'We also need to address that mildly troubling issue.' Chris glanced around the room and settled on Thomas. 'Dear fellow, could you please go into Anna's room next door, reach under the side of the bed nearest the window and bring me the pink and blue items you find.' This polite request was accompanied by a wink and a smile which Thomas had seen before, usually when they were having man to man discussions with a glass or two of whisky.

Thomas walked down the landing to Anna's room and returned a couple of minutes later with two pairs of fluffy handcuffs in pink and blue. Martin raised a quizzical eyebrow. Veronica failed to stifle a giggle. 'His and hers,' explained Chris without embarrassment. 'Needs must in an emergency.' He casually attached the pink cuffs to Paul's left hand, needing to use the highest ratchet because of the slimness of the man's wrist. He repeated the task with the blue cuffs on Paul's right ankle. 'That should help,' declared the ex-surgeon with a look of quiet satisfaction. 'And they're cushioned for comfort.'

The five of them stood in silent contemplation staring at the image in front of them, an emaciated man wearing a child's robot pyjamas, secured to a bed with fluffy handcuffs and an oxygen mask over his face.

'I've seen some bloody strange things since joining The Twelve,' said Martin softly after a while, 'but this is potentially the weirdest.'

'What do we do now?' asked Veronica, thinking that even during her many years in television, she, like Martin, hadn't encountered anything quite like the current situation.

Chris scratched his stubble confidently. 'We wait,' he said. 'And I'll write a shopping list.'

39

Tiffany's oximeter reading had reached ninety-five and, as a result, Monica and Anna had made the decision to release her momentarily from the oxygen mask. This had been a mistake. Almost immediately, the woman had screamed, 'Where's my fucking son?' at the top of her voice and David had had to quickly reattach the mask, not the easiest of tasks even considering that Tiffany's limbs were tied, wrapping it around the back of the hoodie with more tape than the previous occasion. Monica sighed. She had hoped they were making progress with Tiffany but clearly there was more work to be done.

'Okay,' she said quietly. 'Let's try a different tack. Tiffany, do you still believe that we are here to do you harm?' Tiffany grunted in as non-committal way as her situation allowed. 'If we wanted to hurt you or Paul,' persevered Monica, 'don't you think we would have done it by now? We're trying to help you.' She sighed again. Despite napping with Thomas earlier in the evening, the lateness of the hour was having an effect. 'This must be what it's like to have children,' she moaned to nobody in particular. 'I suppose we'll have to sit here until you feel like answering.'

'It's not safe here,' mumbled Tiffany again.

Monica sensed a conversational opening. It wasn't the one she'd been hoping for but under the circumstances the proverbial begging and choosing conundrum was apt. 'Why isn't it safe, Tiffany?' she asked quietly, successfully quashing any sense of exasperation that might be building up. 'I'm going to loosen the mask again so we can try to have a more helpful conversation. Okay? You'll still be able to breathe the oxygen which is helping your recovery but I'll be able to understand you better.'

Tiffany nodded and shuffled slightly, attempting but failing to reposition herself marginally higher up the bed. Monica eased the material holding the mask in place. 'The police are watching,' Tiffany said. 'They watch all the time. Ever since the court case.' She glanced toward the window indicating where she wrongly assumed the surveillance camera was positioned. 'And this fucking headache is killing me.'

Monica brightened. At least they were getting somewhere. 'If the police are watching,' she asked, 'why aren't they here now? Surely they would have seen some people breaking into your house in the middle of the night. Wouldn't they have thought that was worthy of investigation?'

Tiffany considered this for a minute or so, her face contorted owing to the pain which was tearing through her temples and across her forehead. 'They don't fucking care about us,' she said finally. 'Unless we do something criminal. Then they care. Then they take Paul into custody and kick him about until he doesn't know who he is anymore. These days they just watch. The fucking house could be on fire and they wouldn't send anyone. We're better off dead as far as the police are concerned.'

Anna texted Chris to let him know that Tiffany's recovery was progressing well and asked whether it was okay to give her codeine for her headache. *She's now 95 on the oxi,* she wrote. *How's Paul's? xx*

Chris texted back to say that Paul was still stuck on eighty-eight but that he had a plan. *Might need to break a few rules but nothing new there. Yes to codeine Xx.* Chris's text also contained an emoji of a stethoscope along with a red heart which made Anna blush.

At this point, David stepped forward from the window where he had been patiently listening to Monica's steady interrogation. 'Good morning, Tiffany. My name is David Latham,' he began, his voice calm but with a tone of authority. 'I am a friend of Henry and Diana Morris. Their son was Justin Morris. They loved their son as you love yours. They believe that your son was involved in the murder of their son. As a result, I made them a promise that I would kill your boy.'

Tiffany's look of terror returned. She began to thrash about on the bed attempting to work herself free. Monica wondered where precisely David was going with this but decided to let it roll.

David moved towards Tiffany and placed a large, strong hand on her forehead, an action which did nothing to quell her fear. 'However,' he continued, 'I have no intention of killing your son or you. I simply want justice.' Tiffany calmed partially and she started to cry. David found a discarded pair of stockings and delicately dried her tears. 'Now, I know you're scared. I'm scared too. We all are. It's late. Everyone is tired. But whatever you're scared of, we're here to protect you. Nobody is going to hurt you while we're here. Nobody is going to hurt Paul.' He glanced at Anna who nodded almost imperceptibly. 'You have to trust us on this.'

Tiffany went silent and closed her eyes, trance-like. Her

breathing softened and the rapid gulps of oxygen she was inhaling when frightened were replaced by deeper, more considered intakes. Nobody spoke for over ten minutes until Tiffany's eyelids flickered and she returned to the room. She looked in turn at the three retired people in her bedroom, each of them silently willing her to take a leap of faith.

The simple truth was that Tiffany was exhausted, drained by the complications of existence. She was fifty-one years old and had spent the last decade keeping secrets, keeping herself to herself, protecting Paul, nursing Paul, losing friends, losing her will to live sometimes. Since the trial she had become steadily isolated and she hated it. Now, she only lived for Paul but, try as she might, for the last few years she had merely been able to observe as he incrementally deteriorated in every way. Her ageing shoulders could only bear so much weight. Tiffany had been on the verge of collapse for some time.

Anna's phone buzzed. A text from Chris. Paul's reading was up to eighty-nine. 'Your son is recovering well,' she said. 'That was a message from a friend of ours who is looking after him at my house. He was in a bad way but he's strong and he's slowly beginning to turn the corner.'

Tiffany began to weep again, huge sobs of pent-up relief blended with residual fear. Again David wiped her face gently with the stockings.

'If I tell you,' she said feebly, 'we'll need protection because if we don't get it they'll fucking kill us all.'

40

'A re you okay, Dad?' asked Lucinda Tinker. 'I'm still on shift for another hour but the desk said I should phone you urgently.'

Chris had called his youngest daughter on her mobile at 6am without success. She was either sleeping or working. He decided to assume the latter and called St Mary's on the off-chance he was right, in the full knowledge that an early morning call from her father would almost certainly terrify the poor girl. But then he had work to do. And he required certain equipment to do it. 'Absolutely fine, darling,' he said, alarmingly brightly for someone who had been awake most of the night. 'How's your shift been?'

At the other end of the line, Lucinda's voice took on a tone of relief combined with mild irritation. 'It's a Friday night in A&E, Dad. You can imagine how it's been. I've had to change my scrubs three times thanks to almost the full gamut of human excretions. No semen, thankfully, but the day is young. Is this a social call? If I'm brutally honest, the timing could be better.'

Chris noted the faint note of annoyance but he'd make it up to her. 'I need your help,' he said. 'If I send a strange old man in a taxi,' he glanced at Martin and smiled mischievously; the cabbie blew a kiss back, 'would you be able to acquire a few bits and bobs from the supply room, please? I'm looking after someone at the moment and they're not in the best of health. Do you think that might be possible, Lulu?'

The junior doctor sighed. Out of the corner of her eye, she could see a group of four, obviously drunk young men in various states of undress, staggering uneasily through the waiting area. 'It kinda depends on what stuff, Dad. Are we talking surgical gloves? Painkillers? Should be fine.'

'You're an angel, Lulu. I'll need a PN bag, a couple of cannulae, a couple of bags of zero point nine per cent saline, a Medi-Port, some sani-cloth wipes...'

'Dad!' Lucinda was tired and, love her father though she did, this list of requirements would not only get her fired but also struck off by the General Medical Council and possibly even arrested. 'I can't get all that and just sneak it out of the door! And what on Earth do you need it for anyway? You've been retired for seven years, for God's sake.'

'I know, darling,' Chris was turning up the charm, 'but I wouldn't ask if it wasn't an emergency.' Lucinda was silent at the other end of the line. Chris decided to take a chance. 'Who's the consultant on duty at the moment? Can you ask them? Tell them it's for me?'

'It's Duffy,' said Lucinda with an audible shudder. 'She hates me for reasons I don't understand. If I took a biro out of the hospital she'd have me publicly flayed. Sorry, Dad.'

'Duffy? Frances Duffy?'

'The very same.' One of the drunken young men was now urinating into a plant pot.

'Interesting.' Chris had spent much of the previous twenty-four hours making on the spot calculations. Now it was time for possibly the most delicate. 'Could you ask her to call me, please?

She has my number. At least, she used to have it.' Of course, she hasn't needed or wanted to use it for almost ten years, he thought, but hopefully enough water had flowed under that particular derelict bridge. Lucinda said that she would do her best, in between the dozens of other draws on her time in the remaining hour of her shift.

Twenty minutes later, Chris's phone rang, the caller display showing FD. *Here we go, he thought,* inhaling deeply. *Tin hat on.* 'Frances! How lovely to hear from you on this bright and sunny Saturday morning. How are you? It's been ages.'

'Doctor Tinker,' said Frances Duffy with as much formality as she could summon for a man who had turned her life upside down during a passionate but brief fling in her late forties. 'You are familiar, no doubt, with Marfan syndrome?' Chris confirmed that, despite its rarity, he was aware of the inherited condition whose myriad symptoms included extra-long limbs. 'Then I'm sure you'll understand my curiosity at your attempt to obtain, from a junior doctor no less, a list of specialist medical equipment as long as a Marfan sufferer's arm. If I didn't know better, I'd suspect you were planning to treat a very sick patient with a TPN line.'

Chris weighed his options. He could invent some complicated tale about a long-lost relative turning up on the doorstep in poor health and in need of intravenous nutrition, or he could tell the truth. During their torrid relationship, he remembered Frances Duffy had always appreciated straight talking. Plus, at least they had ended it on good terms, both realising that it was what it was – intense, crazy, furious, short. Like a hurricane passing over a small island. He decided to tell the truth. 'Frances,' he began, 'what I'm about to tell you must stay strictly between us.' Chris rattled through a basic overview of The Twelve and then a more detailed summary of the Justin Morris case and the general situation regarding Paul Storey.

Frances Duffy listened with great interest until he had finished.

There was a long pause during which Chris wondered whether Doctor Duffy had perhaps got bored and wandered off to do something more interesting like lancing an anal boil. 'Doctor Tinker,' she said finally, 'do you recall my specialism in the fourth year of medical school?' Chris admitted that he hadn't retained that information. 'It was during a conversation which took place between us in a king-size bed in Hampstead. I don't blame you for forgetting. As I recall you were fairly worn out after what we'd done together. And you were getting on a bit. Anyway. My specialism was inner city malnutrition. Text me a list and your address and I'll be over in an hour or so.'

Chris ignored the dig at his age, breathed an enormous sigh of relief, thanked Frances and ended the call. According to Veronica, Paul's oximeter reading had just crossed into the nineties. Chris pumped his fist, wincing slightly as his shoulder muscle dragged at the remnants of the old wound. 'Still got it.' He grinned and began texting his requirements.

41

Tiffany had pleaded to be fully untied before starting her story but, in the interests of caution, Monica had suggested that her legs would need to remain restrained but that her arms could be made more comfortable. Tiffany had argued that she wasn't planning to run anywhere, largely because she had nowhere else to go and also she felt safer inside, despite her house currently containing three old people who had taken away her son and tied her to a bed using her own clothing. After a few minutes of negotiation, David had carefully untied one hand at a time and tied the two together. Anna wished she had a pair of hers and Chris's handcuffs, unaware that they were already in use elsewhere.

The codeine administered about an hour earlier had had a dramatic effect both on Tiffany's headache and her mood. She'd even offered to make everyone teas and coffees although the consensus in the room was that Anna was probably best placed to sort refreshments.

'He was a good boy,' began Tiffany, her voice faltering as she spoke. 'I know everyone says their kid is good as gold but Paul really was a lovely little boy. He was smart, funny. He used to help the elderly neighbours with their shopping and everything. His teachers used to say what a pleasure he was to teach. I couldn't have been prouder. Then his dad left home when Paul was thirteen and everything changed.

'He started hanging around with the wrong people. They used to come to the house all the time and drink beer and smoke, even though they were all underage. They liked it here because I had food in the cupboards and they just used to help themselves. I always got the impression that they saw Paul as an easy touch who just wanted to belong so he let them use our house whenever they wanted.'

'Why didn't you call the police?' asked Monica as gently as she could.

Tiffany's head drooped. She managed to twist to the right and pick up her mug of coffee from a side table both-handed before taking a long slurp and replacing the mug uneasily back in its position. 'I thought about it a couple of times but Paul said they'd just beat him up for being a grass so I never bothered. Then when he was seventeen, the people he was hanging around with started bringing knives into our house. I came home from work one day and two of them were stabbing my kitchen table. The marks are still there if you want to go and look. I mean, I know it's not the best quality table. It was Matalan. But still, you don't dig holes out of someone's table with a knife.' She frowned at the memory. 'I chucked them out there and then, but later that evening they came back. Paul answered the door and he got a knife held to his throat. I was terrified but they just laughed and went on their way. It was a power thing to them.

'After that I hoped Paul would find a way to edge himself away from this group of thugs but, if anything, his attachment seemed to grow stronger. Looking back, I realise that he was probably looking for male role models after his dad abandoned him but at the time I was working two jobs trying to pay the bills on my own and doing my best to make sure Paul was safe.

'That November night, when the Morris boy was killed; that night will stay with me forever.' There was a silence while Tiffany gathered her thoughts before continuing. 'I wasn't working that night so I was watching *EastEnders* and Paul said he was going out. He'd bought a new jacket with some money he'd got as a birthday present from his nan and he was really proud of it. I heard him leave at about a quarter to eight and I assumed he'd be at the pub and that meant he'd probably roll in drunk about midnight, on his own if I was lucky. Instead, I heard the door go at about ten past eight. I got up and went to check and it was Paul. He was shivering in just his T-shirt and he had the beginnings of a black eye.

'I tried to give him a hug and ask what had happened and where he'd left his jacket but he shrugged me off and said he didn't want to talk about it. Then he went to his room and I didn't see him again that night. The next day, he didn't get out of bed until lunchtime. His eye was quite swollen by then and I wanted to call for a doctor's appointment but he said no. He didn't want any more trouble. It was a Saturday so I only had the evening job that day, I was doing bar work on the high street. I got to the bar just before six and everyone was talking about a stabbing near my house. I hadn't heard anything about it because I hadn't seen the local news or anything, but immediately I had a little warning bell go off in my head, you know?

'I got home around midnight and Paul was sitting in the kitchen eating a bowl of cereal. I asked if he'd heard about the stabbing and he just threw his bowl of cereal against the wall and stormed upstairs. I tried to follow him but he just swore at me and then locked himself in his room. I tidied up the mess in the kitchen and went to bed, although it wasn't easy to sleep with everything that was going on.'

Anna asked if Tiffany would like a top-up of coffee. It was gradually getting light outside and there was the faint sound of birds in the cemetery drifting through the open window. Tiffany nodded. 'Maybe more coffees all round, please, if there's enough,' said Monica.

'If there isn't, there's a café down the road that opens at seven on a Saturday. Anyway, shall I carry on?' Anna managed to scrape just enough coffee out of a jar of Nescafé for four mugs, although a lack of milk meant that two of them had to be black. Tiffany returned to her story.

'I tried not to think about the Morris murder but I couldn't help it. Everyone at work was talking about it and I found myself obsessing over little details in the paper just to reassure myself that it had nothing to do with Paul. Then, after a couple of weeks, the police turned up. Two detectives, both men. They sat at the kitchen table and spoke to Paul for about an hour. Naturally they took great interest in the knife marks on the table. There was a lot of talk about the jacket. It had been found almost burned to a crisp but the bit that had survived the fire had some blood specks on it. Paul said someone had nicked it from the pub when he was in the toilet. The detectives took him away for further questioning.'

Tiffany started to cry again as painful memories flooded back. 'The next day, one of the detectives came back. Detective McMullan.' Monica flinched. 'We sat in the living room and he told me that it was likely Paul would be charged over the Morris murder but, he said, he would be able to manage the case so that Paul would only get a manslaughter charge because there was no proof he dealt the fatal blow. He would get fifteen years in prison but if he showed remorse and behaved himself, he could be out in seven. I didn't know what to think. I knew my Paul could never hurt anyone.

'Then Detective McMullan said that if I agreed to Paul pleading guilty to manslaughter then some friends of his would make sure I got enough money that I never had to work again. He also said that if I didn't co-operate then he couldn't guarantee Paul's safety in prison and he couldn't guarantee my safety here. As threats go, it wasn't the most subtle. He asked me to think about it but also warned me that if I told anyone then he'd make sure I never saw Paul alive again.'

'I can see how that must have been frightening,' said Anna, energised by black coffee.

'I was fucking terrified,' cried Tiffany. 'I'd never had any dealings with the police before. All I cared about was making sure Paul was safe. If that meant him going to prison for a few years, I could deal with that. Of course, because of that jury, he never did time. He got a worse punishment. Imprisoned in his own house just getting worse and worse. And all I could do was watch because I knew that if I asked for help from the outside, I might lose him either to social services or worse.'

42

It was just after seven that Anna's doorbell rang. 'I'd better go,' said Chris nervously. 'Doctor Duffy can be,' he searched for an acceptable description, 'fiery.' Paul's oximeter reading was now a satisfying ninety-one and he was drifting in and out of consciousness.

For the previous hour, Chris had been anxious about many things, notably how Frances Duffy would greet him, how precisely he should greet her, and possibly more importantly, how he was going to fully explain the presence of a severely malnourished young man in recovery from carbon monoxide poisoning in Anna's guest room. Of course, the two of them had been perfectly civil to each other on the rare occasions their paths had crossed at drab medical conferences while Chris was still working, but the last time they had been together alone, both knowing it would be the last time, the sex had been volcanic. He could still recall the intensity of it almost a decade on.

'Good morning, Frances.' He beamed, opening the door to a striking brunette woman with pale skin and bright-blue eyes. She was carrying a well-stuffed doctor's bag. 'You've barely aged. In fact, if I didn't know any better, I'd say you were somehow looking younger than when I last saw you. It's nothing short of a medical miracle.'

Frances Duffy smiled at the compliment and embraced Chris awkwardly. 'Nice place you have here,' she said politely, if a little frostily.

'Oh, it's not mine,' flustered Chris, 'it's... a friend's. We're using it for convenience sake. With the patient. But I've been staying here too. Over the last few weeks.' He didn't want to explicitly advertise that Anna was his lover but equally he didn't want Frances to get the wrong idea. Ten seconds into their reconnection and he was already feeling distinctly uneasy.

Frances raised an eyebrow. 'I understand,' she said efficiently. 'Show me the patient.'

Chris led the senior consultant upstairs to the spare bedroom where he quickly introduced Thomas, Veronica, Martin and Terry, all of whom greeted the visitor with formal handshakes moderated by mild fear – Chris had given them all a succinct briefing during the previous hour, naturally omitting some of the more personal details. Frances's attention meanwhile was drawn to Paul Storey and in particular the fluffy handcuffs attaching him to the bed.

She placed her bag on the floor and stroked her chin. 'You don't change, do you, Chris?' she mused.

Chris blushed. 'He was spasming and we needed to find a way to secure him for his own safety and these were the closest thing to hand.'

'Of course they were,' said Frances impassively. Veronica giggled and then stopped abruptly after a stern look from the new arrival. 'Now, judging by the state of this young man, I'd say he's unlikely to need restraint for a good while but we'll stick with your plan. For now. What's his blood ox?' Terry explained that they'd taken a reading moments before her arrival and it was ninety-one, up from eighty-eight. 'Good. The right direction albeit slowly.' She opened her bag and Chris saw that Doctor Duffy had brought everything on his list plus a few more bits of kit just in case. He gave himself a satisfied smile. 'You'll have to be my surgical assistant, Doctor Tinker. Can you remember how to do that or should I employ your locksmith friend?' Chris's smile evaporated.

'Could the rest of you please go and wash your hands thoroughly,' asked Frances in a commanding tone.

'Will you need us to scrub in?' asked Martin, slightly concerned there may be the risk of bodily fluids on his new jeans.

'Good Lord, no,' said Frances. 'I'll need you to make cups of tea for me and Chris and I don't want grubby fingerprints on my mug!'

'There may be a flapjack left somewhere,' said Terry brightly. 'Possibly in the taxi. I made them last night before we started this operation.'

Frances eyed him suspiciously. 'Were you a baker?' she asked. 'Before you joined Chris's little gang of geriatric superheroes.' Terry replied that no, he had always been a locksmith. 'Then I'll stick to the tea if it's all right with you. Strong, white, no sugar please.'

'Doesn't know what she's missing,' muttered Thomas who then scampered quickly in the direction of a bathroom to wash his hands. Terry, Veronica and Martin followed, keen to be away from the doctor, temporarily at least.

Frances reached into her bag and pulled out a pack of alcohol wipes with which she sanitised the top of the chest of drawers which would have to act as a makeshift work area. She then disinfected her hands and began to place the necessary equipment where it was easiest to reach. She had managed to bring four syringes – Chris had only asked for two – a full TPN bag, multiple alcohol pads, a pack of medical tubing, five sets of surgical gloves, an electronic pump, a miniature sharps container and various vials of what Chris assumed were assorted vitamins and nutrients. 'Have you washed your hands, Doctor Tinker?' she asked in a way that Chris felt wasn't entirely platonic. He confessed that although he had been regularly scrubbing during the morning, the fact that he had touched the door-knob and also the stair bannister meant that he should do it again. 'Off you go then,' said Frances. 'I'll wait.'

When Chris returned to the room, he noticed that Frances had already set up the TPN line into Paul's handcuffed left arm and that the system was ready to go. 'I made the decision to start with a gentle cocktail of multivitamins,' she announced. 'From what you told me on the phone, that should at least begin to help replace what's been lost over the years. The saline solution may feel a little cold for Paul as it's only an hour or so out of the fridge but it'll do him no harm.'

'You don't mess about do you?' said Chris, impressed.

Frances purred, 'I never did, Doctor Tinker. Or have you forgotten?' Chris blushed again and a long-forgotten memory trickled casually but destructively through his mind like molten lava. 'The electronic pump is ready for its button to be pressed. Would you like to do the honours?'

43

'Can I please have a piss?' asked Tiffany. 'One of you can come with me if you're worried, although there's no window in the bathroom so unless you think I'm going to escape down the U-bend, there's probably no need.' Monica agreed but said that she'd have to wait outside to escort the younger woman back to the bedroom afterwards as there was still much more they didn't know about Paul and the Morris case.

David untied her legs from the bed but then tied them together so that Tiffany could walk but only at low speed, shuffling from bedroom to bathroom and back voluntarily before continuing her story. Her mood had brightened further with the dawn and even the absence of Paul appeared to have had an assuaging effect. 'As you know, the Morris investigation was a mess and all of that was down to DI McMullan. Luckily, or unluckily depending on which way you look at it, the lawyer Paul eventually ended up with wasn't anything to do with McMullan. If she had been, Paul would have pleaded guilty and that would be that. But she was a bright young Muslim woman about four years out of law school and she didn't think there was enough evidence to convict and so she said that he should try for not guilty and see what happened. I suspect we got her because the coppers thought the prosecution would eat her alive. They were wrong.

'Thanks to her methodical cross-examination of various witnesses, the jury couldn't decide and so Paul was acquitted. For a few seconds, I was overjoyed. I had my boy back. But then I started to worry about what would happen to us and it didn't take long to find out.

'McMullan did a newspaper interview the week afterwards where he was asked whether he was disappointed in the verdict in Paul's case. He came straight out and said that he knew Paul was guilty and that he'd do everything he could to make sure justice was served, even though he was off the case by that point.

'A few days after the acquittal, he came to the house with another man.'

'Tony Slaven?' asked David quietly.

'Exactly. That conversation was very aggressive. McMullan made it clear that if I went to the police, it would be the last thing I ever did. Even if I got police protection, he would use his contacts inside the force to find us. Slaven said it would be best for Paul if he kept himself to himself for a while. Many members of the public thought he was guilty so he was a marked man. In addition, Slaven said he had friends who wouldn't hesitate to put him in hospital if they saw him. It scared us both. You've got to remember that Paul was never a confident boy. He was an outsider who just wanted to fit in. Everything that happened in 2010 and 2011 would have been too much for anyone, let alone him.'

Tiffany inhaled deeply. Anna asked if anyone fancied another coffee, without milk this time as there was none left and she didn't fancy going to the café in case she missed too much. David and Monica said that sounded good. Tiffany declined and carried on with her story. 'At the time, we assumed that Slaven was making his threats because he was some sort of vigilante but then he offered us money to keep quiet and keep ourselves to ourselves. I thought that was a bit odd but I didn't ask questions. I'd already been fired from one job because of everything that had happened. Slaven said his wife, Janine, would meet me every couple of weeks and hand over cash; enough to keep us going. More than enough, actually. He said she'd be in touch.

'A couple of days later there was a text from Janine saying where and when to meet. She refused to come to the house because she knew it was being watched. Instead she preferred coffee shops as she could sit and relax for a while. Actually, I've changed my mind. I will have a cup.' David went to the top of the stairs to shout down to Anna in the kitchen that another coffee was required. 'The first time we met, it was a very quick meeting. No more than a couple of minutes. We said hello, how are you. She gave me an envelope and I left. When I got home, I opened it up and there was a thousand pounds in crisp twenties. It was more than I'd ever seen in my life. I thought, if this is going to happen every two weeks just for keeping quiet then it sounds all right to me. Paul agreed. He bought a PlayStation 3 which he'd always wanted and then the following year he got the PlayStation 4 on the day it came out.'

Anna arrived with a tray of black coffees and distributed them onto various surfaces near to each person. 'Gradually,' continued Tiffany, 'I became friendly with Janine and I suppose we started to trust each other. One day in about 2017, she was in a foul mood. I asked her if she was okay and she told me she'd had a massive row with Tony and she was thinking of leaving him. We ended up driving in her Mercedes to a pub for lunch and everything just came out.

'According to Janine, it was her son Leo who killed Justin

Morris that night in 2010. He had bumped into Paul outside the pub and taken a shine to Paul's jacket. He asked to borrow it. Paul said no. Leo and one of his mates had threatened to beat Paul up if he didn't hand it over and gave him a couple of jabs to the face as a taster. Paul had no choice.

'After the stabbing, Leo had got home and told his parents. The Slavens had been making money from various criminal activities for years – drugs, guns, you name it – but they'd always managed to keep undercover because of Tony's links with the police. The last thing they wanted was a member of the family involved in a high-profile criminal case. Tony put a call in to McMullan who arrived at their house the following morning. He listened to Leo's story and together they all came up with a plan to frame Paul.

'McMullan took away the bloodstained jacket and burned it. Then he spent a few days tracking down the market trader who originally sold the jacket to Paul and a week or so after that he turned up at our house to question Paul. My son would never have grassed on Leo. He was too afraid.'

Tiffany began to sob once more and Monica put an arm around her shoulder which the woman melted into.

'The partial fingerprint is Leo's,' said Anna. 'And we know he's got a criminal record for beating up a taxi driver. It should be easy to cross-check.' The forensics expert was careful not to reveal how she knew this in case Tiffany clammed up but the woman seemed unconcerned.

Monica extracted herself from Tiffany to check on Paul. She called Thomas who outlined the events of the last few hours, the arrival of Frances Duffy and, after checking with the makeshift medical team, relayed the news that Paul was responding well to the treatment but still wasn't truly conscious, partly because Doctor Duffy had sedated him.

'He'll need his mum when he wakes up,' said Tiffany

impassively. 'And he'll need his medicine in a couple of hours. He takes paroxetine for his anxiety. It's in the locked kitchen cabinet so he can't take an overdose. The key is in a Clarks shoe box under this bed.'

Monica asked what happened to Paul; how did he get into such a state. Tiffany explained that after she'd had the conversation with Janine, Paul finally opened up about what happened on that night in 2010. It had taken him almost seven years. He had been slowly retreating into himself but after he found out the new information, he had really started to decline. 'He stopped eating properly,' said Tiffany, draining her coffee. 'He stopped going outside. He stopped really communicating. Some days were better than others and, on his good days, he used to say that he felt angry that his life hadn't turned out well and that Leo Slaven was still free. He channelled that anger into his video games because he was becoming too weak for anything else.

'The Slavens arranged for him to go on the paroxetine. They offered him heroin too as they thought that might be helpful to keep him docile but I declined. I didn't want to add to our problems by creating an addict. The last year or so, he's only really been eating breakfast cereal and crisps. That's why he is how he is. I read something online about age regression after trauma. He's gone back in years because of everything that's happened to him.'

David held his head in his hands, in despair for the young man he had until recently been expecting to kill.

The room was silent while everyone took in the extent of Tiffany's information. Outside, the late-summer sun began to warm the tops of the stones in the cemetery. Then, wordlessly, David moved towards Tiffany, sat beside her and gave her a hug. 'I'm sorry,' he said. 'For everything.' Both of them began to cry.

'We should pack you a bag,' said Monica, 'if we need to get

you and the medicine over to Paul.' Tiffany nodded. 'I'll text Martin to come and get us. It won't take long at this time of the morning on a Saturday. I'll also see if Terry can come back and fix your door.' Together with David, she helped Tiffany to her feet and untied her hands. The woman responded by giving them both a hug which Anna joined in. 'One final question,' added Monica, 'what was Paul's dream? When he was growing up. What did he want to be?'

Tiffany thought for a moment and then smiled uneasily. 'He wanted to be a zookeeper,' she said, wistfully remembering the eight-year-old boy who used to come home from school with countless drawings of wildlife. 'He loved animals. He still sometimes says he'd like a pet but we just can't. It's too difficult. But he'd love to work in a zoo. It's too late now, though. He's in his thirties, he has no qualifications and he's not well.'

Monica gave her a squeeze. 'We don't have a motto,' she said, 'but if we did, it would be something along the lines of It's Never Too Late. Once Paul's a bit better, we'll see what can be done.'

David looked skywards as he felt more tears form for the loss of not one young life but two.

44

Martin's taxi arrived with Terry just after ten, having stopped off at a local timber merchants for a piece of hardwood which the locksmith was intending to use for the repair of the hole in the Storeys' door. 'It'll only be temporary,' he explained, 'but I'll get you a new door on Monday with better locks and I'll fit it in a couple of hours.' Tiffany asked whether he needed a spare key in case she was caring for Paul, and Terry said, with a devilish wink, that that wouldn't be necessary.

The locksmith asked whether it would be possible for David to stay at the Storey house for the rest of the morning to assist and the plumber replied that not only would it be his pleasure but that it would also provide the opportunity to fit smoke alarms. 'I'll check your pipes as well, just in case,' he added, 'and I'll brief Terry on what's been discussed this morning.'

During the short journey to Anna's house, Monica attempted to prepare Tiffany for what she might encounter when they reached Paul. 'He's been sedated,' she said calmly, 'but only because it's better that he wakes up and sees you there. A friendly face. Otherwise it'll be quite a shock and, as I understand it, in his condition, the last thing Paul needs is a shock.' Tiffany said she understood and asked more about the people who were looking after her son. Monica explained that there were now three more members of her group involved, a former sports coach, a retired TV presenter and an ex-surgeon who was leading the care team. In addition, there was a doctor from St Mary's whom Monica didn't know but she was a friend of the surgeon so there was no reason to suggest she wasn't fully qualified.

'Do you think I can take Paul home when he wakes up?' his mother asked hopefully. Monica tried to manage expectations and suggested that the doctors might be in a better position than a retired chemistry professor to suggest a recovery plan for the next few days and possibly weeks.

Anna fished her door key out of her pocket and let everyone into her home. Veronica was sitting on the stairs waiting for them and looking a little tired. 'We've been grabbing a couple of hours' sleep in between shifts,' she said. 'Thomas is currently having a nap.'

'I recognise you,' said Tiffany, shaking Veronica's hand.

Veronica smiled modestly. 'I was on television a few years back. Daytime shows mostly. Often involving antiques.'

Tiffany frowned. 'No, it's not that. You were in the café when I was meeting Janine. Were you spying on me?' Veronica froze.

Monica decided to step in. 'We were observing you for a while, just to see if we could build a connection without having to take extreme measures. That's all. As it turned out, we couldn't, but we did manage to get enough information to identify Janine. We didn't know who she was before. And that helped to firm up our belief that Paul was innocent. It's nothing sinister.'

Tiffany's face softened as the jigsaw pieces slotted into

place. 'Makes sense, I suppose,' she said. 'Can I see my boy now, please?'

Veronica led the party upstairs to where Chris and Frances were sitting at opposite ends of Paul's improvised hospital bed, Frances monitoring the flow of vitamins into Paul's body via the TPN line. The first thing Tiffany noticed were the fluffy handcuffs. She glanced at Chris who smiled meekly and then back at Monica who shrugged. 'I'm beginning to worry about you people,' she said wearily. Anna attempted to disappear into a corner.

'Trust me, you're not the only one,' muttered Frances and introduced herself and Chris with brisk handshakes. 'Your son is doing extremely well. His blood oxygen is now back to somewhere near normal so we've taken him off the oxygen tank and he's currently taking on an intravenous solution of vitamins and minerals to give him strength. As I'm sure you know, he's severely malnourished. He's also been sedated because we were waiting for you to arrive but he should be waking up in the next hour or so. Why don't you have my chair and you can hold his hand until he does.'

Tiffany slowly moved towards her stricken son and kissed his bony forehead before taking a seat and gently clasping Paul's uncuffed right hand. 'It's okay, baby,' she whispered. 'Everything's going to be fine now.'

Frances placed a hand on her shoulder. 'I would strongly recommend that we admit him to a proper hospital at the earliest opportunity and I will personally make sure he gets a private room with a second bed so you can stay with him.' Tiffany glanced at Monica with a look of renewed fear which Frances registered. 'But we can have that discussion later when he's awake and we can all decide what's best for everyone.' The doctor walked over to the corner where Anna had been hiding. 'Your house?' Anna nodded sheepishly. 'And therefore your cuffs?' Anna nodded again. Frances turned to Chris. 'Your "friend"?'

'Very much so,' replied Chris with a wink in Anna's direction.

Frances turned back to Anna. 'Good luck,' she said, and wandered downstairs to get a cup of tea.

'She's... interesting,' said Monica.

'You have no idea,' said Chris with a sigh.

As it was a Saturday, Monica composed a long text to Suzanne Green with a succinct overview of what Tiffany had told them and suggesting that the forensics team compare the partial fingerprint on the jacket with Leo Slaven's from the database. Suzanne texted back within ten minutes to say that she was just involved in overseeing the policing of yet another protest march through central London but suggested meeting on Monday morning for a full debrief. Monica texted the group to ask them to keep Monday free.

Around noon, while Anna was snoozing in her bedroom, Paul's eyes began to flicker. 'Hey, baby,' said Tiffany, stroking his drawn face, 'it's okay, you're safe. Mummy's here.' The young man tried to lift his left hand but realised he couldn't and raised his head slightly off the bed, looking down to see the furry cuffs. Terror filled his eyes. He inhaled too quickly and began to cough. 'Calm down, baby,' said Tiffany, smiling with tears in her eyes. 'Mummy's got you. We've had a rough night but these old people have been looking after us. They're going to help us. They're already helping you get better. Okay? Is there any water, please?'

Frances passed her a bottle of still water and Paul drank voraciously, finally quenching his parched throat. He looked rapidly around the room at Monica, Veronica, Frances, Thomas and Chris. They didn't look threatening; that much he would admit. 'I'm Doctor Duffy,' said Frances, evenly. 'You've had quite a tough time, haven't you, Paul? Don't worry. We're going to get you back to full strength.'

'Where am I?' asked Paul in confusion, his voice fragile. Tiffany explained where they were and what had happened since the previous evening. She didn't go into detail about what she had revealed about the Morris case. That could wait. The important thing now was for Paul to begin the long process of recovery and for the two of them to try to piece their shattered lives back together.

During the afternoon, and after Terry and David had rejoined the group to confirm that the Storeys' door was secure and their house was fitted with new smoke alarms, it was agreed that Paul and Tiffany would stay at Anna's until the following day. This would allow Frances Duffy time to arrange for Paul to be transferred to a specialist unit at a private clinic connected with St Mary's. 'I would estimate that he will need at least three months of work to get his body back to its full quota of nutrients and we need to increase his muscle mass and repair any organ damage. If everyone agrees, we'll also start cognitive behavioural therapy to work through the PTSD and reverse the age regression with which he's been suffering. If all goes well, I would hope that we'll see a new Paul by the new year.'

'The Twelve will cover all the costs of the private clinic,' reassured Monica. 'It's the least we can do.'

Tiffany, who had spent most of her time in Anna's house holding back tears, couldn't restrain the torrent any longer. 'I can't thank you enough,' she gulped. 'I don't know what we've done to deserve this.'

Before she and Thomas left the house, Monica tentatively outlined to Tiffany what she thought would happen to the

Slavens. 'Assuming the fingerprints match,' she said, 'it's likely Leo and Tony, and probably Janine as well, will be arrested today. If you're able to give evidence then, in all likelihood, the two men will go to prison for a very long time.' Tiffany nodded that she understood.

'What about Janine?'

Monica paused. 'I'm not a lawyer, I'm a chemistry professor, but if I were to hazard a guess then I'd say she would be charged with perverting the course of justice at the very least.'

Tiffany thought for a moment, her mind still reeling from the extraordinary events of the previous few hours. 'There's one thing I haven't told you,' she whispered. 'McMullan. They were lovers.'

Monica's brow furrowed. 'Janine and McMullan?'

'Not Janine. Tony. He and McMullan were shagging. That's what they had the row about in 2017. Janine had caught them in the act.'

45

Suzanne Green had managed to carve out a secretive twenty minutes to meet with The Twelve at a large Georgian townhouse in West Square just behind the Imperial War Museum, chosen by Monica as it was only five minutes' drive from the commissioner's office at New Scotland Yard. According to Monica, the house, which hadn't been used by the group for a while, had four floors including a basement, five bedrooms and was on her long list of places to potentially rent out to the deserving when she eventually got around to focusing on that particular pet project. She had only really managed to narrow this list down to the more residential properties – places like Clarges Mews and Hogarth Court in the City were less suited to comfortable domesticity owing to the lack of any serviceable bedrooms.

The meeting room at West Square was, as usual, a spacious double reception area with a collection of rather austere paintings which Monica had revealed to Thomas as the work of the American artist James McNeill Whistler. 'He lived in Chelsea next door to a member of The Twelve in the 1870s and

80s,' she disclosed. 'They were great friends and so apparently Whistler used to give the chap paintings that he felt weren't quite up to the standard required for his exhibitions. They're not bad though. And they're probably worth a few bob.'

Thomas was examining an unnervingly gloomy painting of a London bridge when Veronica shuffled up behind him. 'One of Whistler's *Nocturnes*,' she said warmly. 'We must stop meeting like this. Near great art.' Thomas relayed the story of how The Twelve came to possess the paintings and Veronica mused that, if she were still working in television, it would be enormously tempting to approach a production company to make a series about the lost art collection of London's secret assassins. Naturally, such a series would be impossible. 'I just feel privileged to be able to see it all for myself,' she said with ebullience. 'I pinch myself on an almost daily basis.'

Polite conversation rarely came easily to Thomas but he had found Veronica a very calming presence since she had joined The Twelve back in the spring. 'Are you enjoying your first case?' he asked, casually waving at the late arrivals Graham and Owen. 'It's my second, as you know, and it's certainly been different.'

Veronica said that she'd found the whole thing absolutely fascinating to be a part of although, even at this late stage, she wasn't entirely sure anyone was going to get assassinated 'which is a great pity as I was so looking forward to that bit.' Thomas raised an eyebrow and momentarily wondered how Mrs Mendoza would react to such a comment.

'I wouldn't bet on that,' said Catherine, overhearing their conversation as she sat on the arm of a large leather sofa casually checking her social media. 'This case has a couple of surprises up its sleeve, I suspect.'

Terry and Anna handed round coffees and teas and Terry

had some butter and sultana cookies which he'd baked on Sunday but apparently were 'better the day after.' Chris provided an update on Paul's progress and reported that he and Tiffany had agreed to formal treatment in the clinic under the personal care of Frances Duffy who had taken the two of them under her hippocratic wing. The doctor had undertaken a full examination the previous day and concluded that, with luck and if he responded well, Paul could be on the mend by Christmas which was something of a miracle considering the state in which they had found him.

'I also have news,' said Suzanne, who was unusually in full uniform. 'The partial fingerprint on the jacket matches that of Leo Slaven. DI Black assembled a team of armed officers yesterday and they raided the homes of Tony Slaven and Leo Slaven early this morning, arresting them along with Janine Slaven and another man who has been released on bail. From what I gather of this fourth individual, he is a male prostitute whom Tony and Janine had procured for the night and has no other connection with the Slavens.

'At Tony and Janine's house, officers found cocaine with a street value of around two million pounds plus a consignment of weapons and ammunition recently arrived from Poland which we suspect were intended for onward sale here in London. There's enough evidence to put them all away for an extremely long time. If Tiffany and Paul also choose to testify in court then we're probably looking at life sentences. All in all, a highly successful outcome. Oh, Terry! Sultana cookies. My favourites. May I take a couple with me when I leave here, please? I have to go straight to the Home Office for a debrief with the home secretary about the weekend protest march. Frankly, I'll need the sustenance to get through it without screaming.'

The locksmith said that she was welcome to take as many as

she wanted; he'd baked plenty and anything left over would be gifted to Mrs Mendoza later in the day – he had his occasional, scheduled chat with the octogenarian psychologist to ensure he wasn't turning into a murderous psychopath. 'As I'm not feeling in the slightest bit homicidal,' he said, 'I reckon it'll just be the usual delightful hour of chit-chat.'

'I'm assuming we don't now need to think about assassinating any of the Slavens?' asked Veronica with disappointment, reaching for a biscuit before they all vanished into Suzanne's pocket. The commissioner confirmed that, barring a total catastrophe in the criminal justice arena, the task of removing the Slavens from the streets of London was no longer The Twelve's concern.

'It's rare not to have an assassination at the end of a case,' said Monica, 'although I checked with Lexington and it has happened a handful of times over the years, most recently in the 1970s when a target died of natural causes before they could be eliminated.'

Suzanne rose from her seat, stashed a couple of cookies and looked with trepidation towards the door. 'Do you all trust me?' she asked, almost in a whisper. The Twelve looked at each other in confusion before nodding and muttering subdued yeses. 'Then you'll know what to do next.' She reached into an inner pocket and retrieved an envelope which she handed to Monica. 'Please open this when I've gone,' she said. 'And, by the way, he still smokes cigars.'

The group sat in silence as they heard the commissioner gently close the front door behind her having skilfully navigated Terry's lock system. Those facing the window watched her chauffeur-driven car set off reluctantly towards Whitehall. Monica stared at the envelope for a moment before opening it, studying the contents and smiling.

'It looks like some of us are going out of town for a while.'

She passed the note, written in Suzanne's handwriting, around the group. Catherine glanced at Veronica who was the last to read the contents which inspired an exuberant smile. 'What did I tell you?' the former journalist said with a wink.

46

With the address, email and phone number of retired detective Brian McMullan in their possession, The Twelve were under no illusion that the case would, as Catherine had predicted, result in a death. A cursory look at Google Maps indicated that the former detective lived in a detached farmhouse in a Malvern Hills valley approximately six miles from the nearest village and nearly two from the closest neighbour. 'Gregarious fellow, clearly,' mused Martin. 'Shall we go and pay a cheeky visit?'

Monica suggested that a small reconnaissance group make an initial trip and asked for volunteers. 'We'll hire a car rather than take the taxi if that's okay, Martin. I suspect a black cab in rural Worcestershire may be moderately conspicuous.' Martin asked whether he could hire a sports car, secretly hoping that Chris would offer to lend his. Monica replied that he could hire whatever he liked so long as he could fit three passengers in it without breaking their legs or causing some sort of arterial thrombosis. Martin scowled and said he'd research something to blend in with pastoral Britain, 'Possibly one of those Range Rover-type things with the heated seats. The ones they have in

Fulham for the harsh and unforgiving terrain of SW6. I've always wanted to drive one of them. Even though it's August.'

Veronica volunteered first, her hand shooting up with breathtaking speed. The former television presenter had enjoyed her first case far more than she had anticipated up to this point and was keen to take advantage of any excursions on the basis that it was 'the sort of thing I used to do, whizzing around the country, meeting people. It'll be like old times.' Graham also put his hand up, with slightly more decorum, and said that he would take a camera with the latest telephoto lenses to bring back images to help formulate a plan. Finally, Catherine suggested that she tag along to keep Veronica company.

'I know what you're like,' said Monica with a grin, her eyes flicking between the ex-journalist and Graham. 'Just don't corrupt Veronica, please. At least not on her first case.' The newest member of the group reddened and suggested that most kinds of corruption had already occurred many years in her past.

By the end of that week, the group had researched Brian McMullan using files provided by Ted Black. They had also studied the layout of his secluded farmhouse using Land Registry documents, and Monica had explained their initial plan to Suzanne who offered to lend them an unmarked police Range Rover on the basis that when it was picked up by number plate recognition cameras on the motorways, fewer questions would be asked. When Monica relayed this information to Martin, adding that the vehicle did indeed have heated seats, he was delighted although also slightly perturbed that Suzanne would think he hadn't already considered the problem of

ANPR and had accordingly figured out a route to the Malverns which largely avoided cameras after leaving the metropolitan area and the motorway network. *It'll take longer but we'll go through some lovely, pretty villages,* he had texted proudly, adding an emoji of a house and a couple of trees. *There are a couple of points where we have to cross an A-road but Graham has said he will assess the risk of being spotted by cameras and advise.* Graham texted the group chat with an emoji of a face wearing sunglasses.

Just after dawn on Sunday morning, the foursome gathered at Martin's house in the East End and set off for the countryside. With barely any traffic on the road, and with the cabbie quickly getting the hang of the Range Rover – 'gorgeous suspension, smoothest of gear changes. I could get used to this' – they were on the motorway by seven. Just under an hour later, Martin took a turn off the M40 just outside High Wycombe and they spent the next two hours weaving through winding lanes and slowing through the tiniest of villages, some of them barely more than a scattering of cottages and a rudimentary shop.

'I could easily retire to a place like this,' said Graham wistfully as they eased gently through an Oxfordshire hamlet. Catherine argued firstly that he had already retired and secondly that he'd probably get bored and even if he didn't then Owen certainly would. 'I'm sure we could always find ways to occupy our time,' he countered, wickedly. 'Especially if you're able to visit on occasion. We could have you on speed dial for emergencies.' Catherine kissed him firmly on the lips.

'I consider myself corrupted beyond measure,' said Veronica, feigning shock. Martin raised his eyes to the sky in despair and incrementally turned up the volume on the 1968 original London cast recording of *Cabaret*.

They reached the Malverns at mid-morning and the Range Rover parked up at the bustling village closest to McMullan's house. Church bells were ringing for Sunday mass as the four of them ambled down the high street and found a quaint tea shop for refreshments and toilet breaks. While Martin, Catherine and Veronica refuelled with coffee and croissants, paid for by using cash as usual, Graham wandered up and down the short high street to assess any CCTV coverage and discovered, delightfully, that the only camera was outside the solitary bank at the western end of the village. 'If we come in and leave from the eastern end then we can't be spotted,' he noted, nibbling a pain au raisin back at the tea shop.

Graham had also figured out the best position to start taking photographs, a hillside around a mile from the McMullan house, and, once sated, they set off again. Martin had to take a couple of dry mud tracks which could only loosely be described as serviceable roads but the Range Rover handled them with satisfying ease. 'Turning circle is good, too,' purred the cabbie in admiration. The only delay was caused by a farmer herding his sheep for ten minutes along one of the tracks. 'First time we've had to factor livestock into assassination planning,' mused Martin.

Initially they parked near the brow of the hill under shelter from some trees, a mixture of oak, ash and hazel. Low cumulus clouds were drifting steadily from the west. Graham pointed out the farmhouse on the opposite side of a small valley and set up a camera tripod to take photographs, focusing in on the door locks and other entry points including windows. There was no movement within the house but an old maroon estate car was positioned outside so it was likely McMullan was at home. Graham noticed what looked like an outside cellar door but had to adjust his position by a few metres to get a clear picture. 'That could be useful,' he muttered to himself.

Back in London, Monica and Thomas were having a rare lazy Sunday morning in bed with newspapers which Thomas had foraged along with fresh croissants from the local café. They had no plans for the day beyond an afternoon visit to the Baker Street house as Monica felt that she needed to accelerate her study of all The Twelve cases stored there. Thomas was happy to tag along as he found the documents fascinating, particularly those from the 1960s and the leadership of Beryl Edwards. 'She reminds me of you,' he said, reaching for a supplement. 'The more cases I read, the more I realise that the Beryl era was pioneering. She made so many innovations and even sold one of the Twelve houses to a charity for wounded service people for a fraction of the expected price. Much like what you want to do with renting them out on the cheap.'

Monica looked up from her newspaper with interest. She had been working through the cases in Baker Street in chronological order from the 1830s and had only just reached the twentieth century. 'Will you let me know if you discover anything else fun about Beryl, my darling?' she purred. 'She sounds like a kindred spirit. Maybe even a soulmate if we'd ever met.'

'She loved chemistry too,' said Thomas. 'Although she was a headteacher, she took a keen interest in all sorts of subjects, especially after her volunteering work during the war. I imagine that's why The Twelve took an interest in her.'

Their phones pinged with a group WhatsApp message from Martin accompanied by a photograph of the rolling hills of Worcestershire with Veronica and Catherine waving in the foreground. 'Time for a shower,' said Monica, stretching. 'And then maybe a half hour playing the cello.'

'Need any help? With the shower part.'

'Always.'

47

That evening, after Martin had returned the Range Rover, albeit with considerable reluctance, to Ted Black, The Twelve met at their Clarges Mews meeting space, a state-of-the-art multimedia room hidden in a grimily nondescript alcove near Piccadilly which boasted a screen on which Graham could project his photographs. Suzanne had been invited but had politely declined as she had a long-standing dinner appointment with the Shadow Home Secretary, a prospect about which she was genuinely excited. In addition, the commissioner had explained to Monica that although she was aware of what was going to happen, equally she didn't necessarily need to know all the details. 'Just try not to leave too much evidence,' the commissioner had warned. 'I know the chief constable at West Mercia well enough to put the brakes on any potential investigation but it would be far easier for all concerned if there wasn't an investigation in the first place.' Monica had said she would bear that in mind.

As it was an evening meeting, all those who weren't driving – everyone apart from Martin – were invited to dip into the drinks cabinet. Catherine, Belinda and Veronica decided to share a bottle of pink champagne as it was just about still summer while the others went for whiskies, gins and, in Terry's case, absinthe because he simply wanted to try it. After one sip, he decided it reminded him of cough mixture from his childhood and reverted to an aged Irish whiskey.

The cabbie explained their route in and out of the Malverns and pointed out that there were only two places where their vehicle could feasibly show up on number plate recognition cameras, both times as it crossed a main road at box junctions. 'I've been anticipating this,' said Owen, 'so I've acquired a jamming device which you can use to remotely switch off the cameras for a few seconds as you pass through. It's illegal, of course, but then the best things always are. Essentially it's like an invisibility cloak for the car when you need it. Don't be tempted to use it on the motorway, though, as you'll be using it permanently and the minute you go past a traffic police vehicle, they'll detect it and pull you over.'

'And that would be embarrassing for Suzanne and for all of us,' said Monica.

Graham's photographs showed the McMullan house from three different angles; the front of the building taken from the hilltop along with images of the side and the back of the house which were less sharp as they were taken from a greater distance. There were close-ups of the locks on McMullan's front door as well as the lock on what was in theory a cellar door. 'All straightforward,' claimed Terry. 'And seemingly no alarms which seems foolhardy in such a secluded spot but maybe the local crime rate is low.'

'Either that or the local criminals know not to go there for their own safety,' suggested Chris ominously.

'He's in his mid-sixties,' said Veronica. 'How dangerous could he be?' There was a brief silence while she glanced around the room at the assembled assassins and everyone else listened for the gentle tinkling of pennies dropping. David whistled, an embarrassed descending note. 'Okay, fair enough.' She sighed and sought refuge in her glass of fizz.

For the next hour, the group debated various options until it was agreed that they needed to get McMullan out of the house so that they could do a proper study of the interior. After that, they would probably need to act quickly to finalise a plan to murder the retired detective. Finally they settled on an idea suggested by Veronica who felt that it was important that she played a significant role in the conclusion to the case.

She would email McMullan saying that she was researching a new television programme, presented by her, in which people with interesting lives who perhaps weren't as well known as they should be, were interviewed. In the email, she would say how much she personally valued the work of the police and felt that he, McMullan, was a perfect example of an unsung hero. 'According to Suzanne,' said Monica, 'he's quite a narcissist so it's something he just might respond to.'

The group that had already visited the Malverns would return along with Terry, and while Veronica and Martin, posing as the series director, talked to McMullan at the tea shop in the local village, the locksmith would gain access to the house and he, Graham and Catherine would do a full survey. Meanwhile, Monica, Thomas and Belinda would stay in London and work on possible ways to complete the job. Martin asked, or rather begged, to please borrow the Range Rover again and Monica said that she felt certain that would be allowed. 'It's a seven seater so there's plenty of room,' the cabbie reassured everyone.

The following day, Owen created a glossy and expensive-looking website for Three Times Four Productions with a contact email address from which Veronica could approach McMullan. The site included a reasonably accurate biography of Veronica which listed all of her television series plus a couple of minor awards as well as a completely fictitious biography for Martin which claimed co-directing roles for various internationally acclaimed but unknown movies and bio-pics. Martin's suggestion that his fake CV included work as a second assistant on the 1976 film *Taxi Driver* was dismissed as a fun idea but potentially damaging to the legitimacy of the operation.

Veronica's email to Brian McMullan was sent around four in the afternoon and then it was simply a question of waiting. That evening, Thomas cooked Monica an approximation of a paella and plied her with white wine in an attempt to take her mind off the case but this didn't stop her texting Veronica every half hour to see whether a reply had arrived. The windows to Monica's apartment were open and the two of them could hear the sound of the last remaining swifts preparing for their long journey south.

'He's probably just thinking about it,' reassured Thomas. 'Either that or he's one of those people who only checks his emails once a day. I don't suppose he gets very many.'

Monica knew he was right but her mind was elsewhere. What if they didn't get a response or, worse, what if Brian replied with a flat "no"? They would need to adopt a plan B. What if someone close to Slaven had somehow tipped McMullan off? Nobody had any idea whether the two men were still in close contact after all these years. And even if he did say yes, getting rid of someone outside of The Twelve's city comfort zone would not be easy.

'Chris says that Paul is doing well,' said Thomas in a further attempt to deflect Monica's thoughts away from McMullan. 'He's visiting regularly with Anna and apparently he's making surprisingly good progress.'

'Huh?' said Monica, distractedly. 'Sorry, I was miles away. Paul. Good.' She drifted back to the whirling tornado of thought, this time focused on the cellar door and how they could potentially use that to bring the case to its satisfactory conclusion.

Thomas cleared away the plates but left the wine glasses on the table and opened another bottle which had been chilling in the fridge. He sat next to Monica at the table and clasped her hand. Monica's head toppled calmly onto his shoulder, her dark hair with grey strands tickling his ear. She closed her eyes in brief contentment. 'It's a tough one,' he said, kissing her forehead and thinking back to their excursion to Baker Street the day before.

'What would Beryl do?' he whispered to himself more than anyone.

Monica's eyes opened with a start. She raised her head from Thomas's shoulder, grabbed his face with both hands and kissed him with an urgency that took him quite by surprise. 'Brilliant!' she said.

48

The following day began at just after eight with a flurry of texts starting with an exclamation-mark-heavy one from Veronica. McMullan had replied overnight. He liked the sound of the television programme and would be delighted to meet with Veronica and Martin at a time and place of their choosing. His email also stated that he remembered Veronica fondly from her *Antique Time Travellers* series in the 1990s and mentioned that he had particularly vivid memories of an episode filmed at Warwick Castle where Veronica wore a low-cut summer dress. Everyone in the group chat found this comment both creepy and unnecessary although all five of The Twelve women agreed that the fact they were dealing with a dirty old man made the case potentially easier. *He's clearly forgotten you're gay,* texted Belinda, *which might work to our advantage.*

From her bed and with a slight headache, Monica texted that she had a new plan. It would presume that the cellar door did in fact lead to a space under the building and could be accessed by Terry and it would involve propane gas. *It's colourless and odourless and we shouldn't need much to blow the whole place to bits,* she texted. Chris asked how easy it would be to get hold of enough and Monica replied that if a retired chemistry professor couldn't surreptitiously acquire a canister or three then there really was no hope for the world. Thomas had, by this point, made the short journey into Monica's en suite to procure some ibuprofen which Monica swallowed gratefully.

The plan would involve two further visits back to the Malverns. During the first trip, Martin and Veronica would meet and distract McMullan at the tearoom while Terry, Monica, Owen and David examined the house and, crucially, the cellar. Assuming everything was as expected, the second visit would entail Martin and Veronica either pretending to film McMullan for the series, the location to be somewhere away from his house, or simply to meet him for final research purposes. At the same time, the other three would place the propane canisters, with the valves open, in the cellar. *We may need to drill holes through the floor*, texted Monica, *but once I've seen the layout of the place, I'll know how much gas we need. It only needs to constitute around five per cent of the total volume of air in the house and up it goes.*

'Won't it require something to ignite it?' asked Thomas, initially in person but then deciding to add his question to the text onslaught.

'Already got a plan for that too.' Monica grinned wickedly to her lover as she tapped away at her phone. 'There are some Montecristo No.4 cigars on the way here as I speak. He's going to think it's his lucky day.' Thomas admitted later that he'd never smoked a cigar and wondered what all the fuss was about. 'Well, these are some of the best in the world and there are ten of them coming so we'll try them if you like.'

'Have you ever smoked a cigar?' he asked, hesitantly.

Monica's sinister grin returned. 'Of course, darling. In my early thirties, I tried just about everything. Experimentation of every kind is what your twenties and thirties are for!'

Later in the day, to give the impression that the imaginary production company was very busy, Veronica emailed Brian McMullan to suggest a meeting at the tearoom in the village the following Monday at 3pm. This would be an initial and informal chat with her and the series director, just to get an idea of what content the retired detective might be able to provide; Martin may, if McMullan was agreeable, record some of the chat on his mobile phone just to show the other members of the crew in advance of any actual filming. At 8pm that evening, Veronica circulated McMullan's reply to The Twelve in which he said that the time, date and location suited him perfectly and reiterated how much he was looking forward to meeting Veronica *in the flesh x.*

Should I be worried? texted Veronica to the group. Martin replied that if McMullan tried anything, he'd end up with a cake fork in his neck and they wouldn't need to bother about the propane. Owen added that they would wire her up with a microphone in case anything happened that required intervention. He would personally teach Terry how to fit the technology. Veronica responded with a pink heart emoji.

Early on Friday morning, two packages arrived at the St John's Wood apartment, one large and one small. The large package contained four ten-kilogram propane cylinders which Martin collected at 10am for storage in his garage until they were required. Monica accompanied the cabbie on the journey to ensure the gas was stored safely and then took the opportunity to pop into Marylebone to pick up some fresh bread and cheese for lunch. The second package, which arrived while Monica was out, contained a box of ten luxury cigars which Thomas studied with interest, carefully extracting one, sniffing it and then rolling it gently in his hands as he'd seen done in movies. It appeared harmless. On her return, Monica suggested they try one and reassured her lover that despite the urgent warning on the box that Smoking Can Cause Impotence, the likelihood of any problems in that area after one solitary cigar were minimal.

'Just to clarify,' said Monica with mild amazement, 'you've never smoked a cigar before in sixty-nine years, or even a cigarette, right?' Thomas confirmed that he had led a relatively sheltered life before meeting Monica but was prepared to let her introduce him to yet another new experience. Monica raised an eyebrow and went to the kitchen to get some long matches and a sharp knife with which she diligently cut the end of the Montecristo.

She settled on the sofa next to Thomas and lit a match then waited for the phosphorus to burn away before putting the cigar to her mouth and gently sucking the flame towards it, rotating steadily. After a few seconds, Monica turned the cigar to blow at the embers before taking a first, slow inhalation. She closed her eyes in concentration as the taste and smell of tobacco enveloped her senses.

'Your turn.' She smiled mischievously, passing the cigar to Thomas.

'Do I just suck?' he asked, staring at it as if it were some sort of ancient artefact.

'You do. But slowly like at the end of yoga class. Not as if you're trying to get a marble through a straw.'

Thomas placed the cigar between his lips and inhaled.

Around five minutes later, after he had partially recovered with a glass of water and a lie down, Thomas looked up through watering eyes and saw Monica, leaning back at the opposite end of the sofa, puffing away happily with the demeanour of a mafia don, albeit a south-Asian, female variation. 'Cigars are clearly not for you, my darling,' she drawled, casually blowing a smoke ring.

49

After ordering coffees and a couple of scones with cream and a local damson jam which could also be purchased by the jar, Veronica and Martin settled themselves into a corner table at the tearoom and waited for McMullan. 'We should pretend to talk about television stuff,' said Martin, attempting to think of something both intelligent and relevant. 'What about that camera work in *EastEnders* last night? That high angle shot over the Queen Vic,' he proffered. 'And I bet they used a dolly for that tracking shot by the launderette.' Veronica suggested, kindly, that he should probably leave the talking to her. Martin nodded and chomped on half a scone, loaded generously with jam and cream. 'Are you okay with this?' he asked, mid-mouthful. 'It's quite a lot to take on for a first timer.'

Veronica beamed. 'I am more than okay,' she said, eyes gleaming. 'I'm really enjoying being bait, as it were. Having you here makes me feel safe and I remember when Lexington used to tell me about the cases before I joined and it all sounded so professional and invigorating. I never dreamed it would be quite like this. It's better than a dream.'

Just after two, the small bell signalling an arrival or

departure tinkled and McMullan stumbled into the café. Veronica recognised him from the photograph taken over ten years earlier although he had aged considerably during the intervening years; his hair was now completely grey and he had put on a fair amount of weight.

Veronica waved in what she thought was the least seductive way possible and the former detective zigzagged uneasily past a couple of tables, almost pushing an elderly lady into a slice of Black Forest gateaux, to introduce himself with the uncertain handshake of a man unaccustomed to regular company. 'Brian McMullan,' he said with an awkward formality. 'Pleased to meet you. Those scones look good.' His accent, despite having lived in the countryside for a decade, had retained a south London twang.

'Please have a seat, Brian,' said Veronica, warmly. 'I'm sure Martin can get some scones and we have plenty of cream and jam for the table. Can we get you some coffee too?'

McMullan looked shiftily around the café. 'Are they expensive?' he asked, wiping a few strands of sweaty hair from his forehead. 'I don't have my cards with me, you see.' Martin assured him that the production company would be able to pay for all refreshments and added that there would also be a fee for his time if they decided on a full interview. McMullan brightened at this news and settled more comfortably in his chair. 'You haven't aged, Veronica,' he said lasciviously while Martin was queuing to order. 'In fact, I'd say you were more delectable than ever.' He reached out a moist hand and caressed the former presenter's finger.

Veronica squirmed internally but, knowing she needed to win McMullan's trust, managed to conceal her discomfort. 'Thank you, Brian,' she said politely, removing her hand slowly from his range. 'That's very kind. It's probably the good genes.'

The faintly uncomfortable silence that followed was broken by Martin's welcome return.

'Did I miss anything?' asked the cabbie. 'Coffee and scones on the way.'

'An interesting discussion about Veronica's genes,' said McMullan, leering at the ex-TV presenter. 'I'm sure they're worthy of investigation at some point when we know each other a bit better.' Martin looked at Veronica whose smile skilfully managed to simultaneously reflect both demureness and revulsion.

A few miles down the road, Terry, wearing latex gloves, had speedily unlocked McMullan's home, surprised by the relative simplicity of his security arrangements, and the four members of this breakaway party were cautiously exploring the house. There was something rebarbative about the interior of the sparsely furnished house as if inhabited by a person with no discernible style or desire to make the place homely. It showed no sign of anyone else's presence although McMullan did appear to keep the place reasonably tidy. A low rumble was emanating from the retired detective's dishwasher in his kitchen. Terry noted that the fridge was full of ready meals with no fresh vegetables and remarked that he could never trust a man who didn't cook, even if it were just for himself.

The main living area consisted of a large space with just a couple of armchairs, a side table and a poorly stocked book shelf with mostly second-hand crime novels from the 1980s and a couple of dog-eared Dan Browns. 'It's sixteenth century,' said Monica. 'Some of it anyway. Someone in the 1950s added an extension to the side. Seems a shame to make a mess of it but we can't be nostalgic. The stone floors in the kitchen should survive so hopefully it could be rebuilt after we've finished. These wood floors on the other hand...'

The ceilings were typically farmhouse low with exposed

wooden beams throughout and Monica was particularly interested in the random pieces of art dotted sparsely throughout the downstairs space. McMullan's taste appeared limited to various poor-quality female nudes which looked like they had either been picked up from jumble sales or painted by a selection of minimally talented artists. She tried to make out the signatures on a couple of them and realised that one of them had been painted by McMullan himself, a particularly unerotic and disrespectful watercolour of a woman tied to a tree with what looked like white knickers around her ankles.

'Come and look at this,' called David from the back of the house, his voice echoing somewhat due to the lack of soft furnishings. Monica and Terry crept through a couple of doors to where the plumber was studying a gun cabinet filled with rifles and shotguns. 'I wonder whether he has licences for these,' he said. There was also a door in the floor which Monica suspected led to the cellar with the other entrance outside the house. This opening wasn't locked so Terry simply unlatched it to reveal a steep set of wooden stairs.

'I'll pop outside and see how easy it is to get in from there,' said the locksmith. Monica temporarily removed her glove and switched on the flashlight from her phone before starting her careful descent with David following close behind. There were only ten steps until they reached the basement floor and, after a few seconds, daylight spread through the space as Terry opened up the exterior door. The three of them looked around them at an area about thirty metres square which appeared to be completely empty apart from a cobweb-covered spade and a similarly adorned garden fork placed against one wall. 'I guess he doesn't have much stuff to store,' mused Terry. They spent a few minutes searching the walls in case there were any hidden exits or tunnels but there was nothing, simply a large empty space with an uneven floor, partly concrete, partly earth.

'How very convenient for our purposes,' said Monica with quiet satisfaction. 'This should be pretty straightforward.' She pulled her glove back on, finger by finger.

'And now you've cursed it,' said David, sighing. The three of them returned to the gun room and Terry secured the trapdoor.

Suddenly, Owen appeared, having had a quick mooch around upstairs. 'Do you want the good news or the bad news?' he asked, a look of mild concern on his face. Monica suggested he start with the good news and then they'd see how they felt. 'Well, if today is typical, McMullan leaves his computer on all the time so it'll be easy to delete Veronica's emails from the laptop and from the cloud so there will be no trace of them.'

'Better and better,' said Monica brightly. 'This is going so well. Do we really need to bother with anything as potentially irksome as the bad news?'

Owen paused for a moment, allowing everyone time to prepare.

'Under normal circumstances I would say no,' he replied. 'Only, there's a naked woman tied to McMullan's bed and I suspect she's been drugged.'

50

'N othing's ever simple, is it?' said Monica with a sigh as the four of them stood around McMullan's bed on which was spread-eagled a very thin woman with a dyed blonde bob and heavy make-up whom Monica estimated was around forty. She was naked apart from wrist and ankle restraints maintaining her unflattering position and a ball gag maintaining her lack of noise. Her arms were flecked with track marks from frequent syringe use and her eyes were closed. 'You've tried waking her up, I suppose?'

Owen nodded. 'She's out cold. There's Xanax in the bathroom cabinet so I suspect that's what's to blame. She could be out of it for ages. There's also some Viagra and some Anusol plus Prinivil for high blood pressure and Glucosamine for joint pain in case you're interested. And he hasn't flushed the toilet. A single old man's life in microcosm right there.'

'We'll have to leave her here,' said Monica, wincing at the mental picture Owen had created in her imagination. 'Much as it pains me. If McMullan returns and finds her missing then he'll know someone's been here and we can't risk the operation.' She moved towards the woman's face and took a photo with her phone. 'Maybe Suzanne can help identify her and we can help the next time we come. If she's still here. It makes our second trip potentially more challenging if she is but at least we now know so we can plan accordingly.'

Martin texted the group to say that the meeting in the café was drawing to a close and so they probably had around fifteen minutes to evacuate the house. 'I think our work here is done, anyway,' said Monica. Terry closed up all the doors including the external cellar and the four of them walked away from the property and up the lane towards the village. After ten minutes, they stopped and hid behind a hedgerow waiting for McMullan's estate car to pass, which it did shortly afterwards. 'That poor woman,' said David softly.

Martin picked them up in the Range Rover a few minutes later and the six of them set off back to London, sharing their gathered information on the way. Monica texted the photograph of the woman in McMullan's bedroom to Suzanne Green who, after an hour, confirmed that she was Natasha 'Tash' Holland, a thirty-year-old prostitute based in Worcester. She hadn't been reported missing and so it was likely that McMullan had simply paid her for whatever he wanted to do with her and she had willingly agreed.

'Thirty?' yelled Terry. 'Blimey! I'd have thought ten years older at least.' Suzanne's text also revealed that Tash was a long-time heroin user who would *do anything for money to feed her habit* according to a source at West Mercia police.

'I thought he was gay,' said Martin, who had slowed down behind a tractor on a winding lane.

Owen explained that McMullan was bisexual 'but well known in the force as a bit of a sexual predator. Clearly his tastes haven't changed over the years. Graham used to know him when he worked at the old Scotland Yard. Not well, I hasten to add, but McMullan was the sort of man whose reputation spread throughout the force back in the day.'

Monica suggested that, if anything, the retired detective's proclivities had become more extreme with age. 'How did you leave it with McMullan?' she asked. Veronica outlined that they had suggested a second meeting in exactly one week at the same location for the purposes of more research in advance of filming. As it had become progressively more apparent that McMullan was attracted to Veronica, she would use this situation to the group's advantage.

During this second meeting, Martin would receive a phone call which meant he would have to urgently return to London at which point Veronica would present McMullan with the gift of cigars and suggest that she meet him back at his house in an hour so they could get to know each other better. 'I'll say I've got my car with me. He won't know. If we keep him occupied for about forty minutes would that give you enough time to prepare the house?' she asked.

'Plenty. Even if there's a surprise visitor which hopefully there isn't,' said Monica.

'If he brings a woman back to his house where there's already another woman tied to a bed then he's, how can I put this delicately, a bit of a sick bastard,' said Terry. 'But whatever happens, we know the ins and outs of the house now so we'll be all good.'

'No pets were there?' asked Martin. 'You know I can't have animals being hurt.' David assured him that they had done a thorough check of the kitchen cupboards and drawers and that there were no pet bowls or food anywhere nor any other sign of animals apart from spiders in the cellar. 'Okay, I can accept that,' muttered the cabbie.

'I think we're good, then,' concluded Monica. 'We'll have a meeting on Thursday or Friday with everyone just in case there's anything we've forgotten. And V, if you could please email McMullan later in the week just to remind him, that would be great.'

The TV presenter was checking emails on her phone as the Range Rover abandoned the country lanes and returned to CCTV camera visibility just outside Basingstoke having taken an alternate route back. 'I don't think he'll need reminding,' she said with excitement. 'He's already messaged me twice to say how much he's looking forward to it. And he's now including two kisses with each email.'

51

'You're quite sure you won't be needing a doctor on this one?' asked Chris, ploughing through a plate of mini chocolate raspberry brownies which Terry had baked that morning because he had some summer fruit to use up. The presence of some vitamin C within the buttery chocolate sweetness meant that the former surgeon could justify eating three on the basis of nutrition. Everyone noticed that Chris's overall mood had lightened considerably even in the last week and his furtive smiles at Anna suggested that there was a reason for this, something which, for now, would remain unknown.

The group had gathered at a detached corner house in a pretty side street just north of Regent's Park for the final meeting before returning to the Malverns to assassinate McMullan. Monica and Thomas had arrived early as it was only a five-minute walk from her apartment and she wanted to refamiliarise herself with it before considering the place for her renting out list. 'I've not been here since the Cooper case,' she said, wandering through the four bedrooms and noting whether any of the décor might require updating before new tenants moved in. Thomas meanwhile was, typically, studying the art, a series of eight small brightly coloured canvases which Monica had explained were 'late Kandinsky from when he lived in Paris. The Russian ambassador to London in the 1930s was a friend of both Kandinsky and the leader of The Twelve at the time, Lionel Waller. They would often lunch together in either London or Paris and Wassily Kandinsky was always very generous with his works. The stuff he didn't exhibit anyway.'

Suzanne Green and Ted Black were in attendance, the younger detective still exhibiting barely suppressed amazement at what was actually happening although apparently unfazed by any of it. They had scheduled the meeting for teatime on the Thursday as both Belinda and Catherine had dental appointments on the Friday; Belinda had even mooted the idea that The Twelve acquire a dentist when the next vacancy presented itself, an idea which was welcomed by many members of the team until Thomas pointed out that although such a person might be handy for personal reasons they would be largely useless during cases 'unless a potential target required root canal work before being dispatched. Besides, have you seen *Little Shop of Horrors*?' Martin commented that the musical was better than the film.

'I did a subtle check on the ANPR on the day you travelled,' began Suzanne. 'Martin has done an exceptional job at avoiding detection and yet I'm going to add one more layer of protection if I may. I'm going to add a temporary number plate to the Range Rover for the outward journey. It's the plate of a very similar car which we're keeping off the road for a while. Only I know where it is. That way, less suspicion falls upon the vehicle if West Mercia get round to doing a check which, in itself, is highly unlikely. They're currently bottom of the constabulary charts for pretty much every type of crime.'

Owen pointed out that they would require two vehicles for this stage of the operation and Suzanne confirmed that she would therefore make another, smaller unmarked car available, probably a Skoda or a Volvo. 'We use them a lot for undercover work as they're fairly nondescript. Again, I'll arrange a temporary plate for extra security. These will both be available for collection on Sunday. I'll leave you and Ted to discuss a suitable location for handover.'

'You're very keen for this to work, Commissioner,' said Graham with a note of wary curiosity.

Suzanne shrugged. 'I just want to ensure nothing goes wrong,' she said casually. 'You're amazing at what you do, so if I can be of any practical assistance then I will be. I also appreciate that venturing outside of London isn't normal Twelve activity so I'm simply covering bases.'

'How long until you retire again?' asked Monica. The commissioner smiled and reached for a brownie. 'One thing we may need to do,' Monica added, addressing Terry and David more than anyone, 'is drill a few small holes in McMullan's living-room floor to allow the gas to penetrate more easily. There are gaps between some of the floorboards but not many. We can position them under furniture so he doesn't notice. There's an armchair in his living room which looks out across the hills, for example.' The plumber and the locksmith nodded and made mental notes to bring the necessary tools.

Chris and Anna had visited the clinic earlier in the week to check on Paul's progress and were delighted to report that even Frances Duffy was surprised by his recovery. Tiffany had burst into tears one afternoon when her son had sat up in his bed and asked whether he could please have a banana, the first fruit he had consumed for about four years. 'Incidentally,' said Monica since the subject of Paul had been raised, 'does anyone have any contacts at London Zoo? Bit of a long shot, I appreciate, but just an idea I've got in the back of my mind.'

'My brother is a council member at the Zoological Society of London if that helps,' said Suzanne. 'He's only been there a year but he's been a vet for over thirty years which is why they approached him. Any good?' Monica gave a mini fist pump and suggested that perhaps she could buy Suzanne and her brother dinner when this McMullan business was over.

After a short toilet break for a handful of the participants, attention turned to Ted Black who related how the evidence was stacking up against Tony Slaven for international drug and arms trafficking and also against Leo after Ellis Richardson, who had originally testified in the 2013 court case, had come forward with fresh evidence. Richardson had been keeping an audio cassette of Leo Slaven and his mates talking about the Justin Morris murder as insurance against being targeted by the Slavens. After reading about the arrests online, Richardson had finally decided that the time was right to clear his own conscience. Monica asked why Richardson hadn't presented the tape as evidence at the trial and Ted Black said he suspected the Slavens had paid him to keep it quiet and then used threats of violence against his family to stop him speaking out. 'Richardson somehow acquired an expensive sports car in 2013 claiming he'd won it in an online competition. Clearly it was a bribe from Slaven or McMullan or both.'

'Just one final loose end to tie,' said Suzanne. 'Monica, may I have a quick word in private, please?' The two women climbed the stairs and found a master bedroom decorated in pale blue with another Kandinsky painting on the wall, this one dated 1939. Suzanne closed the door gently behind her and sat on the edge of the bed while Monica stood by the window, enjoying the late-summer heat on her back. 'You may be wondering why

I'm being so unusually proactive in this case,' the commissioner began. 'Graham certainly is. I can virtually see his detective antennae twitching.' She took a deep breath and then another.

'You don't have to explain anything to me,' said Monica, sensing discomfort. 'We trust each other and that's enough as far as I'm concerned. We don't have to...'

'He sexually assaulted me,' said Suzanne abruptly and then let out a sigh of relief that felt to Monica like a long-forgotten faucet being opened fully. 'McMullan. He molested me when I was twenty-six when I was a sergeant and he was a detective inspector. Not badly. Not rape or anything like that. But he put his hands inside my clothes before I could react and it was enough to rattle me and dent my trust in men for many years afterwards. Hardly anyone knows, just my husband and my counsellor and even they don't know the identity of the person who did it. But that's why I have no problem with what you're about to do. He's an evil, disgusting bastard and I've spent too much of my time over the last few years drumming men like him out of the police force and too much of my time comforting policewomen who have bravely come forward.'

The leader of The Twelve was silent for a moment while she took in the gravity of what she'd heard. 'I'm so sorry,' she whispered. 'Why didn't you mention anything at the time?'

Suzanne Green leaned forward and massaged her temples. 'It wasn't the sort of thing you did, Monica. You know that as well as I do. The culture at the time was weighted in favour of the senior men in the force. I was ambitious and I wanted to rise up the ranks. If I'd made a fuss then the likelihood would have been that I'd have been demoted or worse. So I kept quiet. It was the safest option.'

Monica moved from the window and sat down next to Suzanne to give her a hug, sensing the weight of twenty years of unnecessary guilt being lifted. The two of them remained in a silent embrace for several minutes, the younger woman breathing heavily to restrain tears. 'Is there anything I can do?' whispered Monica.

'Just get rid of him, please, Monica. And try not to get caught.'

52

The four members of The Twelve watched through binoculars from the shade of a hilltop hazel tree, already slightly yellowing at the leaves, as McMullan got into his car and drove slowly away from his house towards his liaison with Veronica and Martin, the final meeting of his life. A pair of pheasants could be heard a few metres away noisily foraging through the undergrowth for seeds and insects. Fifteen minutes later, Martin texted to say that the retired detective had arrived safely at the café which was the signal for Terry, nominated to drive the unmarked Skoda, to set off for the farmhouse with three other members of the group plus four canisters of propane on board.

After picking the lock, which took Terry a matter of seconds, Monica went to search the house for restrained, naked people while the others transferred the canisters with care into the cellar and David made a start on drilling holes in a variety of covert places in McMullan's floor. After deleting the relevant emails from McMullan's computer and the cloud, Owen settled into the armchair overlooking the hills and used his phone to tune into the conversation in the tearoom using spyware he'd temporarily fitted to Veronica's phone.

Today, the former TV presenter was wearing a reasonably low-cut red dress which she felt signified both seduction and danger. In the café, she had opened her laptop and was taking McMullan painstakingly through the various questions she was keen for him to answer; nothing too controversial and certainly nothing about the Morris case or Tony Slaven because that would only scare him off. Veronica needed him to trust her as far as possible this final time and she would stop at nothing to ensure the success of the operation. The focus of the interview would be very much on McMullan's successes, the cases of which he was most proud.

After completing her thorough search of the upper floor of the building which accidentally unearthed a collection of DVDs of extreme pornography which even Monica, broad-minded as she was, found disturbing, the former chemistry professor returned to the main living room to announce that the place was free of unexpected people, even the attic. David finished creating holes in McMullan's floor, having had to ask Owen to move the armchair for the final drilling, and the trap was set.

'Let's just make sure all the lights are off and he hasn't left a candle alight in the kitchen or anything,' said Monica, even though McMullan didn't strike her as the sort of man to even have candles in his kitchen. After they had decided that the ground floor was clear of anything to cause premature ignition, David, Monica and Terry took the steps down to the cellar for the next stage.

'Can you hear me, Mother?' asked Terry, shouting upwards through the newly perforated floor. 'My dad used to say that to my mum,' he added wistfully. 'It's an old music hall catchphrase.' Owen, sitting in the repositioned armchair, replied that the locksmith's voice was so clear that he might as well be in the same room.

'We're ready to go, then,' said Monica. Owen telephoned Martin in the café to let him know that everything was going according to plan and that he could now take his leave of Veronica and wait in the Range Rover which he had parked nearby. The three in the cellar turned the valves on the gas cylinders and climbed the steps to the outside of the building where Owen was waiting by the car. 'Back to our vantage point for the end of the show,' said Monica.

In the tearoom, McMullan's mood had brightened considerably with the departure of the series director, leaving him alone with Veronica. If he wasn't mistaken, the TV presenter was now very subtly flirting with him. 'I heard you're a bit partial to a cigar,' she said, her eye contact now so intense that he was often forced to look away. 'So I bought you a small gift in gratitude for your time up to this point.' Veronica reached into her jacket pocket and retrieved three Cuban Montecristos. 'I hope you like them, Brian,' she purred.

McMullan took the cigars, brushing Veronica's fingers for a little longer than was necessary, and stared at them rapturously as if they were some sort of precious jewels. 'I must admit, though,' continued Veronica as seductively as she could under the circumstances, 'that I do have an ulterior motive for giving you the cigars.'

'Oh yes?' asked McMullan, licking his lips. Veronica leaned closer across the table.

'I haven't been able to stop thinking about you since our first meeting. I'd rather like to get some alone time with you, Brian. If that's all right with you. At your home, if you think it's appropriate.' The old detective's eyes lit up like those of a tiger stalking a retirement home for frail deer. Veronica looked down at her half-drunk cup of coffee and then lifted her eyes upward to peer at McMullan through her eyelashes. 'I could meet you there in half an hour if you like. I just have a few emails to deal with first.'

'I can wait,' said McMullan with discomforting eagerness. 'And then I can drive you.'

Listening in, Owen inhaled sharply but Veronica had already anticipated this eventuality. She and Belinda had spent the weekend running through all possible problems and solutions and the ex-linguist, in her quiet and methodical way, had made sure Veronica had every base covered. 'I'd rather take my own car, if it's all right with you, Brian,' she said. 'We both drove here today, Martin and I. Plus, there's one more thing I think it's important that you should know.' She placed her right hand on McMullan's left and stroked as slowly as she could, resisting the urge to recoil at every veiny bump she encountered. *I should have been an actress*, Veronica mused to herself. *Maybe there's still time.*

McMullan cocked his head quizzically. Veronica was sure he was slightly salivating.

'The smell of fresh cigar smoke really turns me on.'

53

From the copse overlooking the farmhouse, half of The Twelve watched as McMullan's car glided to a halt in his short driveway and the old man levered himself out of the driver's seat and stumbled towards his front door. As soon as he had left the tearoom in a mood which could only be described as ecstatic, Veronica had waited a few moments and then run full pelt to where Martin was waiting with the Range Rover and the two of them had taken a shortcut across dirt tracks and single lane country roads to meet up with the foursome who were already in position.

'How did I do?' she asked Owen. Everyone agreed that for a first case, Veronica's contribution, particularly in these latter stages, had been magnificent. 'I literally can't wait for this,' she said, physically bouncing with excitement.

Monica and David shared a look of moderate concern. 'I'm pretty sure you're going to be surprised at how you feel, V,' said the plumber calmly. 'This generally isn't a moment for elation.'

Veronica gazed at him in surprise. 'Are you kidding? This is my first case and it's been a complicated one and it's reaching its conclusion and I guess I'm just so... what's the word the young people use...? Pumped that we're finally here.'

'When did you last see Mrs Mendoza?' asked Owen, a note of uneasiness in his voice.

'About three weeks ago,' said Veronica nonchalantly. 'Soon after we started focusing on McMullan. She wanted to check how I was coping with my first case and how I thought I was going to be affected by the inevitable denouement.' Monica confirmed that the elderly psychologist had been entirely unconcerned with Veronica's mental well-being, merely noting in her brief report that the former presenter might experience a more extreme reaction than average at the crucial moment but nothing that couldn't be ironed out in a post-event session. 'What does she mean by "extreme reaction"?' asked Veronica, now mildly concerned. 'I'm simply looking forward to the big bang!'

'You're going to feel an unexpected sadness,' said David comfortingly. 'All of us will.'

Veronica's face creased. 'I'm not sure I am, David,' she said with indignation. 'I can feel the adrenaline coursing through me as I speak. It's like the last day of filming a series when you're about to go on set. It's exhilarating.' Monica, with more assassinations under her belt than she cared to recall, placed a comforting arm around her shoulder as Owen rummaged in the back of the Skoda and pulled out six pairs of hi-tech binoculars which he handed round.

'How far away are we here?' asked Martin, raising the binoculars to his face.

'About a kilometre. Just over,' replied Owen.

'And what's that in the old money?' said Terry.

'About two thirds of a mile,' answered Veronica confidently. 'Front row bloody seats!'

Monica checked to see whether Martin and Owen both

knew the escape route; Martin confirmed that he had already plotted a course to the north, avoiding any incoming emergency vehicles which would be travelling from one of two small towns to the south and west. 'We don't hit any cameras until just outside Kidderminster,' the cabbie said, 'so it's a bit of a circuitous route home but the least likely to arouse suspicion. Plus I've changed the plates on both vehicles as Suzanne requested.'

The six of them raised their binoculars and watched as McMullan went upstairs to his bathroom where he spent around four minutes, then he wandered into the kitchen to retrieve a box of long matches before returning to his living room where he poured two glasses of brandy. 'Presumptuous berk,' said Veronica. 'I don't even really like brandy.'

'If my calculations are correct,' muttered Monica, checking the time on her phone, 'the propane percentage in the house should be around seven per cent by now. Maybe eight, which is plenty.' A light breeze dislodged a yellow hazel leaf which fell on Terry's shoulder and distracted him momentarily from the view through his binoculars. Behind them, slightly to the left, a pair of blackbirds were chattering enthusiastically.

McMullan placed the two glasses of brandy on a side table, sat in his armchair and stared out at the hillside in the direction where the group were sheltered. He swirled the alcohol for a moment before taking a sip from one of the glasses then closed his eyes and rested his head back. Life was good. He anticipated that the imminent sex with this TV presenter would feel much more passionate than the unsatisfactory variety with which he was familiar these days.

He reached into the inside pocket of his jacket and extracted one of the Montecristos which he rolled carefully between his fingers and then sniffed all the way down its length, drawing in the raw tobacco aroma. It had been a while since he'd had such a quality cigar and Brian McMullan, former top detective with Scotland Yard, was going to savour every minute of it.

Across the valley, mostly obscured by trees, McMullan thought he could just make out a flash of red, although his eyesight wasn't what it used to be so he assumed it was nothing more than a tractor, parked temporarily on its way from field to farm.

He placed the cigar between his dry, chapped lips, pulled a match from its box and drew it across the striking surface.

From their vantage point beneath the trees, the group witnessed a huge flash followed almost immediately by the sound of the explosion. The blackbirds along with every sparrow and warbler in the vicinity took to the air. Five of the six stood in silence as they watched the farmhouse rage into an inferno, all of them in quiet contemplation of what had just happened. 'We should go,' said Monica after a minute or so. She looked around her at the solemn faces of the four men. 'Where's Veronica?'

'She's here,' said Owen, standing on the other side of the Range Rover and indicating the rear tyre of the vehicle where an inconsolable Veronica was crumpled in a convulsing heap rocking back and forth.

'Thank goodness for that,' said Monica with undisguised relief as she crouched down on her haunches to embrace the sobbing woman, all the time masking her own sorrow. 'For a moment back there I thought we were going to have a problem with you, V.'

Rising unsteadily after a moment or two, Monica felt a comforting hand on her shoulder. It was Martin, a pensive half-smile on his face as he took in the blazing carnage in the valley. 'Auntie Beryl would have fucking loved that,' he whispered.

54

Worcester News Online
Retired Detective Killed In Farmhouse Fireball
By Barry O'Shea

A retired police detective has been killed in what local fire chiefs are calling a 'tragic but avoidable accident'. Brian McMullan, whose forty year career included periods at the Metropolitan Police before moving to West Mercia police in 2013, died after propane canisters, stored in the cellar of his Lower Penfield farmhouse where he had lived alone, exploded last Monday.

The alarm was raised after farmer, Dave Brabham, noticed smoke coming from the valley where the remote farmhouse is situated around six miles from Malvern. 'I was on the tractor sowing barley when I heard an almighty bang,' said Brabham. 'I thought it was a military aircraft because you get a lot of those around here, but then I saw smoke coming from the other side of the hill so I drove up to the ridge to see what was happening and that's when I called the fire brigade. I never really knew the poor chap who lived there apart from the odd greeting. He was the sort who kept himself to himself.'

McMullan, 63, was a key figure in the Justin Morris murder case in 2010, regarded as one of the most controversial cases in the recent history of the Met Police owing to failures in the original investigation. After moving to the local area, McMullan worked for West Mercia for eight years, keeping a low profile, before taking early retirement.

Malvern's fire chief Jeremy Novick said, 'From what we can see, the victim was storing propane in his cellar which leaked, causing it to ignite. There's evidence of a cigar being smoked in an armchair which looks like being the immediate cause of the fire. I would like to take this opportunity to remind the public, especially those living in rural areas, to check how they are storing explosive material and to seek advice from the fire service if they have any questions or concerns.'

'Very satisfying,' said Suzanne Green, reading the online local newspaper report on Monica's phone before handing it to its owner. 'And, if I may say so, a perfect Twelve operation. There's nothing on ANPR to lead anyone towards you. There's no evidence at the location and the local police aren't investigating. I get the impression that McMullan wasn't exactly popular at West Mercia so there's no particular inclination on their part to delve into this at all. Well done, everyone.'

Monica, who had already read the news article when it had been published earlier that afternoon, singled out Veronica for praise, especially as it was her first case. A couple of hours with Mrs Mendoza on the Tuesday after the explosion had helped the former TV presenter work through the tsunami of feelings which had washed over her during the previous twenty-four hours. Veronica blushed and waved her hand theatrically in a pretend dismissive gesture, despite the fact that everyone within the group had already expressed how proud they were of her contribution. 'Belinda helped enormously,' she said, attempting to deflect the attention. The linguist seated next to Veronica on one of the sofas at Minera Mews gave her a congratulatory cuddle.

'I visited Henry and Diana this morning,' said David. 'They're delighted with how things have turned out. Naturally it wasn't what they were originally expecting but then I don't suppose anyone could have predicted exactly what was going to happen. They do feel that they now have justice for their son, which is important. They would like to buy everyone dinner at a Caribbean restaurant in Soho when we can find a date. That includes you, Commissioner.'

Suzanne Green's face broke into a wide smile and she asked David to please thank the Morrises for their patience and their kindness and would check her diary and suggest some dates before Christmas. 'I'm actually a huge fan of curry goat with rice and peas,' she said, licking her lips. 'How is Henry, by the way? Still undergoing treatment?' David replied that his friend was due to finish radiotherapy that week and, if the subsequent tests gave the all-clear, then that would be the end of the treatment apart from regular half-yearly checks in the future.

'How are Paul and Tiffany doing?' asked Monica, contemplating opening some champagne which was chilling in the kitchen.

Anna reported that Paul's progress had surprised everyone and that Frances Duffy was even talking about discharging him from hospital in November, so long as he continued to attend regular outpatient appointments. 'Chris and Thomas and I visited on Monday while you were blowing up a farmhouse,' the ex-forensics expert said. 'We were in town helping Thomas with some shopping.'

'Shopping?' asked Monica with a note of curiosity. Thomas hadn't mentioned buying anything for the flat or indeed his own house. Anna froze. Chris and Thomas looked at each other in a state of subdued panic.

'Window shopping,' said Chris hurriedly. 'Winter fashion. You know.' He gulped suspiciously and pretended to shiver. 'Scarves and that. It's nearly September. The evenings are drawing in. Us oldies have all got to be prepared. Brrrrrrrr!'

Monica's eyes narrowed. She felt certain that something strange was going on but she decided to let it pass. For now. 'I've been thinking about how to help Paul and Tiffany with their futures,' she said, shifting hers and everyone else's attention back to the case, 'and I know she's keen for them both to have a fresh start somewhere. With everyone's agreement, I was going to offer them the house near Regent's Park to live in, rent-free and, in addition, when we have dinner with Suzanne's brother next month, I was hoping that he could help Paul to get an apprenticeship at the zoo. He would be able to walk there in about five minutes from that house and it might be just the thing those two need to get back on their feet after everything that's happened over the last few years.'

The group agreed that this was a perfectly sensible solution and Monica said that she would suggest it to Tiffany after the dinner and also after she had arranged the accommodation issues with Bobby City. 'Lexington might take those Kandinsky paintings,' she said. 'Either that or we'll find another home for them. I don't suppose anyone wants them in their own houses.' A general murmuring and shaking of heads suggested that the collected works of the Russian painter were low on the list of interior design acquisitions for any of the group.

'I have some news,' announced Chris suddenly. Thomas

looked up, concerned. He knew that his best friend was still struggling slightly from the effects of the spring case but had hoped that the ex-surgeon's heroics with Paul Storey had meant that everything was back to some semblance of normality. Chris and Anna stood, arms around each other's waists. 'I'm going to be a grandfather for the first time.'

Thomas breathed a sigh of relief and then quickly remembered where he was and jumped up to join the group enveloping Chris with congratulatory hugs. 'My middle daughter, Freya, and her husband,' he revealed. 'They've been trying for a year and finally they had a twelve-week scan last week and everything is as it should be. It's due in March. They don't know the sex yet but I'll let you know as soon as possible.'

'That's amazing news,' said Thomas, disentangling himself from the group hug. 'And a relief. I thought you were going to tell us you were leaving.'

The former surgeon frowned. 'Leaving?' He smiled with a glance towards Belinda. 'Why on earth would I do something as crazy as that? I love you crazy people.'

'Incidentally,' said Martin as Terry wandered into the kitchen to fetch the champagne and glasses, 'has anyone heard from Lexington recently?'

Nobody had. This was unusual. 'I'll call him tomorrow after yoga,' said Monica. 'He's probably just been busy. You know what he's like.'

55

Two months later, Monica was at her desk as the last rays of autumn sunlight cast shadows across the east wall of the St John's Wood apartment. 'Doing anything fun?' asked Thomas as he enveloped her from behind, kissing her neck just below her right ear.

'Just putting the finishing touches to the report on the McMullan case before I add it to the library in Baker Street,' she replied, smiling and leaning her head to the side to simplify access to her neck for further kisses. 'That local news piece needs to go in but then I'm almost done and we can go and see Lexington in the hospital and after that I've booked dinner at our favourite Spanish place.'

Monica's post-yoga call to the former Twelve leader back in late August had been answered, worryingly, by a nurse named Mia at a private hospital in Belgravia. Mia had quickly reassured her that Lexington was asleep but that he had been bedridden for two weeks after a fall at his home. Apparently he hadn't wanted to bother anyone in The Twelve while they were involved with a case. He would require a new knee and was awaiting an operation which was scheduled for the day after

Monica's call. Mia explained that Lexington had been planning to text the group then – he was aware of the explosion at McMullan's house from the same local newspaper item but chose not to mention this to Mia or any of the other nurses taking care of him.

Needless to say, the group made a dash from their yoga house in Euston to Belgravia and were by Lexington's bedside within half an hour, visiting times being reasonably flexible. Mia had expressed astonishment at the sheer influx of visitors but, with David's help, moved various chairs into Lexington's room to accommodate most of them. After that first visit, and following the successful knee operation, Monica had set up a rota in order that Lexington welcomed at least two visitors a day, unless he texted to say he was too tired and could only entertain one. These single-visit days often coincided with the dates of morning visits from Terry; Mia later explained that the locksmith would always bring huge quantities of something sweet and delicious to eat which resulted in Lexington sharing his bounty with all the nurses in the early afternoon, occasions which became known as Terryware Parties and which left the old man delighted but exhausted.

On that late October day, Monica and Thomas arrived at the hospital just before six and found Lexington in a slightly downbeat mood. 'I was hoping to leave hospital next week,' he said gloomily, 'but now I appear to have contracted a beastly problem with my urinary tract so my escape looks like being delayed a touch. And the worst part,' he grumbled, 'is that I have to lay off the sweet treats for a while until it clears up. Old age is progressively less fun, I'm afraid, but I've had a rich and glorious life and I'm grateful for that.'

For Thomas, this was the first time he had heard Lexington utter anything that could be described as pessimistic and this came as something of a shock. He and Monica consoled him as best they could and Thomas's gift of a new book by the former American ambassador, whom Lexington had befriended in the 1990s, was received with great appreciation. Monica said that next time she would bring the official report of the McMullan case which she'd just completed, purely to give him a lift. 'I've added a lot of description about the countryside,' she said, 'as I realise that it's a bit of an anomaly for The Twelve. Future readers might be intrigued.'

After an hour and a half, Monica could see that Lexington's eyelids were beginning to droop and decided it was time to let him rest. She kissed his forehead; Thomas attempted an uneasy embrace and the couple extended an invitation to dinner as soon as their friend felt up to it.

Just before eight, they were nestled in the candlelight at a corner table of the Spanish restaurant in Bermondsey and had already been given complimentary bowls of padrón peppers and Andalusian olives, gifts from the owner while they perused the menu. As usual on their nights out, the conversation ranged from the recent case, through international politics; various aches and pains; Lexington, of course; how nice Suzanne's brother had been – he had made it his personal mission to find a role within the zoo for Paul Storey by February; Martin's girlfriend, Joanne, whom they had met at a performance of *Wicked the Musical* the week before and who was also delightful; recent government policy regarding social care and their favourite music from their childhoods. Monica had revealed a fondness for the Rolling Stones and Motown while Thomas's tastes were, predictably, more conservative and leant towards Nat King Cole and Perry Como.

'Do you know what day it is?' asked Thomas as decaf coffees arrived. Monica said she believed it was a Thursday. 'Sorry, I meant the date. It's the 23rd of October which means that tomorrow it will be one year since we first met. At my first

Twelve meeting in Notting Hill. Apart from Lexington, you were the first person I met properly. We arrived at much the same time, if you remember.'

Monica clasped his hand. 'Oh, how romantic,' she said, candlelight flickering in her bright eyes. 'And look how far we've come in such a short time.'

'Anyway, I bought you something. An anniversary present. I hope you like it.' Thomas reached into his inside jacket pocket and retrieved a small black box. He handed it to Monica who looked at it in awe, then stared at Thomas before returning her gaze to the box. 'You should probably open it,' he said softly.

Monica gently prized the lid open and inside was a silver ring with a small pale-pastel-green stone. 'It's beautiful,' she said, eyes glistening. 'It's not emerald, though, is it? That would be too expensive. Plus it doesn't look like emerald.'

'It's a precious stone called Beryl,' said Thomas. 'I bought it back in the summer, on the day you were in the Malverns. Anna and Chris helped. Well, Anna helped more than Chris, to be fair but... Anyway, I hope you like it.'

Monica welled up and a couple of joyful tears fell into her coffee. 'It's just perfect. What sort of ring is it?'

Thomas squeezed her hand and stared deep into her eyes with a mischievous glint she knew well from their twelve months together, first as friends and then as lovers. 'I suppose it's whatever sort of ring you'd like it to be, Monica,' he whispered. 'Whatever sort of ring you'd like it to be.'

THE END

ALSO BY PETER BERRY

Lunch with the Deadly Dozen

A secret group of retired experts hunt a methodical serial killer, in this compelling debut crime thriller set in London . . .

BUY NOW

ACKNOWLEDGEMENTS

When the astonishing moment happens and a publisher says that they like your little book and wish to share it with the world, your first feeling is one of profound joy. This is immediately followed by an overwhelming sense of terror. What if nobody buys it? Worse still, what if people buy it and don't like it? Aaaarrrggghhh!

Remarkably, some people liked *Lunch with the Deadly Dozen* and many of those dreamy individuals told their friends either IRL or on their social media platforms, so I'm thanking them all here in the humble hope that they might just consider doing it all again please (oh, and if any of you know anyone in TV/film commissioning... casual whistle. This would be good on the telly, right?). I have doubtless forgotten someone so, if that's you, just let me know and you'll get a mention in Book 3. I need a name for a character.

Brace yourselves. No particular order:

Victoria Bucknell, Simon Ponsford, Caitlin Berry, Ella Berry, Jane Turton, Jo 'very excited' Emson, Mark Potter, Patrick and June Carpmael, Lisa Marks, Lisa Agasee, Chantelle Sturt, Justine Solomons, Tara Donovan, Clare Parker, Claudia Rosencrantz, Kate Bush (not that one), Justin Somper, Alex Hollywood, John Berry, Ian and Sheralyn Bamford, Jonathan and Catherine Bailey, Jill Todd, Snibs and Dave Brabham, Dave and Carol Crowder, Sophia Sheera, Andy and Catherine Sutcliffe, Ben and Rachael Edwards, Steph Seelan, Lisa Howells, Laura Benjamin, Marian Keyes, Simon and Mary Ann

Collins, Val Collins, Owen Bywater, Matthew Christmas, Chris Rowland, Chloe Jackson, Sonia Patel (MBO), Abby Graham, Esther Bultitude, Christina Lankhorst, Luutske Powlesland, Pooja Sharma-Jones, May Bywater, Rachael Parr, Amy Phillips, Nicola Murray, Vanessa Holz, Alison Irving, Nicola Winter, Adrian Lee, Gill Lee, Susan F Crane, Serena Lacey, Pooja Sharma-Jones, The Sandhills Road Book Club, any other Book Club who read and enjoyed Lunch..., Rebecca Rougeau, Sarah Scarr, Richard Farley, Susan Durnford, Ben Hubbard, Gemma Bright, CriminOlly, Katie Bosher, Craig Cunningham, Paul Garnham, Hannah Norris, Hugh Richard Wright, Frances Cottrell-Duffield, Rebecca Ross, Fran Mancey, Debs Cornwall, Sharon Carlyon, Caroline Morrow, Liam Black, Matt Utber, Bob and June Clewley, Etta and John Lazarus, Anu Kumar, Olly Lazarus, Emma Spacey, Lara Spacey, Bethan Spacey, Henry Spacey, Doreen Harbour, Erin Poland, Georgina Hayden, Marston York, Kirstin Chaplin, Natalie Knauer, Francesca Pavis, Katherine Black, Rachael Gray, Natasha Sebuwufu, Nadine Sargent, Mike Gayle, Pauline Bamford, Molly Brabham, Steve Myall, Heather Richards, the lovely staff at New Road Surgery, Dr Robert Brenner and everyone who took a moment or twelve to write positive things either on Amazon or Goodreads or anywhere, frankly. Your kindness creates smiles for all writers. Thank you so flippin' much.

Also thanks to Betsy, Fred, Tara, Hannah and all the Bloodhound crew for their amazing work and general awesomeness and especially to Ian Skewis whose editing skills and encouragement were magical beyond imagination.

And of course thank you to Debi, Caitlin and Ella for just being your incredible selves. I love you always. And to Oatie the dog for valiantly scaring away the squirrels.

A NOTE FROM THE PUBLISHER

Thank you for reading this book. If you enjoyed it please do consider leaving a review on Amazon to help others find it too.

We hate typos. All of our books have been rigorously edited and proofread, but sometimes mistakes do slip through. If you have spotted a typo, please do let us know and we can get it amended within hours.

info@bloodhoundbooks.com

Printed in Great Britain
by Amazon

57544950R00158